PRAISE FOR NANCY BOYARSKY'S NICOLE GRAVES MYSTERIES

"full of page-by-page surprises"
—Kirkus Reviews

"...nail-biting adventure whose thralls are difficult to escape"
—Foreword Reviews

"a hold-onto-the-bar roller coaster of a mystery"
—RT Book Reviews

"a charming and straight-shooting heroine"
—Foreword Reviews

"Well written, non-stop, can't-put-it-down suspense."
—Charles Rosenberg, bestselling author of *"Death on a High Floor"*

"Taut, suspenseful, and fast-paced..."
—Laura Levine, author of the *Jaine Austen* mystery series

THE BEQUEST

a Nicole Graves mystery

NANCY BOYARSKY

The Bequest
Nancy Boyarsky
www.nancyboyarsky.com
nboyarsky@lightmessages.com

Published 2017, by Light Messages
www.lightmessages.com
Durham, NC 27713 USA
SAN: 920-9298

Paperback ISBN: 978-1-61153-190-9
Ebook ISBN: 978-1-61153-189-3
Library of Congress Control Number: 2016956069

This is a work of fiction. All characters, organizations, and events portrayed in this novel are either products of the author's imagination or are used fictitiously.

For Bill,
the love of my life and my partner in crime.

ONE

THE DAY WAS HOT, the sun so bright Nicole found herself digging in her purse for her sunglasses before she stepped out of the international terminal at LAX. Waiting in line for a cab, she got out her phone and tapped in a quick message to her sister. "Just landed. Trip a disaster. Talk later."

She found a cab and got in. Consumed by her tangled thoughts, she was surprised when the cabbie stopped and asked for the fare. They were already in front of her office building, and she had no idea how they'd gotten there.

She was still wearing the clothes she'd chosen for the plane ride home: jeans, tennis shoes, and a pink cotton-knit hoodie. Not the way she normally dressed for an office where the attorneys still wore suits and ties. As she walked in, pulling her carry-on bag, she waved and smiled at the people who looked up. Then she dashed for her office, so no one had a chance to ask about her trip. Breanna, her assistant, got up from her own desk and trailed Nicole into her glass-partitioned office. Nicole set her purse down and flipped quickly through her messages. There was nothing urgent and, more importantly, nothing from Reinhardt. She turned her attention to Breanna and the firm's missing investigator, Robert Blair.

Breanna was pale, her brow furrowed with worry. She was smart and eager to please, but not much of a self-starter. She was easily rattled, at a complete loss when things didn't go according to plan. While Nicole was in London, she'd left Breanna in charge of the office with the proviso that she consult Robert if she ran into something she couldn't handle.

But Robert hadn't shown up at the law firm or answered his phone since the previous Wednesday; today was Monday. This was completely out of character for a man who was never late, rarely missed a day's work, and never without calling. Even so, Breanna had waited until this morning to dispatch a message about Robert's absence to Nicole. That message had sent Nicole straight to the office from the airport.

First, there was the matter of his work. Through the glass, she could see a stack of folders on his desk. As Bascomb, Rice, Smith & Di Angelo's sole in-house investigator, Robert had a sizable caseload. Some he farmed out; occasionally he enlisted Nicole's help if she wasn't too busy.

"For now," she said to Breanna, "why don't you call Wessler. You know, the P.I. we use sometimes? You have his number. Get him and his crew working on Robert's cases." She gestured to the pile on his desk. "Oh, and first make sure there's nothing we need to keep in-house. Ask Hopkins. He'll know. I'll go up to Robert's place and see if he's there. Maybe he had a heart attack or something. "

"I'll go," Breanna said, although her expression said this was the last thing she wanted to do. "You must be completely jetlagged."

"Actually, I'm fine," Nicole said. "I slept on the plane. I'll do it."

As office manager, Nicole had a master key to the desks of the support staff. She unlocked Robert's top drawer. There was his Swiss Army knife, a tool he swore by but rarely carried with him. The next compartment of the desk organizer held several sets of keys. One ring had three keys and a tiny round tag marked "house." She picked it up. Two other key rings were similarly labeled "car" and "cabin" in Robert's small, neat writing. Cabin? She didn't know he had a cabin, although he did take time off sometimes. She always imagined it was for the cases he took on his own, independent of the firm. Maybe he went fishing or even bird watching. She almost smiled. It was impossible to picture him doing these things.

Nicole sent an email about Robert's unexplained absence to Kevin Di Angelo, the senior partner she usually dealt with. Then she printed out Robert's home address. She took one of the firm's loaner cars from the garage and put her suitcase in the trunk. After typing the address into the GPS, she drove from Century City up into the Hollywood Hills. Robert's address was on one of the winding roads several miles above Sunset Boulevard. Her mind was focused on Reinhardt, her missing lover, and the fact that Robert, who was sort of a work buddy of hers, was now missing, too. These distractions sent her sailing by Robert's street twice. Each time, the GPS reset itself, turning her around, then sent her onto the dead end of a cul-de-sac. Exasperated, she stopped, reset the GPS, and at last it took her to the address. She parked at the curb and, after studying the house for a moment, wondered if she'd made a mistake. She looked at the printout she'd brought with her. Yes, this was the place.

The houses on the block were big and looked expensive—very expensive. The street was on the crest of a hill with a panoramic view of downtown, Century City and, if a house were angled just so, the ocean. Robert's property was the largest, appearing to occupy two lots. The house was set back a distance from neighbors on either side. The house itself was screened from view by well-manicured shrubs and tropical, tree-sized plants, which were being whipped around by the wind. All she could see from the street was a long driveway in a diamond pattern of concrete and brick. At the top, Robert's SUV, a shiny black Kia, was parked in a handsomely designed carport. She pulled into the driveway and up the fifty-foot stretch to the top, parking behind him. From this angle she still couldn't see the house, just a gate next to the carport.

She got out of the car and was hit by the fierce, warm Santa Ana wind. It was November, for heaven's sake, but this was L.A.; ninety degrees and windy was possible any time of the year.

As she approached the gate, she glanced up at the trees beating about in the wind. That was when she spotted the security camera. It had been fastened to the top of one of the posts that supported the carport. The camera was broken, dangling from a cord. Bits of broken glass glinted on the pavement below. She wondered what had happened. The tropical shrubs were tall, but their branches were hardly substantial enough to pack much of a wallop. Even in a strong wind, it was unlikely they could hit the camera hard enough to smash it and knock it from its mounting.

The gate to the front yard had a keypad but no visible knob or latch. She thought of the keys she'd brought along. They wouldn't be much help with this setup. The keypad had an intercom speaker with a button next to it. She pressed the button, assuming it would ring a bell inside the house. At her touch, the gate silently swung open. It hadn't been locked. She walked into the yard. She still couldn't see the front door, so she turned left and followed a path of Spanish tiles around the house. This led to a tall, decorative wrought-iron fence that enclosed the backyard, which held a swimming pool and a deck. Beyond the pool was a magnificent view, from downtown to the ocean. The sky above was brilliant blue. Below, hanging over the city, was a pale haze of smog.

She tried the gate, but it was locked. Beyond it, she could see the back entrance to the house. She reversed course. There had to be a front door.

The more she looked at the house, the more questions it raised. How could Robert possibly afford a place like this? He'd been a cop for a number of years. That meant a pension. But it still didn't add up. This house was worth at least three, maybe four, million dollars. House payments, not to mention property taxes, would be more than he earned, even with a pension and the work he did on the side.

Finally, she reached the front door. She rang the bell, but there was no answer. She knocked loudly, then shouted Robert's name. Nothing. The door had three locks: one in the doorknob, a deadbolt just above it, and another deadbolt about a foot from the ground. Looking at the keys in her hand, she decided to try the lock in the doorknob first. The knob turned easily, and the door opened. None of the locks had been engaged. She pushed the door open a crack. The drapes were drawn, and the interior was almost dark. She gave another shout. "Robert? Are you there?" No answer.

She opened the door wider, pulled off her sunglasses, and took a step inside, about to call out again. But as her eyes adjusted to the light, she saw him. He was less than a dozen feet away, across the octagonal entry hall. He was half sitting, half sagging against the wall, and there was a bullet hole in the center of his forehead. On the wall above, at eye level, was a Rorschach splotch of crimson so dark it was almost black, surrounded by a fine splatter of the same color. Below that was a dark smear where his head had rubbed against the wall on its way down. Flies were buzzing around Robert's head as well as near the splotches on the wall. Only now did she notice the smell, a metallic stink mixed with the sweet undertone of decay. She held her breath and studied Robert's face.

He was staring right at her with a deadpan expression, as if he'd just made one of his wry jokes and was waiting for her to laugh.

Nicole felt a wave of shock that almost knocked the breath out of her. During her misadventure in the U.K. the previous year, she'd been forced to kill two men in self-defense, one with a sledgehammer and the second with a flare gun. The sight of Robert's body summoned flashbacks that made her legs go wobbly. She grabbed the doorframe to steady herself, took a step back, and turned to run.

Halfway to her car, Nicole stopped to consider what she'd just seen, or thought she'd seen. She'd taken an Ambien on the plane. It had given her six hours of sleep. Then, somewhere over Salt Lake City, her eyes had popped open, and she was wide-awake, feeling as if she'd had one too many cups of coffee. Ambien was known for its strange side effects. Was it possible she'd been hallucinating?

She forced herself to turn around, walk back to the front door and, after taking a deep gulp of fresh air, lean in for another look. He was still there, along with the flies, the smell, the bloody wall and that incongruous, half-amused expression on his face. It occurred to her that perhaps he'd killed himself, but there was no gun in sight. The entry hall had a wooden parquet floor and a thick, sapphire-blue rug near the door. A single piece of furniture stood against one wall, a handsome, modern console table with an art deco lamp. Both looked expensive. For the briefest second, a thought flickered. Robert shopping for furniture? She couldn't imagine it. Had he hired a decorator? She couldn't imagine that either.

She stepped back into the fresh air and focused on what she had to do next—get away from this place and call the police. A sudden burst of adrenalin, and she was in her car, backing down the driveway. She parked in front of the nearest house and, despite her badly shaking hands, managed to get out her phone and call 911.

TWO

IT WAS ONLY A FEW MINUTES before she heard sirens. Three patrol cars pulled up in front of Robert's house. Nicole had already called the office and told Di Angelo what had happened.

"Holy Christ!" he said. After a few seconds of silence, he told her he was going to send someone out to be with her. She tried to refuse, insisting she was all right, but he wouldn't have it. "Listen. This kind of thing is very upsetting. They'll keep you waiting while they search the place. Then they'll want to take your statement. It could be hours before they let you go."

Nicole sighed. All at once she felt tired, and she realized she'd been shivering since she got into her car. She reached over and turned off the air conditioner. "OK," she said. "Could you send John Gillingham?" He was a new associate—a decent guy, young and married with a new baby. He had a good sense of humor, and she felt more comfortable with him than most of the attorneys she worked with.

She waited while Di Angelo had his secretary check Gillingham's whereabouts.

"He just left for a deposition." Di Angelo said. "I'll send Rick. He was just in here."

"Please don't bother. I have a book to read. I'm fine. Really," Nicole said.

"No, I insist," Di Angelo said. "You may think you're all right, but you're not. Take it from me. Give me the address. I'll send him right up there."

They hung up, and Nicole sighed again. Rick Sargosian was Di Angelo's stepson, and they had an especially strong bond. With Di Angelo's help, Rick had stepped into partnership after a stint in the D.A.'s office and only a year with the firm.

Nicole didn't much like Rick. He was in his mid-30s, unattached, and a resolute skirt chaser. In her opinion, he walked a fine line between flirtatiousness and sexual harassment. When a new female was added to the staff—if she was even remotely attractive—he'd immediately ask her out and proceed to have a fling, if she was willing. Before long, he'd move on. He expended so much time and energy on this activity, it was almost as if he considered it part of his job. He'd worked his way through eight or nine of the women in the office, while openly flirting with others. It amazed Nicole that no one had registered a complaint against him.

She, herself, had managed to keep Rick at a distance. But having him sent up here to provide moral support was a joke. His whole demeanor annoyed her, and she didn't welcome the idea of being the focus of his attention for the afternoon. The firm's stated policy forbade romantic entanglements between employees, but this was never enforced. Nicole, as office manager, ignored these relationships, as long as they were reasonably discreet. People being what they were, it was futile to tell a pool of young men and women who worked together not to get involved. It only made them secretive. So, unless they were disappearing into a utility closet to have sex on the firm's dime—which had never happened, at least to her knowledge—she let these things go.

She did, however, caution the women she hired about getting involved with the firm's attorneys, especially the married ones. In terms of clout, the lawyers were a substantial step above support staff. And fraternization could have serious consequences, the least of which was the awkwardness of working for an ex-lover after a breakup.

By now the police were out of their cars. She started her engine, pulled up behind the last black-and-white, and got out. She introduced herself, then pointed out Robert's house and told them where to find his body.

A tall, burly cop with a red face seemed to be in charge. He assigned a younger officer, whose nametag identified him as Derek Leonard, to wait with her while they checked out the scene.

Leonard was a slight, young man with a hangdog look and an inability—at least with her—to maintain eye contact. Without meeting her eyes, he gestured toward the patrol car.

"I'd be a lot more comfortable in my own car," she protested.

"I have to get your fingerprints and check your ID," he said. "It's easier in the patrol car, if you don't mind."

Nicole did mind, but she settled into his passenger seat and pulled out her driver's license while he went around to the trunk to get a large utility bag. He got out the fingerprint kit and took her prints. Then he took her driver's license and copied the information into his notebook.

"I'm going to sit in my own car now," she said. He seemed about to protest, and she added, "You can come with me if you want." Once they were in her car, there was an uncomfortable silence. She wondered why he felt obliged to sit with her. Was it to make sure she didn't leave before they questioned her?

She rested her head against the back of the seat and thought about the events of the past week. When Reinhardt failed to meet her at Heathrow, as they'd arranged, she'd tried to call him but only managed to get his voicemail.

Not knowing what else to do, she'd taken a cab to his Knightsbridge bachelor pad and let herself in. She'd slept there a couple of nights. Finding the place too lonely, she'd found a reasonably priced B&B and sent him yet another message, telling him where to find her. She kept herself busy with the usual round of museums, shops, and plays between attempts to reach him. But there was no response.

She knew in her heart that he'd eventually turn up, explaining that he'd been called away for work—no details, no whats, whys, or wheres. Yet she couldn't help fearing that something had happened to him. At other moments she felt aggrieved and abandoned. And, as disappointing as this week had been, she now understood that a much larger disappointment lay ahead. Their romance was doomed. He was in law enforcement, and he'd warned her from the beginning that his job came first. He had no control over when he'd be sent on an assignment or when he'd return.

He'd been working for Scotland Yard when they'd met the year before, just as her marriage was coming apart. Since then, she'd gotten a divorce, and she and Reinhardt had met for a long weekend almost every month. The previous holiday had been four glorious days in Majorca before he'd been called away for work.

It was on that trip when he told her he'd left Scotland Yard and was now working for another agency. He refused to say which one.

"Is it MI6?" she asked.

He laughed. "I think you watch too much television," he said, still not answering her question. "This means I'll have longer assignments, but also more time off in between. It will be a good thing—good for us." He told her that he loved her. But what did that mean in terms of the future? She wanted marriage and a family. As far as she could tell, he wanted to keep on doing what they were doing between episodes of whatever mysterious activities he was involved in.

She was startled when someone knocked on her window. It was a plain-clothes detective. Leonard was already out of her car. She opened the door and got out, too.

"We've been through the house and taped it off," the detective said. "Crime scene technicians should be here any minute. Come sit in my car so we can go over what happened here."

She followed him. He was middle-aged, balding, and somewhat overweight. He had an odd way of walking, holding his arms slightly out from his body, like a gunslinger getting ready to draw. She wondered if his odd gait was left over from years walking a beat, when he really did wear a gun on his hip.

When they got into his car, it was uncomfortably hot, the air heavy with old car smell—a stale combination of cigarette smoke and air freshener. He turned on the air conditioner.

He pulled out a notebook and poised his pen over a page. "I'm Detective Frank Miller, and you are?"

She told him her name and handed over her driver's license before he had a chance to ask.

"So how do you know Mr. Blair?"

"I worked with him at Bascomb, Rice, Smith & Di Angelo. It's a law firm in Century City. I'm the office manager. He was our investigator. He didn't show up at work last Wednesday, and he couldn't be reached by phone. So I came out to check on him."

"Yeah," he said. As he jotted in his notebook, he kept talking. "He used to be a cop. On vice. Kind of a famous guy in his day. You know that?" Then without waiting for an answer, he looked up at her. "You have a relationship with him?"

The question took her by surprise. Robert was almost twice her age, tall and gaunt, with thinning gray hair. If he'd been good looking once, those days were long gone. But it was more than that. He was so basically closed off, so emotionally detached she couldn't imagine him having a romantic relationship with anyone.

"No," she said. "I knew him through work. We were friendly but never socialized outside the office, except for an occasional lunch. And I helped him with cases when my own work was slow. That was it."

"O-h k-a-y" he said, drawing out the word as if he didn't believe her. That comment and the skeptical way he looked at her put Nicole on alert. What was going on?

"What kind of cases you work with Blair?" he said.

"The firm mainly represents large corporations," Nicole said, "So we handle their legal matters. For example, we research companies our clients might be in litigation with. We might take a look to see if they're hiding assets through shell corporations. We also handle some matters for executives of the corporations we represent: divorces, prenups, that sort of thing. We do sexual harassment cases. Occasionally we'll take on a minor criminal matter, usually involving someone connected with a corporate client."

"How do you get your information?"

"The usual," she said. "We use Internet searches plus several databases for background checks. We start there, find out what we can. Then we decide if we need to interview someone, locate witnesses—whatever."

"What about this house?" he said. "He own it?"

"I don't know. This is the address we've had in his file since he started at the firm."

"When was that?"

"About six years ago. If you want an exact date, I can check," she said.

"So, how much do you pay your investigators?" He nodded toward the house, his meaning clear.

"His base pay was around ninety thousand plus a year-end bonus, which could be as much as ten thousand if the firm had a good year. He also had his police pension, and he took on his own investigative cases on the side."

He nodded. "But a place like this? What's it worth? Three or four million?"

"Maybe there was family money," she said.

"OK. What about family?" he went on. "Who do we call?"

"I don't know. He never talked about his personal life."

"Could you call your office?" he said "Have them look up his personnel record and see if there's someone we need to notify?"

"Sure," she said. She already knew what his personnel file said, but sensed that the less information she volunteered, the better. Detective Miller didn't seem to believe what she was telling him, and she didn't like his tone.

When Robert first joined the firm, she'd been curious about him. She was always curious about the people she met. But he was such an enigma, she felt compelled to find out his story. She Googled him, then looked him up on one of the firm's databases. It revealed his army record and his career as a police officer. There was no record of marriage or mention of family. Since then, in the years she'd worked with him, she'd never gotten to know much more than that.

He was perhaps the most resolute loner she'd ever met—a self-contained unit with little use for other people and none for small talk with coworkers. The personnel record said he'd been with the LAPD for twenty years, the last ten as a detective in vice. In the line for next of kin, he'd written none, and he'd specified that the forty thousand dollar life insurance policy the firm provided go to a skid-row homeless shelter.

In the rear-view mirror, she noticed several more vehicles pulling up behind them: an aging white minivan, a motorcycle with a helmetless rider, and a somewhat battered Toyota sedan.

Miller glanced out the back window. "Paparazzi," he said, with disgust. "Don't look at them. Keep your head down, or you'll be on XHN in a couple of minutes."

Nicole scrunched down in the seat. "Why would they be interested in this?"

"Are you kidding?" Miller said. "This story is golden. Hero ex-cop, multi-million dollar house, murder. They can't get enough of this stuff," he said. "Of course it would be better if it was a movie star who got whacked, but on a slow news day, this'll do. They'll smoke it up, make it more sensational than it is."

The detective went on to ask more questions: What time had she arrived? How did she get in? She explained that she'd taken keys from his desk but had found the gate and front door unlocked.

"Can I have the keys?" he said. She dug them out of her purse and handed them over.

"Thanks," he said. "Now, do you mind if I have a look in your purse?"

She knew what he was thinking. The bullet wound in Robert's head, with no gun in sight. Silently she handed the bag over. He poked through it and handed it back.

He had more questions: Had she entered the house? Had she ever been inside the house?

When she answered "No," she got that look again. "Did you touch anything?" he said.

"No."

He stared at her a moment, then said, "Do you know of anyone who would want to kill him?"

"No. I only knew him through work. As I said, he took on private clients on his own time. I have no idea what he did outside the office or who his friends or enemies might be."

A memory flickered, then a flashback of a scene she'd witnessed. "Wait," she said, "Something happened a couple of months ago. I was coming back from lunch when I saw Robert heading toward our office building. I was across the street. A man walked up to him and started waving his arms and shouting. I didn't catch what he was saying, but he looked really angry. He gave Robert a shove. This guy was taller than Robert and bigger, more solid. Robert is—was—fit, but thin and wiry. So I was really surprised when Robert grabbed this guy by the front of his jacket and slammed him against the wall. He leaned in close and said something to the man that seemed to deflate him. Then Robert let go and went into the building."

"What did the other guy do?" the detective said.

"He turned and hurried off in the other direction."

"Do you have any idea who he was?"

"No."

"Well, what did he look like?"

"He was heavyset. Dark hair, a little long. Maybe in his thirties."

"Was he white? Black? Latino?"

"White."

"If we showed you some photos, would you recognize him?"

"I doubt it. I'd just walked out of the Century Plaza Hotel coffee shop. Our office is all the way across Avenue of the Stars. That's a pretty wide street. I must have been seventy or eighty yards away. My eyesight is good, but that's quite a distance."

Miller was writing this down in his notebook. Through the rearview mirror, she watched yet another batch of vehicles pull up: a coroner's wagon, a second van with the LAPD insignia, and another two police cars. A couple of uniformed cops made the paparazzi move to the end of the block so the official vehicles could pull forward. Once everyone had reparked, the paparazzi—now numbering eight—scurried toward Robert's house. They stopped just short of where two cops had been posted in front and began shooting pictures.

Just then a shiny black Mercedes sports car with dark windows appeared around the corner and parked behind the fleet of vehicles. The driver got out and headed toward them.

Nicole watched him in the rearview mirror. Miller followed her glance, then turned his head to look.

"Who's that?" Miller asked. "Someone you know?"

"His name is Rick Sargosian," she said. "He's an attorney from work."

"You think you need an attorney?"

"No," she said, wondering why he was being such a jerk. "My boss thought I might be upset after finding a dead body, so he sent someone up here to look after me."

"You upset? You don't look upset."

"Well," she said, trying to hold onto her temper. "It was a shock. Robert was a friend. But I'm OK. I don't think I need Rick. But—whatever." Obviously, she thought, he was playing bad cop, but why? And where was the good cop? Wasn't that how it was supposed to work? Could this guy possibly imagine she'd killed Robert?

"We need you to come down to the station and make a formal statement about finding the body. How about tomorrow morning. Say, around eleven?"

She agreed and he made more squiggles in his notebook. "Now, about the next of kin."

Nicole got out her phone and called Breanna at the office. She asked for Robert's emergency contact information, then put the call on speaker and set the phone on the seat between herself and the detective. They could hear Breanna typing on the keyboard as she brought the record up. After a long moment, Breanna said, "There's no next of kin. But, hey, this is weird. About a month ago, he went into the system and changed the beneficiary of his life insurance policy. It's you, Nicole. He named you."

Nicole felt herself flush. She turned off the speaker and put the phone to her ear. "This makes absolutely no sense. Why would he do that?'

"Don't ask me," Breanna said. "But he was always looking at you. Didn't you pick up on that? I think he had a thing for you, Nicole."

"That's ridiculous," she said. Then she recalled that he had asked her out. Just once, while her divorce was in progress, about nine months before. She'd refused, explaining that she was involved with someone. She remembered what Robert had said. "Fast work. Not even single yet and already taken. Who's the lucky guy?"

"Someone I met in England," she'd said, "when my marriage broke up."

Neither had mentioned it again, and Robert had gone on behaving just as he always had. The perfect gentleman.

"Thanks, Breanna," she said. "I'll be back at the office in a half hour or so."

She turned to the detective. He raised an eyebrow. "Are you sure there isn't anything else you want to tell me?"

She looked at him. "I've told you everything I know." She opened the door of the car and stepped into the hot, gusty wind.

Sargosian was waiting on the sidewalk. By now, the paparazzi had noticed and began rushing toward her.

Spotting them, Sargosian put a protective arm around her and hurried her toward his car. "Don't look at them," he said. "Keep your head down."

The paparazzi began shouting questions: "What's your name, honey?" and "You know the dead guy?" "Who is it?" and "You his girlfriend?"

By now they'd reached Sargosian's car. He opened the door for her, still shielding her from the paparazzi. Oddly, they seemed completely uninterested in Sargosian. As he walked around to the driver's side, the cameras remained focused on her.

"Don't worry," he said, as he got in and started the car. "They can't shoot pictures through the tinted windows. You all right?"

"I'm fine," she said. "Thanks for driving all the way up here. The police are done with me. I want to go back to the office, but my loaner car is parked up near the house, and I don't think I'm going to get to it any time soon."

"Tell you what," he said. "It's almost one. You look like you could use a drink. There's an Umami Burger over the hill on Ventura. We can get lunch, and they have a full bar."

She thought about it. She hadn't eaten breakfast on the plane and was beginning to feel hungry. Her hands were still shaking; she was, in fact, trembling all over. A drink sounded like a good idea. As for having lunch with Sargosian, she knew how to handle men like him.

At lunch he was mainly interested in finding out about the murder. He asked her what she'd seen and what she knew about Robert. He was openly dubious about Robert's ability to afford the big house by any legal means. "A multi-million pad on that hill—doesn't it seem a little strange to you?" he said. "One look at that place, and you know this guy was working some kind of angle."

"What do you mean?" she said, frowning at him.

He hesitated, then said, "I'm just saying. It doesn't add up. He used to be on the vice squad, right? Didn't you hear about the flap last year when the police commission wanted to monitor the bank accounts of officers on the vice and narcotics squads? Those guys run up against temptation every day. Maybe Blair didn't turn over evidence on a regular basis. Maybe he put it in his piggy bank, saving up for his dream house."

She felt indignant on Robert's behalf, even though she'd been harboring the same thoughts herself. "He might have had family money. Did you consider that? Maybe he had a trust fund. Is that so impossible?"

He studied her face for a moment and his expression softened. "You're right," he said. "I was speaking out of turn. He was your friend, and now he's dead. I'm sorry."

To her surprise, Sargosian turned out to be decent company. He seemed on his best behavior, having left most of his big-bad-wolf persona behind. She noticed, not for the first time, his good looks—the dark wavy hair, the expressive brown eyes. His nose was perhaps a little bigger than it should be, but the cleft in his chin made up for it. He wasn't handsome like Reinhardt, of course, who was in a class of his own. Despite Sargosian's effort at good manners, he still showed traces of his smarmy, womanizing self. But he was solicitous of her feelings and struck just the right note as a sympathetic listener.

Before long, the image of Robert's dead body, that wry expression on his face, and—almost as bad—the news about his life insurance started eating at her. Today's events had pushed aside thoughts of her missing lover and her lonely stay in London. But now they surfaced again, and she found it hard to focus on the conversation. She'd taken only a few bites of her burger when she put it down.

She waited for him to finish eating. Then she said, "I just got back from a trip, and I'm really jet-lagged. I think I'll take the rest of the day off."

Sargosian insisted on driving her to her condo. He contended that the police and the paparazzi would still be at the murder scene where she'd left the car. "Besides," he added, "you're too upset to be driving. I'll send a couple of interns up to Robert's house to get the firm's car. They can caravan back to the office."

"But I left my suitcase in the trunk," she said.

"No worries," he said. "I'll have them drop it off at your place."

She thought he was carrying things a bit far, but she was too tired to argue. He waited at the curb in front of her building while she unlocked the door to the lobby and turned to wave at him. He waved back, then drove away. She took the elevator to her second-floor condo and went straight to bed.

Nicole awoke to the phone ringing on her night table. It was dark out, and her alarm clock said 6:00. For a moment, she wasn't sure if it was morning or night.

She picked up the phone and croaked, "Hello?"

"Nicky?" It was Stephanie, her sister. "My god! You sound awful. My friend Becka just called. Take a look at XHN. Did you know that the detective who works for your firm got murdered?"

"Yeah, I know." Nicole said. "XHN? Hang on, let me look." She went to the second bedroom, which she used as an office, and turned on her computer. While she was waiting for it to load, she told her sister about finding Robert's body. XHN—the acronym for the tabloid website Extra Hot News—popped up on her browser. Sure enough, Robert's death was the lead story. The headline read: "Hero Ex-Cop Slain in Multimillion Dollar Mansion." There was a picture of Robert in dress uniform from his days on the LAPD, and another shot of the house, taken from the back. The paparazzi must have climbed down through a neighbor's yard to a spot below Robert's property. He'd used a wide angle shot, and the house looked enormous.

A link labeled "Police Activity at Crime Scene" was next to the photos. When she clicked it, a video appeared, showing the police and crime scene workers in front of the house. Toward the end, it focused in on Sargosian escorting her to his car. Watching it, she was glad he'd warned her not to look at the cameras. A caption popped up, reading: "Mystery woman escorted from murder scene."

The story alluded to several things about Robert's police career that Nicole hadn't known. He'd been cited for bravery and had solved several big cases. As for the house, XHN said he'd bought it seven years before. There was no mortgage on the property, which meant he owned it outright. The house was valued at $3.9 million. It said that police had questioned a woman at the scene and released her.

The story also went into Robert's work for Bascomb, Rice, Smith & Di Angelo, "the city's most prestigious white-shoe law firm." Then in the next paragraph, the article said, "Police refused to comment on speculation that the murder might be related to organized crime, but the assassination-style murder, a single shot to the head, is typical of a paid hit, such as those used by organized crime. No weapon was found at the scene. XHN's calls to the law firm, asking for comment, were not returned."

"My god! How could they possibly find all this so fast?" Nicole said. "Listen, Steph, I've got to go. Someone has to get the partners to issue a statement."

Stephanie was still stuck on the XHN images. "Is that you in the video? I'd never have recognized you." Then, Stephanie added, "But what happened on your trip? This morning your message said it was a disaster. Did you guys break up?"

"Reinhardt never showed," Nicole said. "I spent six days waiting. He didn't call or answer my messages. Look, I have to go. When I'm done, I'll come over to your place and we'll talk."

THREE

NICOLE CALLED THE OFFICE just in time to catch Di Angelo as he was leaving for the day. She told him that the firm needed to make a statement to the press about Robert's death. She urged him to offer a reward for the capture and conviction of the person responsible. Somewhat impatiently, Di Angelo said, "Yes, yes," then added, "I have to go. We have tickets for the opera. This will have to wait until tomorrow."

"The sooner we get something out, the better," she said. "One of the tabloids suggested it was a mob hit and mentioned Robert's connection with our firm. They also said the firm didn't return their calls. It will be in the *Times* tomorrow. We need a statement saying how important Robert was to the firm and that we're giving the police our full cooperation. Maybe offer a reward for information leading to—you know. I'll write it and send it to you. I think we have a couple of hours before the *Times'* deadline."

Di Angelo, like the rest of the attorneys she worked with, didn't regard a call from a journalist worthy of a response. Quite the opposite. His first instinct was to dodge phone calls until the reporter's deadline passed in the hope of avoiding being mentioned at all. "I appreciate what you're saying, Nicole," Di Angelo said. "But one day won't make that much difference. Now, will it?"

She knew from his condescending tone that he wasn't about to listen. If she'd learned anything on this job, it was not to argue with the firm's attorneys. Few of them were satisfied with just winning an argument—which they invariably did, having been trained for this very thing in law school. They also felt the need to stamp the dissenter into the carpet.

"Tomorrow, then," she said.

After hanging up, she got dressed, packed a small overnight case, and headed for her sister's apartment in West Hollywood. The two sisters had been through a lot together in the last year: Nicole's divorce and, around the same time, the sudden death of their father from a heart attack. He'd been in debt, and his daughters had ended up paying for the funeral. They'd had a good relationship before, but these recent events had brought them even closer.

Stephanie met Nicole at the door and pulled her into a hug. "Oh, Nicole," she said. "Nobody deserves such a crappy week." Arnold, Nicole's Australian terrier, who had been staying with Stephanie, rushed up to Nicole and started jumping on her, barking excitedly. Then he turned and rushed down the steps, headed for Nicole's car. Clearly, he thought he was going home. The two women ran after him, catching him before he got to the busy street. Nicole picked him up and carried him inside.

Stephanie ushered Nicole into her living room where two glasses of red wine were waiting on the coffee table.

"Here, drink up," Stephanie said, handing a glass to Nicole. They both took seats on the worn couch with Arnold between them, his head on Nicole's lap. The women took a moment to get comfortable, Nicole tucking her legs under her and Stephanie reclining with her long legs stretched out in front.

Stephanie wanted to know more about the murder. "What did his body look like? Was it really gross?"

Nicole went through the whole story—the murder scene, Robert's huge house, the paparazzi, the police detective's hostile questions, and the way Sargosian had rescued her from the photographers.

When Nicole was done, Stephanie said, "And what about Reinhardt? Have you heard from him yet?"

"Not a thing," Nicole said. "I left him word every way I could think of, but I haven't heard back. When I first met him, and he told me he was divorced, he said women can't take the uncertainty of his line of work. Now I know what he meant.

"On our trip to Majorca in October," she went on, "that last night, he planned a romantic dinner on the beach. We were just starting to eat, when he got a phone call. It was brief, not even a minute. Then he got up and said he had to go. When I went back to the room, his things were still there. A few hours later, he sent me a message explaining that the hotel bill was paid, so I didn't have to bother with checkout. He also told me to leave his things, that someone would be sent to get them.

"I hadn't really heard from him since, except for a few impersonal messages. I had the feeling they were relayed through someone else. And he never responded to my messages asking if we could set up a call on Skype. At that point, I wondered if I'd ever hear from him again. Then, a couple of weeks ago, I got a message telling me to meet him in London, and he sent me a ticket. In all this time, we haven't talked by phone. Before Majorca, we used to Skype almost daily."

"Do you think he's gone off you?" Steph said.

Nicole was silent, mulling it over. "He doesn't play games. He'd tell me. Maybe it's his work or something's happened to him."

"What are you going to do?"

"What can I do? Sometimes I'm really mad and other times I'm just so damned worried. I guess I'll have to wait to hear from him, or not. Whatever comes next."

"You don't seem that broken up about it," Stephanie said. "I thought you were in love with him."

"I thought I was, too. The problem is that he's so damned unknowable. I mean, he can be very romantic, and he's great in bed. But most of the time, it's like he's a million miles away, and I haven't a clue what he's thinking. Maybe I was starting to accept the inevitable, even before this last trip."

The two of them were silent for a bit. Then Stephanie announced, "I'm hungry. How about you?" Nicole shook her head, but Stephanie got up and started poking in her refrigerator for something to eat. Finally, she gave up and sent out for pizza.

While they waited for the food to arrive, Stephanie refilled their glasses and settled back on the couch. "So tell me more about the dead guy," she said. "You never talked about him. Did you know him very well?"

"I guess I never thought about him much outside the office," Nicole said. "But I did work with him, and I knew him as well as anyone can know a complete introvert. He's the one who taught me how to do investigative work. You remember. I wanted to add some variety to my job, so I asked one of the partners if he minded if I helped Robert out when my work was slow. He didn't, but Robert did. In the beginning, he didn't like it one bit. I pretended not to notice how rude he was when he wasn't completely ignoring me. But he finally came around. After that we worked well together, and I could tell he appreciated my help.

"Basically, he was a strange bird. Very closed off. Barely talked to anyone else in the office. He seemed completely oblivious to what was going on around him. But the entire time, he was taking it all in. He was a world-class eavesdropper and knew everything that happened: the affairs, the plots, the backstabbings. He knew a lot about the cases our attorneys were handling, which I never heard much about. He'd tell me stuff when we had our occasional lunch. I was surprised to find out how much was going on under my nose. He was a good mimic, too. He'd repeat conversations he'd overheard. We'd both have a good laugh."

As Nicole thought about Robert and his solitary life, a tear ran down her cheek. "You know," she said, "it's just so damned sad. I think I may have been the only friend he had, and I didn't know him at all." She paused, then added, "And he did the weirdest thing. I found out that he left his company life insurance to me."

"He did? How much is it?" Stephanie said.

"Forty-thousand dollars. Not a fortune, but a nice chunk of change. You know how I've been struggling to make the mortgage payments since the divorce, and the money will come in handy. But I wish he hadn't done it. It will make people think there was more to our friendship than there was. And something about it just feels wrong."

"How so?" Stephanie said. "If he didn't have any family, and you were his only friend."

"I can't explain," Nicole said. "It just feels..." she struggled to think of the right word. "Creepy."

The pizza came, and they ate. Nicole was all talked out. Stephanie poured them more wine while she chattered about the eclectic combination of freelance jobs that kept her afloat. She wrote grant proposals for half a dozen nonprofits, composed and assembled press packets for little theaters, ghosted book reviews for self-published authors, and even, at one low point, did telephone sex. The latter she'd given up, mainly because of the disapproval of family and friends. But she said it was the easiest work she'd ever had and the best paid. The only problem was keeping herself from laughing at her clients and the sounds she had to make to simulate sexual pleasure.

She'd been out of college for almost six years and had never looked for a permanent job because, she insisted, she liked the freedom this arrangement gave her. It was hard for Nicole to understand. Stephanie was stuck in a tiny, rundown apartment. Her car was ancient and unreliable. She was always worried about money and scrambling for new gigs when the old ones inevitably ended.

Nicole dozed off as her sister talked. She woke up when Stephanie jostled her shoulder. "It's 10:00, sleepyhead," Stephanie said. "Let's get you to bed."

Nicole woke up around 5:00 a.m. in her sister's second bedroom—an untidy combination guest room and office.

The dog followed her while she brushed her teeth, retrieved her iPad from its charger, and tiptoed into Stephanie's tiny kitchen. Stephanie and her two cats were still asleep. Nicole fed Arnold, then made coffee.

She sat down at the table and turned on her iPad to wait for the *L.A. Times* website to load. There, the front page screamed a headline almost identical to the one XHN had run the day before: "LAPD Hero Slain in Sunset Hills Mansion." Along with the photo of Robert in his LAPD uniform, the story held many of the same details she'd seen on the web, although it qualified some of the unverified facts, attributing them to XHN.

Nicole scrolled down to finish the story and was startled to see a photo of the building where the law firm's offices were, along with one of Robert's house.

Just then Stephanie walked into the kitchen. "You see the *Times*?" Steph said.

"I'm just reading it," Nicole said.

The *Times* provided a bit more detail about Robert's work as a detective on vice than the tabloids had. "Blair was recognized in 2006 by the Los Angeles mayor for discovering a shipping container with forty women, all illegal immigrants. Two were dead from starvation. The FBI took over the case, and three accused human traffickers were convicted of murder and false imprisonment, as well as immigration-law violations. They received long prison sentences. Blair also uncovered a network of businessmen who lured young girls into prostitution. "He was one of the finest of our finest," said LAPD Chief Ray Spalding.

"It is unknown," the story went on, "how Blair could afford a multi-million dollar house. He was an investigator at the law firm of Bascomb, Rice, Smith & Di Angelo in Century City. Investigators generally earn..."

She closed the iPad and stood up. "OK, Steph. I'm going in early to write that statement for the press."

She got to work around 6:30 a.m., when the office was still deserted. As soon as she walked in, she spotted the flowers on her desk, an extravagant arrangement of yellow roses, white lilies, and blue delphiniums. She knew right away they were from Reinhardt. The arrangement was larger and more striking than any he'd sent before. With a rush of relief, she plucked the card from where it was stuck between the blossoms. But the message was identical to the notes that always accompanied his flowers: "With all my love, R." No explanation, no apology. Here was yet more disappointment. This told her nothing about why he'd stood her up. Worse yet, for the first time, she realized that the flowers she received every couple of weeks were a standing order—not a spontaneous gesture that meant he was thinking of her.

She crumpled up the note and threw it in the wastebasket. Then she went to work on the firm's statement for the press. She included an offer of a $50,000 reward for information leading to the arrest and conviction of Robert's murderer. When she was done, she emailed a copy to each of the firm's senior partners for their approval. Three of them would ignore the message, but Di Angelo would read it and get back to her.

She was catching up on her own email—several hundred had stacked up since she went away—when the staff began arriving. Most of them stepped into her office to say how sorry they were about Robert or to ask how she was doing. She realized, with some dismay, that they were treating her as if she were the bereaved. They really did think she and Robert were involved.

She flushed at the thought. Had there been gossip about them in the office because they lunched together sometimes? More likely it was because he was so unfriendly to everyone else.

Every time she looked up from her work, she noticed a couple of coworkers staring at her. They'd quickly look away, and their attention was making her uncomfortable. Finally, she got up and went to Di Angelo's office.

"I saw the *Times* this morning," he said. "I didn't like the way they hinted about mob connections and mentioned the firm in the next sentence. It makes us look bad. Your statement is fine. Go with it."

"Is the $50,000 reward OK?"

"Sure," he said. "Knowing how the criminal justice system works, we won't have to worry about that for a long time. One more thing," Di Angelo said. "Why don't you take a few days off? With pay, of course. Maybe a week's R and R."

Nicole stared at him. "Why?" she said. "I'm perfectly OK. There's no reason for me to take off work."

"I'm just afraid the press is going to come around and start bothering you," he said. "You know, disrupting things."

"We have security outside. Nobody can even get into our elevator bank. Besides, if they're writing about the law firm, they'll be doing that whether I'm here or not."

"You have a point. Let's see how it goes. We'll revisit it in a day or two."

Instead of going back into her office, she stood in front of the glass partition and announced to the staff, "If any of you have questions about Robert's death, I'll be happy to answer them." Most of them had noticed her return from the partner's office and were watching her. Now the others looked up.

"I don't know much more than what you've seen in the news," she added, "but I'll try to answer what I can."

There were a few solicitous questions—"How are you?" and "What was it like finding him?"

Then someone said, "Is there going to be a funeral?"

"Robert didn't have family, so I imagine the firm will take care of arrangements, but we can't do anything until they release the body. I have no idea when that will be."

Then one of the paralegals raised the question that was on everyone's mind. "Were you and Robert friends or what?"

"We were just friends. Nothing more," she said. "I don't think my love life is anybody's business, but I was never involved with Robert. I am seeing someone who lives in England." She gestured toward the flowers in her office. "I think most of you know about that."

Mindy, Di Angelo's secretary, appeared in the doorway, where she'd migrated from the attorneys' side of the office. She was the cheerleader when it came to office gossip. Nicole had spoken to Mindy about it each time she had a performance review. "What about Robert's life insurance?" Mindy said, her voice all innocence. "Is it true he left it to you?"

Nicole paused a moment. No one knew that but herself, Breanna, perhaps Di Angelo, and, of course, Detective Miller. Had Breanna been gossiping? Well, the news was out, so she admitted it was true, and went on to add, "It came as a complete surprise. I have no idea why Robert would do such a thing, except that he was a loner—you know that. He didn't have many people in his life.

"The important thing to remember is that this is a tragedy," she said. "He was a good person who did his job well and preferred keeping to himself. And these news stories suggest he was mixed up in some kind of criminal activity, which is ridiculous. Now if there's nothing else, I have an appointment. If any more questions come up, I'll be back this afternoon."

FOUR

ON HER WAY OUT of the building, she found a group of paparazzi and reporters waiting in the lobby. The security guards had roped off an area to keep them away from the elevator banks.

"Say, miss," one of them called to her. "Do you work at the Bascomb-Rice law firm?"

"No," she said, averting her face as she dashed for the elevator that went down to the garage. Several others began to follow her on the other side of the rope barrier, yelling "Wait," and "Just a couple of questions." She kept going, ignoring them. Just then another elevator across the lobby opened, discharging three more people. The paparazzi reversed directions, rushing toward them.

Nicole made it to the garage and found her way downtown without incident. In the visitors' lobby of LAPD headquarters, she waited while one of the receptionists, a cop in uniform, picked up the phone and summoned Detective Miller.

Miller came down and escorted her to a small office with a table and three chairs. On the table was a small, white plastic crate containing several plastic bags.

"Have a seat," Miller said, gesturing to a chair. He still emanated the same negative attitude he'd shown the day before.

Nicole took a deep breath, determined not to let him get to her. She took off her cardigan, put it on the back of her chair and sat down while he settled across the table from her. "We're going to videotape this," he said. "That hunky-dory with you?"

"Fine," she said.

"Just explain what happened," he said. "Start with when you noticed Blair was missing and what you did to get in touch with him."

She began by explaining that she hadn't known Robert was absent from work until the previous morning when she'd returned from an out-of-town trip.

"Wait a minute," Miller said. "You didn't say you were away. Where were you?"

"I'd been in London for a week, visiting a friend."

"And you got back—when?"

"Yesterday morning around 8:30. I got a message from my assistant about Robert. So I went to the office, then to Robert's house to find out what had happened to him."

Miller frowned. "I suppose you have proof of your trip, boarding passes or something."

"Not with me, but I can get them. I'm sure it's easy enough for you to check."

He nodded in agreement and said, "Go on."

So she did, explaining everything she could remember up to the discovery of Robert's body. It was hard for her to believe all of this had happened only the day before.

"And you still maintain that you and Blair were not romantically involved," Miller said. "And you were never inside his house before yesterday. You didn't enter it at that time, except maybe a foot or two inside the front door."

"That's right."

"Then let me ask you this," he said. "Was he stalking you? Sexually harassing you?"

"Harassing me?" she said. "No. He wouldn't do that."

"OK," he said. "Then explain this." He took three plastic evidence bags from the white crate and placed them on the table in front of her. Each held a framed photograph of her. One showed her in a bikini, leaning back on her elbows and smiling at the camera. She remembered when it was taken—on the trip to Majorca with Reinhardt. They were on the beach behind the hotel, and a waiter had used her phone to take it. In the original, Reinhardt had been sitting next to her. But in this version, he'd been deleted. There was another photo of her at an office party, and a third of her alone. She couldn't figure out where this one was taken. She seemed to be standing on the sidewalk, waiting. Her head was turned so her face was in profile.

"Where did you get these?" she asked.

"They were in his bedroom," Miller said. "We also found these items." He cleared his throat, then held up three more evidence bags, one containing a sheer, blue, print nightgown. Two others each held a pair of frilly bikini panties. "Are these yours?"

Nicole was speechless. These were hers, all right, sexy lingerie she'd bought for her visits to Reinhardt. Several hundred dollars worth of filmy nothings. When she'd packed for her most recent trip, she'd been unable to find some of her lingerie. She'd wondered if she'd left them in Majorca, then remembered seeing them when she'd unpacked and tossed them into her laundry basket.

A realization hit. "He was stalking me," she breathed. Then louder. "He must have broken into my place and taken my clothes." She rushed on to explain. "In September, a few days after I got back from a trip to Majorca, my condo was broken into." She shook her head, as if trying to dislodge the memory. "I called the police, but they didn't come out because nothing seemed to be missing, and there was no damage to my place. I didn't think to check my underwear drawer."

"What made you think there was a break-in?"

"Things were out of place. The photos on my bookshelf had been rearranged. My bedspread was wrinkled, as if someone had been sitting there. And the toilet seat was up. That was the tip-off. That hasn't happened since I separated from my husband. Actually, it was the first thing I noticed." She remembered thinking at the time that whoever had been in her condo had marked his territory with that raised toilet seat.

"Look," she said, pointing to the photo on the beach. "My boyfriend was in the original of that photo, but he's been edited out. The second picture looks like it's from last year's office Christmas party. Robert must have taken it, although I don't remember seeing him there. He never went to office events outside of normal business hours. I've never seen that third photo before."

She was wondering how she could have been so stupid. The man she was feeling sorry for—poor lonely Robert Blair—was a nut job with some kind of weird fixation on her. "We found this stuff on the floor of his bedroom," Miller went on. "The whole house had been tossed:--every drawer, cupboard and closet pulled apart. You notice that?"

"I told you," she answered. "I didn't go into the house. I stepped into the entry hall, saw the body, and started to leave. Then I went back for another look. I touched the door and maybe the door frame, but I never went inside."

"Why did you go back?"

"Because I couldn't believe my eyes. Listen. I didn't give these pictures to Robert, and I certainly didn't give him those clothes or leave them at his house, if that's what you think."

"Tell me this: Did Blair have a computer in his house?"

"I guess so. He'd need one for work, especially outside cases. He wouldn't work on those at the office."

Blair looked up from his notebook. "I asked this before, but maybe you've remembered. Did he give you any hint about the kind of outside work he took on, who his clients were?"

She shook her head. "I have no idea. He never talked about it."

"You didn't give any of your things to Blair," he said. "And you never noticed anything inappropriate in his behavior or indication of a romantic interest. Is that what you're saying?"

"Right," she said. "Oh. He did ask me out to dinner once, when I was going through my divorce. I told him I was involved with someone else."

"How did he react?"

"I don't remember much of a reaction," she said. "He never brought it up again. He was always very formal, courteous, never even remotely flirtatious. That's what makes this so strange."

"What about his life insurance policy? Did you know he'd made you the beneficiary?"

"No."

"And you say you don't know anyone who'd want this guy dead." For the first time, he gave her a smile. It wasn't a pleasant one. "OK," he went on. "I think that's enough for now. But I have to ask you: Did you kill Robert Blair or arrange to have someone else kill him?"

"No." Nicole felt a little sick.

"Do you own a gun?"

"No."

"And you weren't involved with him except as a coworker."

"Absolutely not. We knew each other at the office and that was it," she said. "Sometimes we had lunch together if we were working on a case."

"What did you talk about?"

"Office gossip, shoptalk. Nothing personal."

"Look-it," he said, "maybe this guy was stalking you while keeping his interest in you a secret. It usually doesn't work that way, but—just for the sake of argument—let's say that was the case. I still think there's something you're not telling me."

He was quiet a moment, then added, "I'm going to be straight with you. If I think that, then it's likely that the person or people who killed your friend will come to the same conclusion. His place was searched from top to bottom, and from the state of it, I don't think they found what they were looking for. It would be in your best interest to tell me everything you know before they decide to come after you."

"But I don't know anything," she insisted. Then, after a moment, she added, "Are you saying I need protection?"

"Who knows?" he said, as if it were no concern of his. "But if I were you, I'd be careful. And if you do decide you have something to share with me, give me a call." He handed her his card.

She understood what he was doing—trying to scare her into telling him whatever he imagined she knew about Robert's murder. "OK, then," she said. She got up, put her cardigan back on, and headed back to Century City.

To save time, Nicole had planned to leave her car with the valet in front of the firm's office building. But, as soon as she turned the corner onto Avenue of the Stars, she saw the chaotic scene on the street—the handful of media representatives had swelled to a crowd with the addition of five TV vans. Tightly packed into the valet lane were several dozen men and women, most of them holding cameras with microphones attached. Five burly security guards stood in front of the double doors centered in the curved glass facade of the highrise. The guards were standing shoulder-to-shoulder to keep the unwelcome visitors out. She drove around the block to the building's self-park garage entrance. After parking, she took the stairs, which brought her to the rear of the elevator lobby, out of sight of the herd.

Once in her office, she put her things down and went to get some coffee. Three of the attorneys' secretaries were in the break room. Their conversation stopped as soon as she walked in. She greeted them curtly, then poured a cup of coffee, taking her time adding cream and sugar. Meanwhile the trio stood and watched. After she left, the hum of voices resumed. She couldn't make out what they were saying.

She managed to settle down to work. There were performance reviews to be filled out, a stack of invoices to approve. God, this was boring, she thought. She had to find something else. She'd never planned to make this her life's work. It was just a stopgap after college, a favor to a friend whose job this used to be. Her friend needed back surgery, but after she'd recovered, she'd decided she wanted nothing more to do with Bascomb, Rice, Smith & Di Angelo.

At the time, Nicole was newly engaged, and this job was a comfortable perch when she was busy planning her wedding. Then she and Brad bought the condo and were fixing it up. The people at the law firm were pleasant and seemed to appreciate her efforts, and the money was good.

It wasn't until the last year or two that Nicole had become fed up with the job. She'd come to the realization that the work done by the firm was the antithesis of what she believed in. Sure, they handled domestic issues in which each side probably deserved what the other was handing out. But the firm's main income came from large corporations, protecting them from lawsuits. She didn't see anything wrong with that. Some were nuisance suits from those looking for a payout from deep-pocket corporate America, and some of the litigants were simply giant corporations trying to get an edge on one another.

But much of the firm's work was done on behalf of big companies being sued by people who appeared to have genuine grievances: cars that malfunctioned and crashed, killing or maiming people; processed meat or vegetables containing bacteria that made people sick; class action suits for polluted water that, litigants claimed, caused genetic damage. Nicole wasn't privy to the legal documents in these cases; her job had little to do with casework. But, from what she gathered from the news and from Robert, a good number of the people who sued giant corporations had solid proof of their claims. Up against unlimited money for lawyers and court costs, these little guys usually lost. They simply could not afford to keep up the fight as long as the corporations could.

She also objected to some of the smaller cases the firm undertook. These were often scrapes with authorities by the sons, daughters, and others connected with Bascomb, Rice, Smith & Di Angelo's major clients. Minor offenses, like cheating on college exams and drug use on campus, for example, were often mitigated with big donations to schools that had threatened to throw the offenders out. For those who'd been arrested for offenses like rape or drug dealing, Rick Sargosian and a couple of others with criminal law experience often could work out a deal for community service or get them off completely by vilifying the victim.

She knew that the accused had the right to a defense. But in too many cases, Bascomb, Rice, Smith & Di Angelo were simply on the wrong side, the side of the moneyed class, the one percenters who just about always won.

At this point, with condo payments to make on her own, she couldn't afford to leave. Not unless she lined up something that paid as well. No good-works nonprofit was going to match her current salary. She'd once hoped to become a writer or an editor; of course, those jobs, at least the ones that paid, had all but disappeared. More recently, she'd thought about getting her P.I. license and assisting Robert with his investigations. Now that Robert was gone, they were in the process of bringing in an outside firm to do his work on a temporary basis. Maybe, she thought, when all this died down…

She told herself she was too tired, too stressed out to think about the future. So she buckled down, trying to focus on her work.

She'd told Breanna to hold her calls unless it was an emergency, or Reinhardt, or her sister, or someone with legitimate business. In the first ten minutes, however, two reporters managed to get through, one posing as her doctor's receptionist, the other as her stockbroker. "Stockbroker!" she told him. "I don't even have a stockbroker." After that, she had Breanna double-check caller ID, if there was one. Then, if the caller was legitimate, Breanna was to get a name and number for a callback.

The phone rang around 3:30 p.m. It was interoffice, and the caller ID display said "Sargosian." "So how's it going?" he began.

"Not that great," she said.

"I can imagine," he said. "That mob outside would be enough to wreck anyone's day. How about dinner? I know a little place—"

"Sorry, Rick, I'm just not up to it. And besides, I'm in a serious relationship. I want you to understand that."

"Yeah, I know. The one who sends you all those flowers. Well, where is this guy anyway?" he said. "You're going through hell, and he's nowhere to be found."

"He's in England." Several heads turned to look at her through the glass wall of her office, and she realized she'd raised her voice. She swiveled her chair around, so she had her back to them. Then she added more softly, "He lives in England."

"Well, if I were him…" He left it unsaid. "It's just dinner. I promise. It would cheer you up."

"I don't think so," she said. "But I do have a question."

"Yes?"

"The police are acting like they think I might have had something to do with Robert's murder. Or that I know something about it, which I don't. They found framed photos of me and some of my clothes in Robert's place. The only way he could have gotten this stuff was by breaking into my place. I told Detective Miller that, but he doesn't seem to believe me. He seems to think I was sleeping with Robert. I need an attorney. I know the rule: It would have to be someone outside the firm. Do you have any recommendations? The police aren't threatening to charge me at this point, but I do need advice."

"Well, sure," he said. "I can recommend a defense attorney, but you won't be able to reach anyone until tomorrow. Look," he went on, "I started out as a deputy D.A. Six years on the job. I can answer your questions. You don't want to sit home tonight worrying about this. How about we talk about it over dinner?"

Nicole was quiet for a long moment, then said, "OK, but please understand: This is not a date." She paused, but he didn't say anything. "Just tell me where the restaurant is," she went on, "and I'll meet you there. It'll make getting home easier."

"Sure," he said, naming a restaurant less than a half mile from their office, a half mile that no one in L.A. would dream of walking.

She had the feeling he was trying to maneuver her into his car for the ride. The restaurant was so close, she imagined him thinking, what problem could she have with that? But she did have one. "Fine," she said, "Six-thirty. See you there."

FIVE

RICK SARGOSIAN WAS MORE ATTENTIVE at dinner than he'd been at lunch the day before. Clearly, he'd taken a fancy to Nicole, and she didn't like it.

When she told him about Robert's fixation, he said, "You're a beautiful woman. This can't be the first time you've gotten unwanted attention."

"No," she admitted, "it's not. But I've never had anyone stalk me. I thought Robert was a nice guy. But he wasn't—he was some kind of perv. This whole business is creeping me out."

Nicole wasn't a great beauty, she knew. She'd always thought of herself as "pretty enough." And she was good at making the best of what she had—highlights to brighten up her mouse-brown hair, time and care with her makeup, clothes that made the most of her figure.

But there was more going on—pheromones or something. Because, even when there was a truly gorgeous woman around, men were drawn to her. In high school, she'd had plenty of dates.

But she'd also been pursued by boys whose attention she didn't want, and she had a hard time discouraging them.

And there was the matter of her dimples. The slightest smile made them appear, and they had an odd effect on people. Those dimples made people jump to the conclusion that she was sweet, that she liked them. Would-be boyfriends seemed to interpret her smile as an indication that she thought they were special, even when nothing could be farther from the truth.

Her sister had teased her about being a nerd magnet. And it was true. Compounding the problem was her reluctance to hurt anyone's feelings. For a while, she tried different strategies: agreeing to meet for a Coke after school, then failing to show up. Next time, the boy would appear at the door of her classroom so she couldn't escape. Once she'd accepted the offer of a ride home from a would-be suitor, then invited five of her friends along, directing him to her house first so she wouldn't have to be alone with him. That made the boy a little angry, but not to the point that he stopped calling and asking for a date. Finally, she figured out that it was easier on everyone to simply say she already had a boyfriend, even if it wasn't true. This usually worked.

She'd told Rick she had a boyfriend, and he didn't care. He'd edged around the booth so he was sitting close to her. She scooted over to put some distance between them. He winked at her, as if her moving away was a little game they were playing. That wink really annoyed her. "Rick," she said. "I have two words for you to consider: sexual harassment. I thought I made it clear that I'm involved with someone else and am not interested in you except as a coworker and a friend. I accepted your dinner invitation because I need advice."

"Whatever you say, Nicole," he said. "We aim to please." He winked again. "OK, here's my advice. Don't discuss this with anyone. Above all, do not talk to the police or the press." He said this last sentence slowly, as if he were talking to a child. "Once you make a statement to a reporter, you lose control. There's no telling how he will use it or twist it around to get himself a more sensational story. Talk to no one. That's the most important rule here. Your attorney will do all the talking for you. Meanwhile, I'll call over to the D.A.'s office—I still know some people there—and see what I can find out. This Miller guy is just probably making noise to scare you because he thinks he can squeeze information out of you."

As she sipped her chardonnay, she began to feel less anxious. Sargosian had also relaxed, seeming to realize he was getting nowhere being aggressive, and the rest of the meal passed fairly pleasantly. They had just enough common interests to keep the conversation afloat for as long as it took to eat—movies, TV, and, of course, office gossip.

Afterward, when they retrieved their respective cars, Sargosian insisted on following her home, "Just in case." She took this to mean in case the press was waiting at her place. After she got in her car, she wondered if he might be thinking she'd change her mind and invite him in.

She slowed as she turned the corner onto her street. In front of her building was a contingent of reporters and cameramen as well as a couple of TV news vans. Several vehicles were blocking the entrance to her underground parking. She drove past them, Sargosian close behind, and turned into the alley, heading for the building's guest parking. But that was no good either. Four men with cameras were stationed there. My god, she thought, they were acting like it was the biggest story in Los Angeles, and how could it be? She drove a block or two away and pulled out her phone to call Stephanie and ask if she could spend the night again. In her rearview mirror she watched Sargosian get out of his car. He walked up to her window, and she lowered it.

"Look, you can spend the night at my place. I'm not far from here. I have a perfectly nice guest room, and I promise not to bother you."

"Thanks, but I'm calling my sister. I'll stay there."

He raised his hand, as if taking a pledge. "The guest room has a lock on the door. Scout's honor." She laughed, and he smiled, too, as if he'd won his point.

"I'll see you tomorrow," she said. She closed her window and turned back to her phone. Sargosian stood there a moment. Then, somewhat deflated, he trudged back to his car. She almost felt sorry for him––almost. She understood there was one sure way to get rid of him: All she had to do was give him what he wanted. Then she'd be the old cow—as the theory went. He'd immediately lose interest and start looking for a new cow.

It occurred to her that he was like the paparazzi, only they were more constant. As long as the story had some life in it, she could count on them to be there.

§

Nicole awoke in Stephanie's office and reached for her iPad. Her only thought was to check tabloid websites, starting with XHN. This morning she was shocked to see that not only was the story still prominently displayed at the top of the page, but her picture was there, too. The photo—the one from the Christmas party that Robert had framed—was displayed next to another shot of Robert in uniform when he was about her age. The headline shouted, "Murdered Ex-Cop's Girl Won't Talk." The National Enquirer site had a similar story with the addition of a short video from the day before that showed her rushing for the elevator with several reporters chasing her, shouting questions. The way she had her head averted made her look like someone about to be arrested and trying to avoid publicity. All she lacked was a jacket pulled up to hide her face. There was a small item next to this story about a big drug deal that had gone bad because of an LAPD crackdown the previous week. *The Enquirer* said the police refused to speculate whether this development was related to the "hero ex-cop's murder."

The Times had much the same story, without the drug crackdown angle. Instead, it included the fact that Robert had recently designated Nicole the beneficiary of his life insurance policy. It also mentioned that Robert's house had been searched and trashed, presumably by the murderer.

The last paragraph read, "An inside source, who asked not to be named because he isn't authorized to speak for the LAPD, said a cooperative witness has come forward. 'We have hope this person will be able to help with the investigation.'" Nicole had a hunch this was a reference to her and that Detective Miller was the source. He'd leaked the information to put pressure on her.

There was also a profile of Robert, which Nicole read with great interest. An enterprising reporter had located a couple of Robert's ex-colleagues on the vice squad. One of them said he wasn't a team player and tended to bend the rules. He described a case where Robert had ignored his partner's advice to get a search warrant and had instead picked a lock. He'd found evidence that had led to the arrest of a major drug dealer. But the dealer had been freed, the cop said, because of that missing search warrant.

Another retired colleague said, "I don't like speaking ill of the dead, but Blair was a loner, and he wasn't well liked. It was his way or the highway. That was his M.O. If you got assigned to a case with him, and you didn't like his methods, he'd disappear on you and do what he wanted. But you've got to hand it to him: He was one smart dude, and he got the job done."

Nicole left for work wearing the same outfit she'd worn the day before, now slightly rumpled: a short black skirt, a pale blue silk blouse, a cream-colored cardigan, and black heels. She was a little worried about her wardrobe situation. With the media tracking her, she dreaded the idea of going home to get more clothes. She couldn't borrow anything from Stephanie because she was almost six inches taller than Nicole and two sizes larger. Image was important at work, and she couldn't keep showing up in the same clothes.

When she arrived at the office, she encountered an even larger media presence than the day before. This time several of the paparazzi had figured out where the garage entrance was, and she found them waiting there. She drove past the building, heading west to the underground parking of Century City's shopping mall. Once there, she called Breanna. "I'm parked in Gelson's lot," she said. "Can you pick me up? I can't deal with that mob in front of our building." About ten minutes later, Breanna appeared in the corner of the lot reserved for the upscale market's customers, the legions of affluent foodies who live in West L.A. and Beverly Hills. Nicole got in the back of Breanna's Honda and scrunched down to hide from the cameras when they drove into the law firm's garage.

On her desk was a note with "From the desk of Rick Sargosian" at the top. Under the heading, he'd scrawled, *Give me a call as soon as you get in.*

"I've found a defense attorney for you," Sargosian said when she called him. "Sue Price. She's a partner at Lombard, Price & Thompson. They're a couple of blocks east of the county museum. She's really good. I talked to her, and she's expecting your call." He gave her the attorney's number.

She thanked him and was about to hang up, when he said, "Don't worry about the cost. This legal problem is directly related to your work; you found Blair's body while carrying out your duties as office manager. Besides, he was sexually harassing you, and that relates to the workplace as well."

Nicole stopped listening for a moment. She hadn't even thought of what a defense lawyer was going to cost, but she was grateful that this, at least, was one thing she wouldn't have to think about.

"So how about it?" Sargosian was saying.

"Sorry?"

"I asked if you'd like to have lunch?" he said. "You know— just friends."

She sighed. She didn't need this right now. Yes, he'd been really nice to find her an attorney, and no, she still wasn't interested. "Sorry, Rick. I'm busy."

"What about—"

"Let's talk later, OK? I want to see if I can get an appointment with this lawyer today. Thanks again for your help, Rick. I can't tell you how much I appreciate it." She hung up before he could say any more. She immediately called the defense attorney's number and spoke to a receptionist, who said Ms. Price would be available at 4:00 that afternoon. Nicole alerted Breanna that she was going to need a ride back to her car at 3:15.

After they hung up, Nicole had an idea. What if she talked to the head of the XHN, the biggest tabloid in L.A., and asked him to call off the dogs? He was an attorney, and from what she'd heard, a perfectly decent human being. She looked up the tabloid's "hot tip" phone number and put in a call. After a single ring, a woman said, "XHN tip line."

"This is Nicole Graves," she said. "I wonder if I could talk to David Griffen."

"May I say what this is about?"

"Just say I'm the lead story on XHN today, and I want to talk to him."

There were a few clicks on the line. Then a man's voice said, "This is David. Is this really Nicole Graves?"

"It is."

"What can I do for you?"

"Actually, I need some advice," she said. "The paparazzi are making my life impossible. They're stationed outside my workplace and outside my home. I've had to move somewhere else, and it's an ordeal getting to work every day. I know you're just one news agency, but you're the most influential in L.A. I'm wondering if you can tell me what to do to get them to ease up."

He was silent a moment before he answered. "I'm really sorry," he said. "I can ask the shooters"—she noticed he didn't call them paparazzi or even photographers—"not to be so aggressive. But this is a very competitive business, and it attracts a certain kind of person. They probably won't listen. Again, I apologize. I know how hellish it is to get caught up in a sensational story. But I can assure you this is only temporary. Once the next big story hits, you'll be old news, and they'll leave you alone. Meanwhile, can I talk you into giving us an interview? We'll let you look at it before it runs."

"I can't," she said. "My lawyer has advised me not to discuss the case with anyone."

"I understand," he said. "But if you change your mind, would you give me a call?"

She sighed. "Sure. Thanks for taking the time to talk to me."

After they hung up, she buried herself in work. This morning five new investigation requests had been sent to her. One of them was for "babysitting" a witness. This involved looking after someone, usually very young or old, who had limited life skills and needed help with basic needs like finding a place to stay, stocking food in the refrigerator, or buying clothes appropriate for the courtroom. Sometimes the individual needed medical attention or social services—the investigator was responsible for handling these things as well—while waiting to appear in court as a litigant, a witness, or the accused. In other instances, a person needed to be kept out of trouble until the current case was concluded.

Nicole, herself, had picked up this duty several times, taking care of young women. Once she'd been sent to France to look after a client's underage daughter who'd somehow managed to end up in Paris without a passport. How the girl had pulled this off was beyond Nicole's imagination. She seemed barely able to take care of herself. The job, which at first sounded glamorous, turned into a headache because the girl was spoiled, seemed to truly hate her parents, and refused to leave Paris. After straightening out the passport problem, Nicole managed to persuade the girl to return home. She'd sulked on the long flight. But they were flying first class, so Nicole read a book and enjoyed the ride. As for the women in the other cases, who generally did not have wealthy parents waiting for them, she wondered what became of them when the trial or hearing was over and they were cut loose to fend for themselves.

Two of the new requests involved tracking down the assets of individuals or corporations who were being sued—tracing money through shell corporations—to make sure the suit was brought against someone who could actually pay if the case was settled favorably. Another request was to locate a witness who'd disappeared after agreeing to testify.

Only one case was earmarked for "in-house" handling. This was a minor investigation that Di Angelo had requested. The case involved a corporate CEO's son who was accused of raping a young woman in his frat house at USC, where they both were students. Nicole was supposed to look up the victim to see if there was anything in her past the firm could use to discredit her.

She started by looking on Instagram and Facebook in case the girl had posted slutty pictures of herself, or anything that might make her look bad. Nicole found nothing of the sort. The girl's Facebook page, which she hadn't bothered to make private, showed a long list of her friends. Nicole made note of those identified as "close friends." She'd contact some of them and see what she could find out. God, she thought, how she hated this kind of research, looking for ways to smear the victim of a violent crime.

She looked at her watch. It was almost noon. She emailed the four other requests to the outside P.I. agency.

Nicole got up from her desk and looked out the window. While the crowd in front had thinned a bit, it was still big enough to keep her from going out for lunch. She was their prisoner. She called the building's coffee shop and asked them to deliver a tuna sandwich and a Coke.

A few minutes later, someone knocked on her open office door. She turned, expecting her lunch. Instead, it was a young man—clean-cut and baby-faced—holding a huge vase of red roses. There must have been four dozen buds, just beginning to open.

Nicole stood up and directed him to her credenza, where Reinhardt's flowers had been consigned.

"What's the big occasion?" the man said. "Should I be wishing you a happy birthday?"

"It's not my birthday," she said, reaching for her purse to get out a tip.

"Say," the man said, as if just recognizing her. "Aren't you the one whose picture was in the paper today?"

"No," she said. "You have me confused with somebody else." She handed him a five-dollar bill.

He took it, and then said, "Actually, I'm not the delivery boy. I gave him something to let me bring the flowers up. I'm with Fox News. The way the media is portraying you is making you look bad. People need to hear your side of the story. All you have to do is talk to an interviewer for a half hour. You can let the public see who you are and tell them what really happened."

"I have nothing to say. Please leave," she said.

"Listen. You're missing a great opportunity. If you'll grant Fox an exclusive interview, we'll show it to you before it's aired, so you can make sure there's nothing to embarrass you. No other news outlet would do that."

"I'm not granting any interviews," she said. Then, louder, "You have to go, or I'm calling security."

He still didn't move. "This is being tried in the court of public opinion," he went on. "All people know about you is what they're seeing in the tabloids."

Nicole glanced through the glass partition that separated her from the rest of the office. The place was deserted. She picked up her phone, dialed 09, which got her the desk in the lobby, and said, "Let me speak to security."

At that, the man turned and hurried out of the office, still clutching her five-dollar bill.

She looked at the flowers, then pulled out the card and opened it. The flowers were from Sargosian. The card read:

Great time last night. I'd like to see you again outside the office, but I don't want to push. Let me know when you're ready to get together. Rick

Nicole tossed the card in the wastepaper basket. A few minutes later, her sandwich arrived. While she ate, she turned back to her work.

§

Sue Price's law firm was in a much more modest suite than the one where Nicole worked. It was cozy rather than elegant, and Nicole imagined it would be more pleasant to spend her time here than in the sterile glass highrise in Century City. She had to wait only a few minutes before she was shown into her new lawyer's office. Sue Price was tall and strikingly beautiful, with a creamy complexion and a cloud of red curly hair. She smiled at Nicole, introduced herself as "Sue," and almost cooed with sympathy. "You poor thing," she said. "Rick told me what you've been going through. It's a nightmare when an innocent bystander gets swept up in one of these high profile cases and the media goes crazy. I'll ask Margo to bring us some coffee and then we'll sit down and figure out how we're going to handle this."

While Sue was ordering the coffee, Nicole looked around. The office had a corner fireplace, and the shelves around it held a figurine collection instead of law books. The figures ranged from pricy Lladro china to pipe-cleaner creations, all of cats, some cute and cuddly, some comical.

Sue's secretary walked in, carrying a tray with a white china coffee pot, cups, and saucers. There was also a dish of chocolate cookies. She set the tray on the coffee table and left, quietly closing the door. Sue sat in a chair next to the table and motioned for Nicole to sit in the chair on the other side. After Sue poured her a cup of coffee, Nicole helped herself to a cookie.

At the lawyer's invitation, Nicole recounted everything she could remember about Robert's death and even shared the heartbreak of her lonely week in London and her concerns about her missing lover.

"Well, one good thing," Sue said. "I just spoke to Rick, and he says the D.A. doesn't have a case at this point. No murder weapon, no evidence, no leads. That doesn't mean they won't try to make a case—the forensics haven't come in yet. But they're not going to find your DNA if you've never been inside Mr. Blair's house."

"I haven't, but they did find my underwear and a nightgown in his bedroom," Nicole said. "At some point Robert seems to have broken into my apartment and stolen my lingerie. The detective showed it to me. Robert also had some framed photos of me." She explained that Robert had removed Reinhardt from the one at the beach.

Sue was quiet for several moments, seeming to consider what she was going to say. "Now I'm going to give you some marching orders," she finally said, "and I want you to listen very carefully. Whatever you do, do not speak to the media or the police. About the media, the only words to come out of your mouth when a reporter asks anything—even 'How are you?'—is this: 'I'm referring all questions to my attorney, Sue Price, at Lombard, Price & Thompson.' And when they call me, I will tell them, 'We have no comment other than to say Nicole Graves had no involvement in this crime.'

"I want you to go about your business as you normally would. Do not hide from the press. Remember, you've done nothing wrong. Sure, if there's a back door and you can easily avoid them, do so. If not, just hold up your head and—this is important— avoid being defensive, no matter how aggressive they are.

"Besides, once you tell them you have an attorney and give them my name, they'll be calling me. Just present your best self. Try to smile. Show those pretty dimples and act like you're really sorry you aren't allowed to talk to them. Let them see what a nice person you are. Keep in mind that it won't be long before the next big story comes along, and they'll forget about you."

"What if the District Attorney decides to charge me with Robert's murder?" Nicole said. "What if they think I hired someone to kill him for his life insurance?" she paused. "Forty-thousand dollars—wouldn't a hired killer charge that to do the job?"

"I doubt they'll put together such a case," Sue said. "But in that unlikely event, we'll see what evidence they have and take it from there. You don't own a gun, do you?"

"No." Nicole thought of her sister, Stephanie, who did, in fact, own a gun. As a female, living alone, she had a permit, but never took the weapon out of her apartment. Nicole disapproved of the gun, warning Stephanie that it was more likely to be used against her than to protect her. But her sister said all her single friends owned guns, and it made her feel safe.

"Good," Sue was saying. "Now, if Detective Miller calls and wants to talk to you, refer him to me. Meanwhile, I'll let him know I've advised you not to make any more statements, and that should be the end of it. If he calls you and tries to convince you that you're not a suspect, and he only wants to meet with you as a possible witness or to help with his investigation, do not believe him. That's an old trick. The police lie, you know, to get people to talk. Don't fall into that trap. Tell him to talk to me.

"There are only two rules the police go by: Either they have a case and they arrest you, or they don't, and they won't. If they have evidence that convinces them you're guilty, nothing you can say will change that. On the other hand, if you're innocent, and you change your story, even in some minor, inadvertent way, they can use that against you. You can't imagine how difficult it is to tell the same story twice in exactly the same way. It's so easy to trip yourself up. You have nothing to gain by telling them any more than you already have."

Sue stood up. "I think that's all for today. If you have questions or anything comes up, I'm giving you my cell phone number, so you can reach me any time, day or night." She jotted the number on the back of her card and handed it to Nicole. "Don't hesitate to call. Now be aware of what's going on around you. You may be followed, probably by paparazzi, or maybe the police. I'd avoid going out much, except to work, mainly because of the media. It isn't pleasant having them pop up everywhere you go. Stick close to people you know and trust. Have you somewhere to stay other than your own place?"

"I can stay with my sister."

"Perfect. Best keep away from home for a bit. You'll just be pestered by reporters. And one more thing. About Rick—he has a good heart but usually there's an ulterior motive. When it comes to the ladies, he's a bit of a bad boy."

"You didn't have to warn me," Nicole said. "He's not too subtle about it."

They both smiled, and Sue surprised Nicole by reaching out and hugging her. "Take care," Sue said. "You're such a sweet little thing, I don't want to see you crushed by this."

"You'd be surprised," Nicole said. "People who make the mistake of thinking I'm sweet find I'm not sweet at all. When it comes down to it, I can really kick ass."

Sue laughed, revealing one imperfection: a slightly crooked incisor. "Glad to hear it."

Nicole arrived back at the office around 5:15. The media pack had shrunk to a mere two dozen or so and a single TV van. She drove past the paparazzi into the valet lane that ran close to the building, gave the key to the valet, and stepped out. They all rushed at her with their cameras. She looked around at them, trying to keep from scowling. It wasn't easy. She was being pushed and jabbed by elbows and camera gear; the reporters clustered around her, sticking their microphones in her face. "How do you feel about the murder of Robert Blair?" one said, while another asked her to describe the murder scene. "Did you kill him?" a sweet looking young woman said, without appearing the least bit embarrassed.

Nicole managed what she hoped was an apologetic smile and referred them to Sue in the words she'd been told to repeat. Then she walked through them—forcing them to step aside—past the guards and into the building with her head held high. It made her feel empowered, and for a brief moment, she was almost enjoying herself. She thought of turning and waving goodbye. But, no, that would be going too far.

When she got back to her office, Breanna handed her a telephone-call slip. It was from an attorney named Daniel Freeman. "I looked him up on the web and the phone number listed there is the one he left," Breanna said. "He looks legit."

Nicole went into her office, closed the door, and made the call.

"Hello, Ms. Graves," the voice on the line said. "I'm Robert Blair's attorney, and I need to speak with you as soon as possible."

"About what?"

"His estate and his final instructions," Freeman said. Then, as if in response to her silent confusion, "About disposal of his body."

Her stomach knotted. "What has this got to do with me?"

"Let's make an appointment and I'll explain. We can't discuss it on the phone. There's been too much publicity, and you never know who might be listening."

"OK," she said. "Where are you located, and what's a good time?"

"I'm in Studio City," he said, "I have time at 11:00 tomorrow morning, if that's convenient."

She said it was, and he gave her his address. After she hung up, she began to feel uneasy. What if this Freeman person wasn't who he said he was? But if he was, and he was handling Robert's estate, what did that mean? Robert had left her his life insurance. What if he'd also left her something in his will? The possibility made her feel queasy, but she had to find out. She'd drive to Studio City, scope out the scene, and decide what to do.

62

Six

THURSDAY MORNING WAS PRETTY MUCH the same as the previous day. Nicole got to work at 8:00, an hour early, only to encounter the same crowd of paparazzi and TV crews as the day before. She left her car with the valet and fought her way through the pack, who were again assailing her with questions. She told them to call her lawyer. The building's entrance was fortified with security guards, who made her show her pass before they'd let her in. She cringed at the idea of facing the same mob in a couple of hours when she left to meet with Robert's lawyer. But there was nothing to be done about it.

Before settling down to work, she couldn't resist checking XHN. Sure enough, there was a new story. This one went into her divorce from Brad and the fact that he'd spent time in prison in the UK for money laundering. Oh, no, she thought. This is really bad. She went to the other tabloid and newspaper sites, including the *Los Angeles Times*. They all had the story. In fact, the Robert Blair murder had gone viral, and every news outlet she checked seemed to have at least a few paragraphs about it.

She looked at her email and was upset to find it filled with messages from friends, acquaintances, and people she didn't even know. Her friends offered sympathy and support, while the rest seemed motivated by morbid curiosity. What had happened? What had she seen? Was she a suspect? It occurred to her that some of these messages might be from reporters who'd found her email address on the law firm's website.

When Nicole looked at her watch, she was surprised to see it was time to leave for the meeting with Robert's lawyer. She'd blown most of the morning and accomplished nothing. She grabbed her purse, then retraced her route back down the elevator to the valet station. She handed her parking ticket to the valet, then slipped back into the building to wait. Security guards kept the paparazzi at bay. When her car was brought around, she came out again and shoved her way through the forest of microphones and barrage of questions. The media was especially aggressive today, demanding to know more about her ex-husband and his conviction. They pressed against her as she tried to open the car door, and she had to squeeze her way in. She started the car, then remembered Sue's instructions. Lowering her window, she told the reporters to call her attorney.

As soon as she pulled out of the valet lane, a contingent of paparazzi on motorcycles was close behind. She drove quickly, weaving through side streets, but she couldn't shake them. On Sunset Boulevard, she planned to turn left onto Beverly Drive, which would take her into the San Fernando Valley via Coldwater Canyon. But she knew she couldn't arrive at Freeman's office with these jerks on her trail. She slowed, signaling for a left, allowing the paparazzi to pull up beside her in the outside lane. When the light turned green, instead of turning onto Beverly Drive, she made a 120-degree left turn into the driveway of the sprawling grounds of the Beverly Hills Hotel. Meanwhile, her pursuers flew past her up Beverly Drive. Traffic was so thick at the intersection that it was impossible for even the most audacious of them to make a U-turn. She passed the giant pink hotel, then exited the grounds and wove her way westward through back streets. When she reached Beverly Glen, one of the few streets that lead into the San Fernando Valley, she turned north, emerging several miles west of her destination. She was running late, but at least she'd lost the paparazzi.

Freeman's office was on Ventura Boulevard, as were countless restaurants, shops, medical buildings, supermarkets, and other businesses that line the eighteen-mile main corridor of the valley. She realized that the attorney's office was not far from a street that wound its way up to Robert's house on the hill.

She parked across the street from the lawyer's address and walked a long block to the traffic light to cross the busy thoroughfare. A man was waiting at the corner, leaning against the post that held the button to activate the "walk" signal.

"Excuse me," she said. "I just want to push the button."

He moved away from it, then smiled at her and said, "You know, I *did* push it." She pressed the button, taking note of his looks.

He was about her age, tall and lanky with sandy hair and a light sprinkling of freckles. He had a square jaw, a generous mouth, and an interesting angle to his face that went from chin to cheekbones. His blue eyes were fringed with long, fair eyelashes.

She smiled at him. "Well, maybe you don't have the golden touch," she said. Already, the light on Ventura Boulevard was starting to blink yellow, warning traffic to slow down.

She looked back at the man. "You see?" she said.

"Thanks," he said. "If you hadn't come along, I'd probably be standing here all day."

She smiled at him again. Stop doing that, she told herself. Didn't she have enough problems without picking up strange men on street corners? What was she thinking?

The pedestrian light was now green. She looked both ways before stepping off the curb. At that moment a dark gray SUV appeared on the adjacent side street. It revved its engine, sped up, and careened around the corner, as if aiming directly at her. The guy she'd been talking to grabbed her shoulders and pulled her back onto the sidewalk. "My god!" They both said it at the same time. Nicole's heart was thumping in her throat.

"Th-thank you," she managed to say. "I think you just saved my life."

He shook his head. "I can't believe he did that. It looked like he really meant to hit you."

She watched as the car disappeared in the distance, too far away for her to read the license plate. She remembered the detective's warning that Robert's killer might decide she knew something and come after her. On the other hand, she'd had similar close calls when she was crossing a street. This was L.A., where no one walked, and cars were oblivious to anyone foolish enough to attempt to cross a street.

"Are you OK?" the man said. "You've gone all white. Maybe you should sit down." He gestured toward a bench at the nearby bus stop.

"I'm fine," she said.

"Josh Mulhern," he said, putting out a hand to shake hers. "You work around here?"

"No. I have an appointment." She gestured across the street and glanced at her watch. "And I'm late." The pedestrian light had turned red again, and she pressed the button, impatiently hitting it twice.

"How about getting together a little later for lunch?"

"I can't," she said. "I work in Century City. I have to get back."

"What about a drink after work?" he persisted.

She almost agreed, then remembered. She was planning to ask Stephanie to brave the paparazzi and drive her to her place this evening to get her clothes.

"I'm sorry, but there's something I have to do tonight," she said.

He looked disappointed, and she felt she was being ungracious, especially after he'd pulled her out of the path of that car.

"Look," she said, taking her card out of her purse and noting her cell number on the back. "Here's how to reach me. Give me a call, and maybe I can meet you later in the evening."

He beamed at her, taking the card.

He seemed about to say something else, but just then the pedestrian light turned green again. She gave him a wave and took a careful look around before she hurried across the street. When she reached the other side, she looked back at him. He was still standing on the corner and seemed to be studying her card. She wondered if he'd recognized her name from the news and was deciding further contact was a bad idea. Whatever, she thought. Yet she did find herself thinking she wouldn't mind meeting him for a drink if he did call.

The address the lawyer had given her was in a series of small, individual bungalows, each with its own entrance, like an old fashioned motor court. Low rent, she thought. From the sign on his door, DANIEL FREEMAN, ATTORNEY-AT-LAW, he appeared to be a solo practitioner.

She could understand why Robert wouldn't use any of the attorneys he worked with. He was too secretive for that. And if—god forbid—Nicole was mentioned in his will, he wouldn't want the firm to know.

She opened the door to the office and peeked in. There was a small reception room and a secretary sitting at a desk. An elderly woman reading a magazine was the only occupant of the small waiting area. Nicole stepped inside.

She introduced herself to the secretary, who asked her to take a seat. The other woman went in next but didn't stay long, and Nicole was soon shown into Freeman's office. Middle-aged, with thinning, dark hair and rimless glasses, he was almost nondescript, the kind of man who could easily fade into a crowd. She was sure she'd never met him before, but something about him was familiar. His desk was clear, except for a computer and a single folder. The office had a tidy, settled look.

His first words were, "I'm sorry for your loss."

She stared at him, digesting this. He was talking about Robert. He, too, thought she was Robert's girlfriend.

"Thank you," she said, deciding not to bother explaining.

"Mr. Blair was a new client," Freeman said. "He came in on—," he paused to look in the folder on his desk, "October 14, about five weeks ago, and said he wanted to establish a trust. He said he'd be turning sixty on his next birthday and thought it was time. Then he came back to sign the papers, about a week later. He wanted to keep the matter private and paid in cash."

She didn't say anything, just waited.

He cleared his throat, removed his glasses, polished them, and put them back on. "Now, for the business at hand," he finally said. "You are the sole beneficiary of Mr. Blair's estate." Freeman looked back in the file. "That means he left you his house, worth an estimated $3.9 million; a checking account worth roughly $30,000; a small cabin in the Owens Valley worth an estimated $80,000; and an investment account of $380,000.

"The total value is below the threshold for estate tax, and Mr. Blair set up a testamentary trust to be effective immediately upon his death. This means you won't have to wait for probate or other legal procedures before you assume ownership. There will be a short delay before you actually receive the property, only because the coroner must first issue a death certificate. That can take a week or so. I'm named as trustee, so I'll take care of these matters." He smiled, apparently under the impression he was delivering good news.

Nicole was speechless. How could Robert have done this to her? It appeared to give her a motive for killing him. Would the police be taking an even closer look at her? And what would the news hounds do with that? She didn't want to think about it, nor did she want anything to do with his house or his money. But who would believe her? People have killed for less.

"Mr. Blair's body," the man went on. "Do you know when they'll release it? I have his final instructions." He held up a piece of paper.

"I have no idea."

He smiled again. "Don't worry. I'll find out and let you know when they do. Meanwhile I'll just keep this in his file."

She felt herself flush. "Is the trust going to be filed with the county? Is it public record?"

"No," Freeman said. "Mr. Blair wanted these arrangements to remain private. He didn't want to embarrass or cause you inconvenience in any way. He was very clear about that."

She sat there a moment, absorbing this. Robert didn't want to embarrass or inconvenience her. What a joke! People were going to find out. There was no way around it.

Freeman waited patiently, his hands folded on his desk. At last, realizing their business was concluded, she got to her feet. Freeman handed her his card and offered her his services if she needed anything. "Now that you're a woman of property," he said, "it might be wise for you to make out a living trust."

She thanked him, and they shook hands again. This time, he covered their interlocked hands with his left hand in a gesture of sympathy. It was at that moment she thought of who he reminded her of—a funeral director. Still stunned by the news he'd delivered, she found her way out of the office.

When she was back in her car, she called to make an appointment with Sue. She had to tell her about the inheritance, and she didn't want to risk doing it over the phone. The secretary immediately put her through.

"I'm free until after lunch," Sue said. "Why don't you come now?"

By the time Nicole arrived, Sue's receptionist had gone to lunch, and Sue herself greeted Nicole in the waiting room. In Sue's office, a small table had been set with two places and a platter of sandwiches, as well as a coffee pot.

The sandwiches looked good, a choice of Brie with watercress and apple slices, pastrami on rye, and tuna on wheat. "I didn't know what you like," Sue explained, "so I decided to give us some choices.

Nicole reached for half a pastrami and explained to Sue about Robert's attorney and the bequest.

Sue was quiet for a moment, munching on her apple and Brie sandwich and washing it down with a sip of coffee. "Well," she finally said, "here we have a perfect example of good news and bad news. That much money could completely transform your life and give you some wonderful opportunities. On the other hand, in the eyes of a lot of people, Mr. Blair's bequest would give you a motive for wanting him dead."

She pressed a napkin to her lips and continued, "Here's what I'm wondering: Mr. Blair appears to have believed his life was in danger. The fact that he set up this trust a few weeks before his death is just too powerful a coincidence. So why would he leave you his estate, when it could make you a suspect?"

"I have no idea," Nicole said. "The fact that he was stalking me shows he was more than a little nuts. Maybe it never occurred to him that he was putting me in a bad position. The bottom line is that I don't want his money. It makes me sick to think that he had feelings for me. He never should have made me his beneficiary. And here's what I want to know: What if I refuse to accept the inheritance? What happens then?"

There was a pause while Sue thought it over. "You could do that. Then the money would go to the state. But, Nicole, I want you to think very carefully before you make a decision. This man obviously had mental problems, and if he'd lived, he might have— no, probably would have—become a nuisance, or worse. Believe me, having a stalker can wreck your life. But that didn't happen. Instead, he was killed and he left you a substantial amount of money. At the same time, he's disrupted your life in a big way. That money, whether you claim it or not, will cast suspicion on you. Refusing his bequest isn't going to change that.

"If you really don't want it, think of the good you could do if you contributed to some worthy causes. When everything settles down, you could sell his house and use the proceeds plus his other assets to set up a foundation. It's not like you have billions to give away, but you could make a difference. Or you could keep the money. As I said, it could change your life. Frankly, after all this man's behavior has put you through, you deserve some kind of compensation."

Nicole had finished her sandwich and was pouring herself more coffee. "What would you do?"

"The decision is yours, Nicole," Sue said. "I'm just laying out the options."

Nicole gazed out the window for a long moment. This wasn't just about Robert and whatever creepy delusions he was harboring about her. It could determine how she lived her life, what her future might be.

Finally she said, "Do I have to tell the police about it?"

"No," Sue said. "Certainly not. This is a private matter, and it's none of their business. The way Mr. Blair set it up, it shouldn't even come to their attention. Even if it does, they have no case against you. They would need evidence. According to Rick, his source in the D.A.'s office tells him they have nothing to build a case on. If they did, and you were an actual suspect, they could put a hold on the transfer of Mr. Blair's property until you're no longer under suspicion. But I don't think that's likely."

"OK," Nicole said, "but it would get ugly if the media found out about it."

"Very ugly," Sue agreed.

Nicole thought about it for a moment and said, "Why didn't Rick himself tell me what the D.A.'s office is up to?"

"Well," Sue said, "I hope I wasn't talking out of turn, but I did suggest to Rick that he back off for a bit. From what you said, I gathered you didn't like the attention he was giving you—especially after your experience with Mr. Blair. I thought you'd appreciate some peace and quiet in that department."

"You're right," Nicole said. "It's a relief not having to worry about being hassled right now."

"Don't expect it to last," Sue said. "He seems to have his sights set on you. He isn't used to women who say 'no' and mean it. That just makes you more desirable."

"Thanks for the warning," Nicole said.

Seven

Twenty minutes after leaving Sue's office, Nicole was in Century City, pushing her way through the paparazzi to get into her building. Back in the quiet of her office, she tried to focus on work, but her mind was abuzz with all that had happened since she'd returned from London. She thought of her close call that morning, and the guy she'd agreed to meet for a drink. He'd probably Google her and see what the tabloids were saying. Considering today's story, she doubted he'd actually call. Even so, she was curious about him. Why not check him out on one of the firm's databases? A thorough search would give her a lot of information about him, including judgments and liens, property titles, professional licenses, marriages, divorces, and police and court records.

On the California Architects Society's site, Josh's photo popped up. He was smiling. What she liked about his looks was his open, honest gaze, his square jaw, and his rather sensuous lips. He had a warm smile that was somehow both sweet and sexy.

A quick look at his profile seemed to indicate he was an upstanding citizen: a licensed architect with a masters in architecture from U.C. Berkeley. Next she looked him up in one of the firm's subscription databases, which went deeper into individuals' backgrounds. Here she learned that, for the past fourteen months, he'd been living alone in a house he owned—estimated value of $650,000—modest by L.A. standards. But, she noted, he held title to three other houses in Studio City and nearby Van Nuys. No marriages on record. She looked at his previous address, which had been a rental. He'd lived there for a couple of years with a woman, Eleanor Winter. Nicole left Josh's profile to look up Eleanor. The single photo of her—it looked like a professional glamour shot—showed a sexy brunette with sculpted cheekbones and a seductive smile. Her listed occupation was as a realtor. Aside from Eleanor, she also used the name Elle. The record confirmed that this woman had moved from her earlier address—the same as Josh's—about the same time he'd moved into his house. Huh, she thought. This was an ex-girlfriend. She stared at the woman. Elle looked cool and sophisticated, and in no way did she resemble Nicole. She wondered what the story on that romance was and why they broke up. Unfortunately, this information—the kind she was most curious about—wasn't available on any database.

She went back to Josh's record. He'd never been arrested or had a judgment against him. His credit rating was good. He was born in 1986. This made her hesitate. He was 29, almost four years younger than she. She'd never dated a younger man. But she wasn't going to date him, was she?

This wasn't the first time she'd searched the web to check on people she knew. She used it every time her sister started up with yet another nightmare boyfriend. Stephanie was tall, blonde, and truly beautiful. She was cynical about men as well as about marriage, and the men she dated seemed specially selected to confirm her cynicism. To Nicole, they were all hopeless losers.

Several things they had in common: They were tattooed—some all over, some to a lesser extent. To a man, they were muscular and shorter than Steph. Another shared trait was that they were all slackers, either unemployed or underemployed. Her current flame had dreadlocks, even though he was a fair-skinned Caucasian. Stephanie said he got the effect by washing his hair and treating it with gelatin. Stephanie thought it looked cool.

Nicole had been surprised, perhaps a little disappointed, when she'd done a background search on "Mr. Dreadlocks," and he'd come up fairly clean. He didn't have an arrest record, but there had been several red flags. He had forty unpaid parking violations. More alarming, at least to Nicole, was that, at the age of twenty-six, he was twice divorced and the father of a seven-year-old boy. He'd been in trouble several times for failing to pay child support. When she told her sister about this, Steph had laughed. "I'm not going to marry him, Nicole. How dumb do you think I am?"

After rereading Josh's record, Nicole decided her first instinct had been right. He wasn't a criminal, a married man, or (worse yet) a member of the press. It would be perfectly safe to meet him for a drink. She smiled at the idea of possessing such powerful tools for checking out what was basically a blind date. If she ever was out on that meat market again, she'd be able to eliminate a lot of men without bothering to meet them for coffee.

Sue had been right about Sargosian. Returning from the break room, Nicole found a note from him on her desk. *Come to my office. I want to talk to you*, it said, in his oversized scrawl.

She was just leaving her office to see him when her cell phone rang. To her surprise, it was Josh Mulhern. "About that drink tonight," he said, "where do you want to meet and what time?"

"How about the V Wine Bar?" she said. "It's a little place just off Santa Monica Boulevard in West Hollywood. But it would have to be around nine. Does that work for you?"

"The V Wine Bar, 9:00." he repeated. "Sure. I'll see you then."

When she arrived at Sargosian's office, his door was open. She stood in the doorway and said, "You wanted to see me?"

He smiled, "Always. Come in—have a seat." He gestured toward the small couch across from his desk. He got up to close the door, then sat down next to her. The couch was a tight fit for two people, and Sargosian was pressed against her a little too snugly. She felt a wave of annoyance.

"I wanted to clue you in on what's happening," he said. Then he repeated what Sue had told her about the investigation. "Now there's been another development," he added. "The police are going in a new direction, following the money to see if one of Blair's private clients killed him or had him killed. We just got word that they want us to turn over Blair's office computer. They have a warrant, but I've filed an objection based on attorney-client privilege. Over the years, Blair used that computer to research confidential matters for the firm. The police would be gaining access to them. That's our objection. Now it's up to the court."

"What do you think will happen?" she said. Tired of being crowded, she got up, moved to the window and looked out. The media was still in front of the building, apparently waiting for someone to come out.

"I think we have a good argument," he said. "Meanwhile, make sure no one touches his computer. Any research done in-house should be from another desk. Blair took on private cases of his own, didn't he?"

When she nodded, he said, "Do you know if he used his office computer to work on them?"

"I doubt it. He had a pretty heavy caseload," she said. "Whenever I looked over his shoulder, he seemed to be doing work for the firm. Of course, I wasn't watching him every minute, and he may have come in after hours or on weekends."

"Did he ever talk to you about his outside cases?"

"He never talked about anything he did outside the office," she said.

"You used to go out to lunch with this guy. What did you talk about?"

"Basically, we shared office gossip," she said. "Everyone thought he was completely tuned out, but he knew everything that went on in this place. He was also a great mimic. For example..." Despite the ill will she was feeling toward Robert, she couldn't help smiling. "He told me how you used to come into the staff break room to flirt with Melanie. Said he walked in on you one time when you had her backed up against the wall—just this side of in flagrante." She held up her thumb and forefinger about an inch apart. "You both jumped when you sensed his presence. He did a hysterical imitation of your come-on and the way she batted her eyes at you."

Sargosian actually blushed. He cleared his throat, then said, "That didn't happen. He was exaggerating."

"No doubt," she said. "It was still funny. He should have been an actor. He had everyone's mannerisms spot on. Even yours."

"So you don't know what he was doing on the side?" he said, changing the subject. "What kind of cases he took on?"

"No," she said. "Is that it?"

"How about dinner tonight?"

"I'm busy," she said. "Thanks for the update, Rick. I really appreciate it."

§

That evening, Nicole said nothing to her sister about the inheritance. She didn't want to think about it, much less talk about it. While she and Stephanie were eating a quick dinner of cold, leftover pizza, Nicole mentioned she was meeting someone later in the evening for a drink.

"You mean a date?" Stephanie was surprised.

"Not really," Nicole said. "This guy rescued me from a speeding car when I was crossing the street. Then he asked me out for a drink."

"Good for you," Stephanie said. "Getting right back on the horse." Stephanie said.

Nicole frowned. Stephanie seemed to think this was the beginning of a new romance, right on the heels of Reinhardt's disappearance. "Oh, for heaven's sake," Nicole said. "It's just a drink."

Stephanie looked at her. "Sure. Don't get so defensive. I'm just saying it will get your mind off what's been happening."

After they finished eating, the two of them piled into Steph's ancient Volkswagen bug and made the drive to Westwood. Nicole had brought along her garage door opener. She was hoping they could slip into her condo building's underground garage in a car the paparazzi wouldn't recognize. But parked vehicles lined the street, with several blocking the entrance to her garage. Stephanie had no choice but to park in the only available spot, directly across the street.

There were a dozen photographers waiting. The two women got out and walked determinedly toward the building's main entrance. Nicole took Stephanie's arm to steer her through the paparazzi. As they walked, Nicole was ready to repeat her line about contacting her lawyer. But no one was asking her questions. They were much more interested in Stephanie. One said, "What's your name, sweetheart?" Another wanted to know, "What's your connection with Nicole?" The third wondered if Stephanie, who was a good deal taller than her sister and more substantial in build, was her bodyguard.

"You've got that right," Stephanie said. "Leave us alone or I'll beat the crap out of you," The photographers laughed, and Stephanie laughed with them.

"Steph!" Nicole warned, unlocking the door to the building's lobby and pulling her sister inside. "I told you not to talk to them!

They're taking video and recording your voice. Now you're going to hear yourself saying that on the XHN."

"Don't worry about it," Stephanie laughed. "My friends will be thrilled they know a celebrity."

The two of them worked as a team, packing up Nicole's things for what she guessed would be four or five days. Nicole was in the bathroom, getting her toothbrush and other toiletries, when she happened to glance at the window and saw a face looking in at her. It was a paparazzi holding a camera. Her mouth fell open in surprise. How in the hell had he gotten up there? Her condo was on the second floor, and there were no trees outside. She quickly pulled down the shade. Then she hurried to the spare bedroom and, without turning on the light, peered outside. The man was standing on the top of the six-foot cinderblock wall that ran behind the building. He was assisted by someone else, standing in the alley. She could see the pair of hands holding onto the man's ankles. Deprived of his view inside, he was in the wobbly process of getting down.

She checked to see how Stephanie was doing. "I've got my makeup," she said. "I'll get some outfits for work and my sweats. Why don't you pack some underwear and a nightie?" By the time Nicole and her sister left the building, another dozen photographers had joined the original group. The two women walked toward the car, Nicole carrying her suitcase. The men shot pictures and demanded to know where Nicole thought she was going and if she was "skipping town." This time she didn't bother to answer.

Driving away, the two women watched in amazement as yet another photographer arrived on a motorcycle and sped after them for several blocks—at what seemed to be great peril—trying to position himself between their car and the one in the adjacent lane so he could get a photo of Nicole in the passenger seat.

"Holy crap," Stephanie said. "That guy's going to get himself killed!"

"These people are excitement junkies," Nicole said. "They actually enjoy risking their lives like this. You know, protecting the public's right to know."

They both laughed. By now the paparazzi was far behind them.

As soon as they got back to Stephanie's, Nicole began to spruce up for her meeting—she refused to think of it as a date—with Josh Mulhern. She looked through the clothes she'd brought to Stephanie's. Her choices were between several skirts and blouses, as well as a flower-sprigged dress and a fitted navy number she'd bought in London but hadn't yet had a chance to wear. Nicole held the flowered dress up to herself and looked in the mirror. This would do. She pulled off the skirt and blouse she'd been wearing and hung them up. Getting out Stephanie's iron, she gave the dress a quick once over, then put it on. She carefully reapplied her makeup. Still not satisfied, she borrowed her sister's hot rollers to put more bounce in her hair.

She was late arriving at the wine bar. Looking around, she saw him in a corner booth and waved. He smiled and waved back. As soon as she sat down, she decided to get the whole thing out on the table. No pretending she was unattached and that her life wasn't a mess.

"This is just a drink and conversation," she said. "I want you to understand that."

He smiled, putting his hands up in mock surrender. "OK, OK," he said. "What exactly have I done?"

"I want to be sure you know a couple of things about me. No elephants in the room."

He stopped smiling and leaned forward on his elbows, chin resting on his hands. "Shoot."

"First of all, I'm in a relationship. I should have told you when you called."

"Are you engaged?"

She shook her head.

"Living together?"

"No," she said.

"So, where's this guy at the moment?"

"In England. He lives in England."

"Huh," Josh said.

"What?" she said. From his tone, she got the feeling he didn't think it was much of a relationship.

"Nothing," he shrugged. "So, what's the other thing you want me to know?"

"I'm in the middle of a—what should I call it?—media blitz."

"I know," he said. "I looked you up. It was a bit of a shock to see all those tabloid stories. I can't imagine how that makes you feel."

"Ah," she said. "Would you have brought this up if I hadn't?"

"Probably. Look, can I get you something to drink? It seems to be self service here tonight." He gestured around him. There were just a few couples in the mostly empty bar. No waitress in sight.

She told him she'd like a glass of chardonnay, and he went off to get it.

What now? she thought. She wanted to know more about Josh. True, she was curious about everyone she met. But with this guy it was more intense. She was attracted to him, and Reinhardt was pretty much out of the picture. She'd stopped trying to reach him, reasoning that she'd already left plenty of messages; that was enough. Even if he called and begged her forgiveness, she was done. He was too much of an enigma for a long-term relationship. Yet, for reasons she couldn't explain, she was feeling guilty about meeting this new guy for a drink. That was ridiculous, right? She wasn't going to sleep with him—was she? She lingered on that thought until she realized Josh was back, handing her a glass of wine.

Once he was seated, she asked him about himself, and he told her pretty much what she already knew. He also said that, since he'd started his architectural practice in the middle of the Great Recession, business had been slow. He'd gotten a loan from his father and bought a derelict house, fixed it up, sold it, and bought another. Now he had three rental houses in addition to the one he lived in. He'd loved doing that, but had no time for it now that his practice had picked up. As far as his personal life, he said, "I'm not presently involved with anyone. I had a bad breakup a little over a year ago, and I'm just coming out of it."

She thought of the woman, Eleanor a.k.a. Elle, who'd been living with him the previous year. She must be the relationship he was talking about.

He put his hand on hers and said, "But what's happening with you? I mean, this is pretty nasty publicity. How are you dealing with it?"

"I hate it," she said. "I can't wait for it to be over."

He asked her about Robert's murder. She told him the basic details. It had all been in the paper.

"Was he a close friend?"

"Not really," she said, withdrawing her hand. "Look, if you don't mind, I'd rather not discuss it. I came out tonight so I wouldn't have to think about it."

"Sure. Sorry."

They were both quiet, and she began to think perhaps the evening had been a mistake. Maybe she should call it a night.

"Read any good books lately?" he said.

"I wish," she said.

They both laughed, and her mood lightened. The conversation turned to books they'd both enjoyed. She was surprised by the similarity in their taste. She'd never met a guy who read the same books she did. He even liked the Victorians—Dickens, Trollop, Thackeray—who were her special favorites. They chattered on amiably like old friends, discussing movies, plays, the news, politics.

All at once she noticed they were the only people left in the bar. She looked at her watch. It was almost midnight.

"Oh, my god," she said. "I've have work tomorrow."

"I'll walk you to your car," he said, getting up.

It wasn't far. She was parked about a half block from the bar. But it was a side street, and the lights in nearby businesses were off. She was glad for his company.

When they reached her car, he walked around to the driver's side with her. She unlocked the door, pulled it open, and turned to say goodnight when he leaned in and lightly brushed his lips against hers. Meeting no resistance, he pulled her toward him and kissed her. After a few seconds' hesitation, she found herself kissing him back. Finally, she gently pushed him away.

"I've got to go," she said. She got in the car, closed the door, and lowered the window.

"Can I see you again?" he said.

She nodded. "I have to get on the other side of this whole ugly episode before—" she paused, not quite knowing what to say, then added, "before we get together again."

"I'm a good listener," he said. "I can even offer a shoulder to cry on."

"Maybe so, but remember what Nelson Algren said: 'Never go out with a woman whose troubles are worse than your own.'"

"Um, I don't think you've got the quote quite right," he said. "What he said was: 'Never play cards with a man called Doc. Never eat at a place called Mom's. Never sleep with a woman whose troubles are worse than your own.'"

They smiled at each other for a long moment.

Then Nicole said, "Look, I'll call you when I—when my life gets back to normal."

She put her key in the ignition to start the car, but he said, "Wait! You don't have my number." He pulled out his card and handed it to her.

EIGHT

WHEN NICOLE GOT TO WORK the next day, the scene in front of the building was relatively quiet, with only a few paparazzi keeping watch. There had been no new stories about Robert, although the tabloids managed to build an article on the somewhat tenuous news peg that there were no new developments in the case. To her, it appeared to be a lame attempt to keep the story alive and run Robert's photo yet another day.

She was still jet-lagged, her fatigue compounded by the late evening with Josh. She couldn't remember ever being so grateful that it was Friday.

The day was a busy one, and not in a good way. She completed the paperwork on the performance reviews and, by late morning, began delivering these evaluations to the staff. It was a yearly unpleasantness, dreaded by everyone, especially Nicole. Staff members came in one by one, and she had to explain what they were doing wrong or what they could do better, or in several happier cases, how well they were doing. Raises depended on these ratings, and she'd taken a lot of time to look at each employee's work and be fair, even generous, in her assessments. But there were always slackers, those whose work was below par, and others who she thought must have "job suicide" with work so spectacularly bad that it appeared they were determined to get fired and collect unemployment.

She'd told Breanna to hold her calls while she was conferring with each person, but to take a message from Josh Mulhern or put him through if she was free. Breanna raised her eyebrows. "Not a word," Nicole warned. Breanna made a motion of zipping her lips, and they both smiled.

From her glass cubicle, she watched the usual parade of clients making their way to conference rooms to meet with their attorneys. The billing rates at a firm like this ran close to $1,000 an hour for a lawyer's time—$700 for a paralegal. While most of the work was for big corporations, some cases involved family law—prenuptial agreements, the subsequent divorces, negotiations over the settlement of property, and renewed fights over the initial prenups. It was a perpetual-motion machine. Obviously, in order to employ a top-drawer firm for these matters, the clients were either executives of corporate clients or the superrich. More often than not, the husband was a good deal older than the wife.

Once in a while, a husband or wife would call on the firm's services to investigate a spouse he or she suspected of infidelity. These investigations were usually conducted by an outside firm, since Robert was always quick to hand them off. It had seemed to Nicole that he felt these cases were beneath him. He was a cynic about marriage and refused on principle to be party to such stupidity. But now, given his unwanted interest in her, and the age disparity between them, she wondered if it might have been something else.

The firm's other non-corporate work involved estate issues, wills, trusts, inheritances, and the like. Such cases were often filed by heirs who objected to whatever had been left to them, or—to be precise—what had not been left to them. Many of these litigants had been trust-fund babies, had never had to work for a living, and never would. Still, they seemed in such bad need of more wealth that they were willing to spend what—over the years—amounted to hundreds of thousands of dollars fighting for money that had been left to someone else. In the offices of Bascomb, Rice, Smith & Di Angelo and their $1,000-an-hour fees, billable hours could add up quickly. In Nicole's view, the whole exercise was a ridiculous waste of time and money. An estate could be depleted before the case was settled, which was exactly what had happened in Dickens's Bleak House with the case of Jarndyce and Jarndyce.

On her way to Stephanie's that night, Nicole detoured west to check on her condo. The front of the building was deserted, and she felt safe enough to stop and pick up her mail.

When she got back to the car, she gave into an impulse and called Josh. He picked up after one ring. "Really?" he said. "Things back to normal already?"

"I wouldn't say they're normal," she said. "But nothing bad happened today, so I decided to call you."

"It's 6:00," he said. "Can you meet me for dinner?"

"I have to stop at my sister's apartment in West Hollywood first. I've been staying there since my condo became paparazzi central. But I could probably meet you at 8:00."

"How about the Café Marie. It's just off Ventura near Laurel Canyon," he said. "Does that work for you, or do you want me to come over the hill to West Hollywood?"

It was clear they were negotiating over what might happen after dinner. If they met in West Hollywood, they couldn't go to her sister's. "Café Marie is fine," she said. "I'll see you at 8:00."

Nicole put her foot to the accelerator and made it to Stephanie's in record time so she could shower and freshen up before driving out to the valley. At the same time, she kept asking herself what she thought she was doing. It was as if she'd lost control and some kind of possession had taken hold of her.

She pulled her new navy dress from the closet, held it up to herself, and looked in the mirror. It had a scooped neckline, just short of daring, and was fitted to the hip, where it flared into soft folds. The dress was flattering—no doubt about it. She decided it would be fine to wear to dinner. She selected fresh underwear, grabbed a towel from the linen closet, and went into the bathroom. Before she closed the door, she told her sister that she was going to shower.

"OK, but I'm next," said Steph. "Remember: I've got a date, too."

"This isn't a date," Nicole corrected her. "It's just dinner."

She took her shower and had just slipped into her bra and bikini panties—a matched set in sheer black lace—when Steph knocked. "Can I use the shower now?" she said.

Nicole opened the door. Steph had her change of clothes over her arm—jeans and a hoodie. No use dressing up for Mr. Dreadlocks. Usually, Nicole had observed, they just retired to Stephanie's room, from which sounds of noisy sex would soon emanate.

"Huh," said Stephanie, taking note of Nicole's lingerie. "I guess this Josh guy is pretty hot."

"Stop that," Nicole said, playfully punching her sister in the arm. "He's never going to see me in this. Besides, you're the one who packed my undies. Remember? And this is what you packed."

Nicole arrived at the restaurant first, a pretty little French bistro. The hostess had Josh's reservation and seated her in a booth at the back. Nicole ordered a glass of wine. She sat uneasily for what seemed like a long time, constantly checking her watch. All kinds of things were going through her mind, especially the idea of being stood up. Again.

Then there he was, beaming at her and handing her a single, perfect red rose. "Sorry I was late. I got stuck at the office."

She felt herself flush. "No worries," she said. "I've already eaten. I was just waiting for the check."

He laughed and sat down, then put up his hand to get the waitress's attention. "Come on," he said. "I wasn't that late."

"Fifteen whole minutes," she said. "Don't say I didn't warn you about women with more troubles than your own."

"I consider myself warned," he said. "Next time I'll call if I'm going to be even a minute late."

Looking into her eyes, he reached out and took her hand. Her hand tingled; another tingling started at the inside soles of her feet and was working its way upward. *Unbelievable*, she thought, *I hardly know this guy and look what he's doing to me.*

The waitress arrived and had to clear her throat to get their attention. Josh ordered a drink, and they both studied the menu.

They ordered—a steak for him and glazed salmon for her—and chatted about their day, the latest news, schools they'd gone to, their first romances. By the time they ordered coffee and a single molten chocolate cake to share, they'd both scooted to the center of the booth and were sitting close together. She was all too aware of the warmth of his thigh against hers.

Josh told her about his breakup. "We were engaged and starting to plan the wedding when she told me she'd met someone else. I found out later that she'd been seeing him for some time. I was ready to settle down and start a family, and I thought she wanted the same thing."

He paused a moment and seemed to be considering it. "Maybe she did, but not with me. Looking back on it," he added, "it wasn't so much losing her that bummed me out as the betrayal."

Nicole told him about her divorce—the short version—and admitted that Brad, her ex, had been into wholesale betrayals.

The waitress appeared, cleared away their empty cups and dessert dish, and placed the check on the table. "We're closing in a few minutes," she said.

Nicole looked at her watch. "11:30? I had no idea it was so late."

Josh paid for dinner, and they walked out of the restaurant to the street where her car was parked. His was a few spaces ahead. Every business in the area seemed to have closed; the block was pretty much deserted.

"My place is just a few blocks away," he said. "You could stop for a drink."

"Anymore and I won't be able to drive home," she said.

"I've got a couch."

They both smiled. It was pretty much what Rick had said, but coming from Josh it was something else entirely.

"I'll follow you," Nicole said, gesturing to her car.

His house was a small craftsman-style bungalow, the front yard smartly fitted out with a picket fence, a stone path bordered with flowers, and glass-haloed garden lights. When they stepped inside the house, Josh closed the door and reached over to push a button that turned on dim, recessed lighting. He pushed another that closed the blinds in the living and dining rooms. Then he pressed her against the door and kissed her. She kissed him back, putting her arms around his neck. With surprising speed, he took off his sports coat, tossed it behind him and began unbuttoning his shirt. Nicole started on the small buttons that ran down the front of her dress.

While this was going on, he still managed to keep kissing her. Nicole had begun to giggle, realizing it was a race to see who could get undressed first. When most of her buttons were undone, she kicked off her shoes and let her dress drop to the floor, leaving just her sheer, lacy bra and panties.

"Whoa!" Josh said. "Stop right there. I think the next step requires my personal supervision." They both laughed as he pulled her toward the couch.

Afterward, he grabbed a throw blanket from the back of the couch and pulled it over them. They held each other, dozing.

A while later, Nicole woke with a start and sat up. He stirred. "What?" he said.

"I've got to call my sister," she said. "She'll wonder what happened to me."

"Can you spend the night?" he said. "I have to leave tomorrow morning for a family get-together. But I'd really like it if you stayed."

She regarded him for a moment. She really did like this guy, his earnest blue eyes, his easy smile.

"OK." She got up and sent her sister a message saying she was spending the night with "the new guy." She thought Steph probably had figured it out already. With that out of the way, they moved up a short flight of stairs to his bedroom and made love again.

Nicole woke up at 9:00 a.m., confused at first about where she was. When Josh came into the bedroom, he was already dressed. He'd brought her a cup of coffee, which he put on the night table next to her. He also had her clothes, neatly folded over his arm, her shoes dangling from two fingers. He placed them on the bed.

"I have to go, and I wanted to say goodbye," he said. "My folks have a place up at Tahoe, and we're going to spend the weekend skiing. I wish I could cancel and spend the day with you, but it's a family get-together that's been in the works for months."

"Oh," she said, "I have to get back to Stephanie's anyway." This wasn't true, and she felt disappointed, even though she hadn't given any thought to what would happen next when they'd ended up in his bed the night before.

"Stay as long as you'd like," he said. "Breakfast is in the oven, keeping warm. The key is on the table next to the front door. Just lock up and drop the key in the mail slot."

He leaned over to kiss her. "Can we have dinner Monday night? We can eat here. I'll cook."

"Sure," she said. "Have a great time."

Josh kissed her again, and after another round of goodbyes, he was gone.

She got up and put her clothes on. Then she walked around, getting her first good look at the house. This was a sample of his work as an architect, and she was impressed. From the area, she knew it had probably been one of the many identical tract houses built after World War II. He'd made it cozy and charming, with a floor-to-ceiling stone fireplace in the living room; hardwood floors; and a surprisingly large, well-equipped kitchen. The furniture was spare, modern, and tasteful. Everything looked new, and the house was tidy and clean—another point in Josh's favor.

She found her breakfast in the oven, a plate of French toast and bacon, lightly wrapped with foil to keep it from drying out. She smiled, thinking about the previous night with Josh. *He cooks, too.* He was almost too good to be true.

After Nicole ate, she took another tour of the house. She had a strong impulse to snoop around but limited herself to opening closet doors and checking bathroom cabinets and dresser drawers for any sign of a woman staying here or leaving things to mark her territory. She found no such evidence, just that Josh was neat and given to storing his possessions in boxes, lined baskets, and other organizers.

When she ended up in his office and saw his computer, the temptation was too much. She sat down in front of it and turned it on. To her surprise, it wasn't password protected. What a trusting soul he was—leaving her alone in his house with free access to his computer.

His files all seemed to be work-related: plans and proposals for architectural projects. She looked at his email account. Among the messages he'd already opened were a number from friends, several offering to fix him up. Then she noticed an unopened one that had come in that morning. The "from" line—eleanorwinter@ palmyra.com—caught her eye. It said, "I miss you. Please call me."

It was signed, "All my love, Elle." Nicole closed it and took care to mark it unread, so Josh wouldn't know she'd been snooping. Then she saw an earlier message from Elle, dated ten days before. It said, "Why don't you return my calls?" One more was dated a week before that. It said, "I broke up with Tate. I realize now I made a terrible mistake. I'm still in love with you. I know you're angry, but can't we get together and talk?"

She clicked on Josh's outgoing mail. He hadn't replied to any of these messages. Even so, Nicole didn't like this development. Maybe Josh hadn't answered his ex, but that didn't mean he wouldn't eventually do so. Well, Nicole told herself, this was what she got for snooping around. She quit out of his email and turned off the computer. Then she put her dishes in the dishwasher, made the bed, and left.

She got to Stephanie's at 10:00 a.m. As soon as she opened the front door, Arnold's excited barks woke up Steph.

"So how was it?" she wanted to know. Nicole smiled and felt herself flush. "That good, eh?" Steph said.

"Truly," Nicole said. "God, I am such a slut."

"Don't be ridiculous. You had a good time. That's exactly what you needed." Stephanie regarded Nicole for a moment, then went on, "You know, when someone's life is completely upended like yours has been, it's natural to look for a way to ease the pain. This guy was it. I can't imagine why you'd feel guilty about it."

"Oh," Nicole said, eager to change the subject, "things have quieted down on the media front. The paparazzi have pretty much exhausted the story and abandoned me for fresh kill. So I'm moving home today. Would you mind keeping Arnold until Sunday? I just want to go home and sleep."

"Sure," said Stephanie. "Arnold likes it here. He's asked me to adopt him. I'm seriously thinking it over."

Nicole laughed, then went to the room she'd been using and started packing.

NINE

BACK HOME, NICOLE SPENT the rest of the day in bed, catching up on her sleep. She got up to eat dinner—leftovers she found in the freezer—then went back to bed with her book.

She woke up at 7:00 a.m. on Sunday, pulled on some old jeans, a T-shirt, sunglasses, and a floppy-brimmed hat for a trip to the nearby supermarket. She badly needed to restock her kitchen, but she didn't want to run into anyone who might recognize her from the news.

When Nicole got back to her place, it took two trips from the garage to carry up the groceries. She was just putting them away when her phone beeped, and she looked at her messages. There were two, both from Daniel Freeman. One was from Friday. She wondered how she'd missed it. It said, "Blair's death certificate came. Drop by after work to sign the papers for his bequest."

In the second message, which had just come in, Freeman said he was in the office this morning catching up on some work, and she could drop by if she wanted to take care of the paperwork.

Nicole called him. "I'm still not ready to accept the money," she said. "I need more time to think about it."

"All right," said Freeman, "but he did leave an envelope of material for you. He said it includes a personal letter and information about the property. I should have given it to you when you came in before, but it slipped my mind. Perhaps there's something in it that will help you decide."

"What time should I come by?" she said. She looked at her watch. It was 10:30 a.m.

"I'll be here until noon or so," Freeman said.

Nicole quickly changed into something more presentable—a red sweater, short navy skirt and heels—and went down to get her car. As she reached the street, she noticed a gray SUV pull away from a nearby no-parking zone. It looked just like the one that had almost run her down the day she met Josh. It was clearly following her, and whoever was at the wheel wasn't trying to be subtle about it.

Once again, she remembered her interview with Detective Miller. He'd thought she was Robert's girlfriend, and that she knew more about Robert's murder than she admitted. He'd warned her that the killer might draw the same conclusion. Robert had photos of her in his house, which the detective said the killer had searched. Photos identifying her and where she worked had been in the news. The man following her could be with the media. But he might also be Robert's killer. Whoever he was, she had to get him off her tail.

She tried the trick of turning into the Beverly Hills Hotel driveway, but the man seemed to anticipate this and followed her in, along the road fronting the hotel and out again. She wove around the residential streets for perhaps ten minutes, passing one mansion with sprawling gardens after another, but she couldn't shake him.

Finally, as Nicole was turning back onto Sunset Boulevard, she managed to sail through the light just after it turned red.

She almost got into a wreck, and several cars that had jumped the green light screeched to a stop. But the maneuver was successful. Cross traffic trapped the gray SUV in the middle of the intersection, sending up a prolonged chorus of honking. She turned on Beverly Drive and made her way over the hill and into the valley, driving as fast as she could. Traffic was relatively light. By the time she reached Ventura Boulevard, she was sure she'd lost him.

If it was the same SUV she'd seen a few days before, she reasoned, he would know where she was headed, even though he might not have the exact address. She took the extra precaution of leaving her car in a parking structure near Freeman's office so it wouldn't be seen on the street.

To Nicole's annoyance, Daniel Freeman once again tried to talk her into signing the papers and accepting the inheritance. "I could have the money transferred directly into your account," he said. "It would be available to you tomorrow."

"As I said," she told him, "I'm having a lot of hesitation about accepting it. I'll let you know as soon as I decide."

"Of course," he said. He placed the papers back in their folder. Then he got up and went over to a framed landscape hung on the wall. He slid it aside, revealing a wall safe. He put in the combination, then opened it and took out something. He closed the safe, spun the dial, and straightened the picture. When he turned back to her, he was holding a large, tan mailing envelope. "Given the notoriety of this case, I'm keeping Mr. Blair's file locked up." He sat down again and placed the envelope on his desk, pushing it toward her.

"As I mentioned, he left this envelope for you. He said it included a letter explaining certain matters he wanted you to know if anything happened to him." He paused to take two sheets of paper out of a desk drawer and put it on top of the envelope. "Here are his instructions for burial and his death certificate."

"Didn't you think it was odd?" she said. "I mean, how often do people walk in here out of the blue and make out a will?"

"At the time, I didn't think anything of it," he said. "In my experience, people are uncannily aware when it's time to record their last wishes. Of course, as things turned out, it was very strange, considering the way Mr. Blair died. I've never had anything like that happen before."

"He knew someone wanted to kill him," she said, almost to herself. "Someone must have threatened his life, and he took it very seriously."

Freeman gave the envelope and papers another push toward her, and she picked them up. The envelope was fat and seemed packed full. A square object inside gave it an irregular shape.

They both stood up. She thanked Freeman and told him she'd be in touch. He walked her to the door and, once again, shook her hand while sandwiching his left hand over hers.

Back in her car, she made her way along Ventura Boulevard, remarkably devoid of traffic, even for a Sunday morning. She turned onto Beverly Glen, heading home.

Just before she reached Mulholland Drive at the crest of the hill, she saw, with a shock, that the same gray SUV was behind her. How on earth had he found her? While they were stopped at the signal, she got a look at him in her rearview mirror. He was big with jowls and a shaved head. The light turned green, and she started up so fast her tires screeched. He was just as fast, close behind her as they sped past Mulholland and down the sharply twisting road. She could see he was deliberately tailgating her, forcing her to go faster. Using the shoulder of the road, he pulled along the passenger side of her car and sideswiped her. The maneuver pushed her car toward the line of cars on the other side of the road and the steep cliff beyond it. She corrected her steering just in time to avoid a head-on collision. She sped up until he was behind her again. *Holy shit*, she thought, *he's trying to get me killed and make it look like an accident.* She kept ahead of him with her foot on the accelerator, going a terrifying sixty, then sixty-five down the winding road.

At last they neared the bottom of the hill at Sunset where cars were waiting at a red light. Nicole spotted a gap in the flow of cars on the other side of the road where traffic was headed in the opposite direction. She wasn't sure she could manage it, but desperation prompted her to execute a quick U-turn. She barely made it into the space between two cars. This prompted loud honking from the drivers behind her, who had to hit their brakes. She was now headed back to the valley. Meanwhile, her pursuer was stuck between other cars waiting at the signal, facing south.

She'd planned to reverse directions again at the small shopping center at the crest of the hill and head home to Westwood. But by the time she got there, she realized what a bad idea that was. Whoever was tailing her knew where she lived. It was too dangerous to go home. She got out her phone and, once again, called her sister to ask if she could stay a few more days. Not wanting to alarm Stephanie, Nicole explained that she was still being hassled by paparazzi.

Nicole came back down the mountain, this time through Laurel Canyon. Construction crews seemed to be working on every major street. It took a while for her to battle her way into West Hollywood. Before she went into Stephanie's apartment, she opened the trunk of her car and pulled out one of the tote bags she kept for grocery shopping. She dropped Robert's envelope into it.

Once inside, she greeted her sister and Arnold, who was as excited as ever to see her. Stephanie was sitting at the table eating lunch.

"Hey," Stephanie said. "You hungry? I have leftover tuna casserole."

"Sure," Nicole said. "I'll be there in a minute." She disappeared into the room where she slept and put the tote bag in the closet.

While they ate, Nicole told her sister about the inheritance, swearing her to secrecy. She didn't mention the man in the gray SUV. Stephanie would demand they call the police, and Nicole wasn't up for that. So far the police had been less than helpful, and they weren't about to assign her a bodyguard. Nor did she say anything about Robert's envelope. Stephanie would insist on opening it right away, and Nicole wanted to put it off as long as possible. Most especially, she didn't want to read Robert's letter. Maybe she would turn it over to her lawyer so she wouldn't have to deal with it. She had decided, however, that Stephanie might as well know about the bequest.

"Oh, my god," Stephanie said when she heard the news. "You'll never have to work again in your life. Tell me again: How much is it?" Then, after Nicole repeated the amount, Stephanie said, "Oh, my god" again. She was even more flabbergasted when Nicole told her she didn't want the money. "It makes me sick to think about it," Nicole said. "His crazy fixation on me."

"What difference does that make?" said Stephanie. "This could be so great for you! You know Marja, this friend of mine? She helped out a neighbor, an old woman who didn't have any family or friends. Then the woman died and left Marja almost a million dollars. She bought a little house, and she travels. She took a job that she loves with an art gallery. It doesn't pay much, but that doesn't matter because she doesn't need the money. It's a total win-win!"

"This is not the same," Nicole said. "It just feels wrong. I mean, where do you think he got all that money? Helping out in a soup kitchen or visiting cancer patients? It was probably something like dealing drugs or arms trading. He could have been a hired killer.

"And Robert was actually stalking me. He broke into my place and stole my underwear. That's really sick. How could I bear to spend that money or live on it? My lawyer said I could give it to charity. That's what I'm thinking."

"Right." Stephanie sounded disappointed. "The money is just a big pile of trouble for you."

"Exactly," Nicole said.

"So what about this new guy?"

Nicole hesitated before answering. Then, "I really like him, Steph. He's fun, and he gets me. He really gets me."

"I'm guessing Reinhardt doesn't."

"Exactly. Like, sometimes he can't tell when I'm joking. I have to explain. And, basically, he's a very serious person."

"Like what's-his-name in Wuthering Heights?" said Stephanie.

"Heathcliff? Oh, god, no. Reinhardt isn't moody and brooding. But I always have the feeling he's thinking deep, serious thoughts when we're not talking or interacting in some way. He's not much into small talk. With Josh, I have his undivided attention, and we never run out of things to say. Of course, after just two dates, I can't pretend I really know him. But what strikes me about Josh is that he's a real grownup. Maybe the first truly grownup man I've ever been with."

Stephanie laughed. "Grownup, Nicole? What do you mean? We're all grownups. Even Brad was a grownup."

"No, he really wasn't," Nicole said. "The only reason he married me was because I gave him an ultimatum; I was going to leave him if he didn't. He never did get to the point where he wanted kids. And he was always dreaming up get-rich-quick schemes. Do you know how immature that is? He had a successful career, but it wasn't enough. He had to up the stakes, look for shortcuts. And Reinhardt, with his cloak and dagger routine—that's kind of the same thing, isn't it? A refusal to live in the real world like everybody else, an excuse to avoid responsibility and commitment.

"On the other hand, Josh knows who he is and what he wants out of life," Nicole went on. "He loves his work, and he's ready to settle down and have a family. He was engaged, but his fiancée cheated on him, and they broke up. But he really does want marriage and children. Of course, it's way too soon to know if we're really a match. And there's Reinhardt—"

"I thought you were through with him."

"Right," Nicole said, "but there are moments when I'm still conflicted. Like: What if he called and had a good explanation for failing to show up in London?"

"Like he was kidnapped by space aliens? Give me a break." Stephanie's voice was heavy with sarcasm. "No matter what happens with this new guy, you've got to dump Reinhardt. You'll never make a life with a guy who," she paused and started counting on her fingers, "lives in another country (one finger), won't commit (two fingers), puts his job first (three), stands you up in a foreign country (four), doesn't bother to call and explain or apologize (five), refuses to tell you where he works (six), and— oh, yeah—is a spy (seven)."

"We don't know he's really a spy," Nicole said. "He never said that."

"Of course he is, dummy," Steph said, with great certainty. "Why else would he keep disappearing like that? Even if he isn't a spy––what about the rest?"

"You're right. He's a lost cause," Nicole said. "But that Josh—I mean, wow!"

Stephanie laughed. "I think that's great," she said. "Good for you!"

Later, when they retired to their rooms for the night, Nicole got out Robert's envelope and sat on the bed—a single bed disguised as a couch with a fitted red-and-blue slipcover and matching cushions. She poured out the contents of the envelope. Inside were two smaller tan envelopes. There was also a white letter-sized envelope with her name written in Robert's neat hand and a small, light-blue drawstring pouch with Tiffany printed in silver letters. She could tell that it held a small box.

The blue pouch caught her eye, but first she reached for one of the tan envelopes. It held a printout of a map with an *X* marking

Robert's house and the address written at the top of the page. It also held a set of keys on a key ring. It was just like the key ring she'd taken from his desk. Stapled to the map were five pages, the first of which was a floor plan of the house, which Robert had rendered to scale, he'd noted, on graph paper. The other pages were what appeared to be a detailed inventory of each piece of furniture and its value, as well as an explanation of the house's other special features, such as the intercom and security system. She leafed through it quickly and stuffed it back in the envelope.

The second envelope held keys and a printout of a map of the Owens Valley, which was about 250 miles east of L.A. The map had an X marking the location of his cabin. An address was noted at the top of the sheet. She felt something else in the envelope and reached in. It was a photo of Robert, holding a fishing pole with some kind of fishing-gear backpack hanging from his shoulder. Behind him was an A-frame cabin, probably a prefab—cream-colored with red trim. She stared at the picture of Robert for a long moment. He looked so harmless, and she'd thought he was her friend.

She figured the cabin in the photo must be his place in the Owens Valley. It looked nice. She couldn't really imagine Robert enjoying himself in the out-of-doors—fishing, of all things. And who had taken the picture? Perhaps he'd used a tripod. Had the police taken a look at the cabin? Did they even know about it? Did the murderer? Maybe it would bear checking out.

Finally, she opened the white envelope containing Robert's letter. In a way, it wasn't as crazy as she'd expected. It was coherent and written in his usual careful hand. But it also showed how delusional he was. It said:

Darling Nicole:

If you're reading this, it means I'm dead, and all of my dreams for the two of us will have come to nothing. As for the ring in the box, I was going to give it to you as soon as your Brit-cop boyfriend was out of the picture.

The unspoken words between us made me understand that somewhere, deep inside, you knew we were destined to be together. That's why I took the step that put my life in danger. I was playing some dangerous games, and I had to bring these projects to a conclusion and cut all ties, no matter what the risks. Otherwise, you could never be mine.

I want you to have my house, my cabin, and my money. As for the computer you'll find at the house, please erase the hard drive, remove it, and destroy it. You can burn it or bash it in with a hammer. Either will work. Then dispose of it somewhere far from my house. Above all, be sure it never falls into anyone else's hands. I don't need to tell you to be discreet about this. You're an intelligent and practical woman, Nicole. Those are just two of the things I love about you.

–Robert

After putting the letter back in its envelope, Nicole shoved all three envelopes into the big one, leaving just the small Tiffany pouch on the bed. She picked it up, and pulled out a small blue jewelry box and a folded piece of paper. She held the box away from her, as if it might explode, and forced herself to open it. The box was lined with royal blue velvet, and the ring was breathtaking. It held a huge, brilliantly sparkling diamond set in yellow gold, the classic Tiffany solitaire. She closed the box, then unfolded the paper. It was a sales receipt, dated six weeks before. The diamond was two and a half carets, it said, and had cost $41,000. If the ring had been from anyone else, she would have tried it on. But she didn't want anything to do with Robert's obsession. She put the receipt and the box back in the pouch and shoved it into the large envelope and closed the clasp. Then she put it back into her tote bag and the tote bag into the closet.

Nicole lay awake most of the night, thinking about the letter. Around four in the morning—even though she knew it was crazy—she began to wonder if Robert had something to do with Reinhardt's disappearance.

TEN

SHE'D SET HER ALARM FOR 7:00 a.m. to get ready for work but was jolted awake at 6:30 by loud knocking on her door. It was Stephanie. "Holy fuck, Nicole," she called. "Get up! You've got to see this."

Nicole struggled out of bed. Arnold, who'd been sleeping with her, jumped down, too, and they both followed Stephanie down the hall to the small dining room where Stephanie had set up her computer. She pointed to the screen.

"The tabloids know about your inheritance. Look!"

Nicole sat down in front of the computer, where XHN's headline screamed "Murdered Ex-Cop Leaves Millions to Nicole." It showed a picture of Nicole and Stephanie from the night they went to her condo for her things. She was carrying her suitcase. The photo's position, right under the headline, suggested she was toting away some of the loot. The caption read, "Nicole Graves, newly named heiress to mysterious fortune of murdered ex-cop, Robert Blair, leaves Westwood condo with sis, Stephanie Graves."

Nicole paused and reread the caption, noticing the error in Stephanie's name. It was Stephanie Barnes, not Graves. Barnes was Nicole's maiden name. Graves was her ex-husband's name. This was a bit of luck. The tabloids would have a hard time tracking down Stephanie if they didn't have her right name.

The story claimed that the details of Blair's will were released exclusively to XHN. It mentioned the value of Robert's two properties—although it didn't give the location of his cabin—along with the amounts he had in his bank and retirement accounts.

Nicole was horrified.

"How did they get this stuff?" Stephanie asked.

"I have no idea." Nicole paused and thought about it. "The only ones who knew about the will were you, me, and Robert's attorney, maybe his secretary. You didn't tell anyone, right?"

"Of course not. I promised."

"Then it had to come from Freeman's office. He made a big show of locking the file up in his safe." She looked at her watch. "I wonder what time his office opens." She quickly typed in Freeman's name and occupation on Yelp, pulling up his office information. It didn't open until 9:00 a.m.

"OK," Nicole said. "I have to get dressed and leave for the office. Damn. All those reporters will be back. I'll call Freeman from there, not that it will do much good. Now the whole world knows about the bequest."

As she was leaving Stephanie's, Nicole remembered she'd left Robert's envelope in the closet. She thought of Stephanie's boyfriend and realized it might not be a good idea to leave it unattended, especially with that huge diamond ring inside. She retrieved the envelope, still in the tote bag, and put it in the car. She planned to lock it in her desk drawer. That way she'd be sure it was safe.

Nicole was on edge as she drove to the office, watching for the gray SUV that had followed her the previous day. It was nowhere in sight. It occurred to her that the man might be driving another vehicle, but no one seemed to be following her.

She slowed down when she turned onto Avenue of the Stars and saw what was waiting in front of her office building. It was the biggest media circus yet—about fifty foot soldiers armed with cameras plus five TV vans. The paparazzi were blocking the valet lane despite efforts by three of the valets to force them onto the sidewalk. As soon as the men with cameras spotted her car, they rushed at it. She kept it moving slowly, forcing them out of her way. When she reached the valets, one of them summoned two security guards, who helped her out of the car and cleared a path for her. Meanwhile, the paparazzi were shouting things like, "How does it feel to be an overnight millionaire?" and "What did you have to do to get him to leave you everything?"

Surely, she thought, they didn't expect answers to such questions. Nevertheless, when she reached the door, she turned and recited her litany yet again, referring them to her attorney. This time she made no effort to look sorry she couldn't stop and chat.

She secured Robert's envelope in her desk drawer. That done, she called Sue's office. She hadn't arrived yet, so Nicole called her cell. "I'm just on my way in, dear," she said. "Terrible traffic. What's going on?"

Nicole explained, and Sue was quiet for a moment. "Well, that's a shame. I was hoping we could keep this matter quiet. You'll probably have that police detective calling you again. Remember, now: You're not going to talk to him. Tell him to call me. I'll deal with him. And don't talk to the press."

Next Nicole rang Freeman's office. She didn't have to explain why she was calling. "I'm so sorry the media got hold of Mr. Blair's file," he said. "My office was broken into last night. As far as we can tell, his was the only file taken."

"But you had it in the safe."

"The safe was open when I got here. I was sure I'd locked it. You saw me do that, didn't you?'

"Yes."

"I keep the combination on my computer. But that's password protected."

"Do you know how easy it is for someone to hack into a computer?"

"I guess I do now," he said. "I never thought it would come to this. Now I have reporters in front, wanting to talk to me, and my phone has been ringing off the hook. I'm sure it's much worse for you. I'm really sorry."

"I know you are," she said. And she could see he really did feel badly about the media frenzy he'd stirred up.

Around 10:00 a.m. there was more bad news. It was delivered in a call from Stephanie. "Look at XHN now!" she said. "Oh, my god. It was Becka. I know it was her. I'll bet she called and gave them that information. Maybe she sold it to them."

Nicole was already pulling up the site on her computer. The top story had been pushed down to second place. Now it led with the photo of her on the beach in Majorca. She looked awfully bare in her bikini. Then she realized they'd retouched the picture to make the swimsuit look even skimpier than it was. It was the same photo the police had found in Robert's house. But in this one Reinhardt had not been erased; he was sitting next to her. The headline over it read, "Nicky, Brit, and Murdered Cop in Love Triangle?" She hated the way they'd taken to calling her "Nicky," as if they actually knew her. Under the photo, the caption read, "Just a few months ago, Nicky was sunning with an unidentified man on a Majorcan beach." Her scalp prickled, and she felt suddenly chilled.

But as she looked more closely, she realized it would be pretty hard to identify Reinhardt from this photo. He was always camera shy, and she'd yet to get a good picture of him. In this one, he was wearing sunglasses and a Panama hat, its brim shading his face. In addition, his head was tilted in her direction, and he was grinning broadly, as if she'd just said something funny. The angle of his head, the glasses, the hat, even the smile, made him fairly unrecognizable.

As she read the story, it was clear XHN had no idea who he was. But they had done a good job digging up dirt about Nicole, herself. The story repeated the news of her divorce and her ex-husband's time in a British jail. It said, "One source disclosed that Nicole is romantically involved with a man living in England." They didn't have his name or occupation. Thank god for that, she thought.

The article disclosed the details of her most recent trip to London, explaining that she was supposed to rendezvous with her British lover on October 25th, but he had stood her up. "She returned to L.A. a week later," the story went on, "several days after Blair's death." It identified her as the office manager of the law firm where Blair worked and repeated that she was the one who discovered Blair's body and called the police.

"Nick, are you still there?" Stephanie said. "It's my fault. I'm so sorry. I mentioned your romance to Becka, and I should have known better. She's a tabloid junkie, but I never dreamed she'd do anything like this. You've been living such a glamorous life, and she was always asking about you."

"You didn't tell her about the inheritance, did you?" Nicole said.

"No, I didn't mention that to anyone. I promise," Stephanie said. "I just told her you were involved with a Brit you met in London, but I never said he stood you up. I swear. I don't know where they got that."

"Wait," Nicole said, after considering it a moment. "They must have hacked my phone. They didn't need anyone to tell them about Reinhardt. That's where they got the photo. When Reinhardt didn't show, I kept messaging and emailing him. But I never use his full name in messages—he asked me not to. I just used 'R.' His phone has no caller ID, and the location function is blocked, so at least they didn't get an inkling who he is. The people I work with know I have an English boyfriend, and at least one of them is a real blabbermouth. It probably wasn't your friend at all. They hacked my phone and pieced it together with scuttlebutt from my office."

"I'm so sorry, Nick."

"So am I. I just hope this doesn't get back to Reinhardt's bosses, whoever they are. You can be sure this story and the photo will turn up in the English tabloids. And it wouldn't help his career."

After they hung up, it occurred to Nicole that in all of her misadventures in the UK the year before—she'd been assaulted, kidnapped, and nearly killed—her name had never made its way into the news. She hadn't even considered the possibility or realized how fortunate she'd been, at least in this regard.

She spent the next hour going over various tabloid websites, then looked at the Associated Press, which had a more restrained version, leaving out the suggestion—never embellished upon—of a love triangle.

The Los Angeles Times' coverage came as a surprise. The reporter, Greg Albee, had been struck with an original idea. He'd contacted a couple of people who worked under Nicole. They refused to be identified because they weren't authorized to speak for the firm—in other words, they were afraid they'd get fired for talking to a reporter. They spoke highly of her, with comments like, "Nicole is great to work for. I consider her a friend," and "I don't know anyone in the office who doesn't like and respect her," and "I never saw any indication she was mixed up with Blair. She was nice to him because nobody else could stand him." Apparently he hadn't contacted Mindy, the office gossip.

The reporter also had found a woman she'd gone to college with—someone Nicole didn't even remember. She described Nicole as "a wonderful person, funny, bright, and genuinely nice." Finally, they'd interviewed Brad, her ex-husband. Seeing his name made her stomach knot. But, as she read it, this part of the story surprised and saddened her: "Nicole is incapable of what the papers were suggesting," said Graves. "She'd never take advantage of someone to get money, much less kill anyone. She just isn't made that way. The worst mistake I ever made was not fighting harder to keep her. I screwed up, and the worst thing that came of it was losing Nicole."

Next to the story was a photo of her, one she'd never seen before. Brad must have given it to the paper. It showed Nicole playing with his niece when she was small. She was smiling into the little girl's face, and the child was smiling back. She felt tears well up. She'd never go back to Brad, didn't even want to talk to him—he'd messed up their lives and their finances pretty badly. But she did appreciate his good word. And, as for the reporter, Albee, she felt like sending him a thank-you note.

Around 2:00 p.m., she received a call from Freeman. "The coroner is releasing Mr. Blair's body. You mentioned that your law firm would take care of the arrangements." He gave her the number of the coroner's office, and she sent a memo to the partners. Then, after double-checking with Di Angelo, she arranged for a funeral home to pick up Blair's body from the morgue.

Nicole chose a place in Culver City, because it was the closest to the firm. She explained to the undertaker what Robert had requested in his final instructions, a small nondenominational service with a closed casket.

"You can't put an announcement in the paper or let any word of the funeral slip out," she said. "It would attract a crowd of curiosity seekers and the media. He had no family, so the event will be strictly people from the office. We'll need a small room, one that would fit about…" She paused to think about it, "twenty to twenty-five people." The date was set for Wednesday, two days away. She sent Breanna with the company's credit card to choose a coffin and make arrangements, explaining once again that, under no circumstances, should anyone outside the firm hear about it. She'd just settled at her desk again when she remembered her dinner date with Josh. He was at work and probably hadn't seen the day's news. With a sinking heart, she realized she couldn't possibly go to his house. The paparazzi would be even more intent on following her, and she didn't want them to find out about Josh. The "love triangle" headline would morph into something worse. She could imagine how it would make her look. And she couldn't inflict this misery on Josh.

She started to call him on her cell. Then, remembering it had been hacked, used her office phone instead.

"Hi," he said. "Only three hours and," he paused, apparently checking his watch, "thirty-three minutes until I see you. I can't wait."

"I'm really sorry, Josh, but I can't make it," Nicole said. "Look at the latest on XHN and you'll see why. Robert Blair left me money, rather a lot of it. Believe me, I don't want it. He was a nut job. The tabloids found out about the inheritance and some other stuff. So now the whole hornets' nest is back on my doorstep. If I come to your place, they're sure to follow. I can't drag you into this mess—for both our sakes."

"Why don't I drive out there and pick you up? You can arrange for the building to let me into the garage, and I'll meet you there. The press won't know my car."

"I really want to see you," she said. "But it's just not going to happen tonight. I'm sorry."

He tried to persuade her, and she had to keep repeating the same thing. "You don't want to get mixed up in this. I can't let you." At last he seemed to realize that she wasn't going to change her mind. "Look," he said, before they hung up, "call me later, OK?"

Nicole said she would and added, "Promise me you won't believe everything you read in those stories."

As soon as she hung up, the phone rang again. This time it was Detective Miller. Before she had a chance to tell him to call Sue, he said, "Listen, I know your attorney told you not to talk to me. But I'm calling about something completely different. We're looking at the money in this murder case. We have reason to believe someone Blair was doing business with had him killed. We're hoping you can help us figure out who it might be. Maybe he told you something you don't even realize is important."

She repeated, word for word, what Sue had told her to say.

"Yes, yes," he said, impatiently. "But that was when you might have been considered a suspect. That's not what we're talking about here. You're no longer a suspect. You're a witness. You see the difference?"

"I'm sorry but you'll have to talk to Sue."

"Don't you want to help us find the person who killed your friend?" he said.

What she really wanted to say was that Robert was no friend of hers. Instead she repeated what she'd just said.

"All right," he said. "If that's the way you want to play it." It sounded like a threat. He hung up without saying goodbye. Another blow fell at 3:00 p.m., when Kevin Di Angelo called her in to see him. To her surprise, all four of the firm's senior partners were sitting on the couches in Di Angelo's large corner office. She'd had very little contact with any of them except for Di Angelo. There was Richard Bascomb, a bespectacled professorial-looking man, who always wore a bow tie. On the other couch was Rex Smith, a polite and soft-spoken man who was the firm's point man on tax loopholes. Next to him was Jonathan Rice. Rice was a white-haired, unmade-bed of a man, whose scruffy appearance belied the fact that he was a major behind-the-scenes political force, one of the city's most powerful kingmakers. He rarely came into the office except when he had an appointment to meet with his single client, the billionaire financier and philanthropist,

Ernest Pizer. Pizer's name was on museums, hospitals, theaters, and at least one building on every college campus in L.A.

Looking at the lineup, Nicole had the feeling she was about to be fired, or perhaps something worse, although she couldn't imagine what. She felt a little faint.

"I'm really sorry, Nicole, but we've talked it over, and we have to insist you take time off—a few weeks at least. With pay, of course. The media presence, as I'm sure you're aware, has become unmanageable. We have to let it run its course. These idiots will get tired of hounding you and move on. Once the story dies down, you can come back."

She was quiet, thinking it over. Maybe they weren't going to fire her this minute. They might be planning to wait until later and tell her not to bother coming back. As she thought about it, she realized she didn't really care. Di Angelo was right, of course. Under the present circumstances, work had become impossible. Just getting into the building and out again was physically and mentally exhausting.

Di Angelo mistook her silence for hesitation. "You can use the time to get out of town. You won't want to fly a commercial airline, of course, but we have an agreement with a private airline at Santa Monica Airport. You can go somewhere on the firm's dime. I know, why don't you fly to Hawaii? Soak up a little sun. Or go to London, or even Majorca, if you prefer."

The reference made her cringe. He'd been reading the tabloids.

"Thank you for being so considerate," she managed to say. "You're right. Things are completely out of control. I'd welcome some peace and quiet."

"The attorney we've hired for you—Sue Price, is it?—will take care of the details, expenses, and the like."

The four partners stood. Di Angelo came over to shake her hand, while the other three, being more restrained, nodded in her direction.

"Oh, and why don't you use the executive elevator to avoid—um—unwanted attention. It goes directly to the garage."

"I left my car with the valet," she said. "Even if I have them bring it to me in the garage, the paparazzi are going to recognize it the minute I drive out."

"Take one of our loaner cars. Get your things, then come back and let Mindy know I told you to use our elevator. She can take you there. After you've left—let's say an hour from now—I'll have someone go downstairs and let the media know you've taken a leave of absence. Hopefully, they'll go away."

Nicole went back to her office to arrange for the loaner car. Then she got her purse, as well as the tote bag with Robert's envelope, and returned to Di Angelo's outer office. She explained to Mindy what he'd said about the elevator. She made it a point to give Mindy as little information as possible. Hearing what Nicole had to say, Mindy forced her little rosebud mouth into a smile and said, "Well, we're really going to miss you around here, Nicole."

I'll bet, thought Nicole. *Who else could possibly furnish you with such juicy gossip?*

Mindy got up and motioned for Nicole to follow. They walked down the corridor toward the executive elevator, Mindy leading the way. She was plump and given to wearing tight dresses that emphasized her many curves. Today she was wearing a print jersey knockoff of the classic Diane Von Furstenberg wraparound. The gently draped folds of the skirt swung as she walked. The floor-to-ceiling windows to their right gave a startlingly clear view of the Century Plaza Hotel across the street and the city stretched out behind it. The day was sunny, the sky bright blue, and the air so clear they could see the snow-capped San Gabriel Mountains miles to the east.

They both stopped when they saw who had just pressed the elevator's button and was waiting for it to arrive. It was Rice's billionaire client, Ernest Pizer. Nicole had never seen him in person but recognized him from pictures in the paper and on the news. He was roly-poly and bald with a fringe of white hair. With a white mustache and beard, he would have made a perfect Santa Claus. What surprised her was that he was short, not much taller than she.

Mindy grabbed Nicole's arm and stopped. "Let's wait," she said in a whisper. Her meaning was clear. Nicole, a lowly office worker, couldn't possibly ride the elevator with the likes of Ernest Pizer.

But Pizer had other ideas. He looked at Nicole and said in a kind voice, "Well, what are you waiting for young lady? Why don't you ride down with me and keep a lonely old man company?" Behind his glasses, his eyes twinkled, and he smiled.

Nicole smiled back and stepped forward to wait with him.

Mindy, her behind swaying in rhythm to her walk, departed back along the hall. When the elevator came, Nicole and Pizer got in. It started down, in smooth, almost silent motion.

"I know who you are," he said, matter-of-factly. "All that news coverage?" He shook his head. "What a mess this unfortunate event has made for you. You have my condolences. I've worked all my life to keep that mob away from me. I have any number of media representatives, media consultants. They're not much help. Once something goes viral…" He shook his head. "Dreadful, just dreadful."

"It really is," she agreed. "But eventually it will stop, and I'll get my life back."

He looked at her and said, "I certainly hope so." But the smile had disappeared, and his expression had soured, as if he thought it unlikely that this would turn out well. A moment later, the door opened at the garage level, and they both got out. Pizer nodded toward her, "Goodbye, young lady," he said. "And good luck."

ELEVEN

NICOLE HEADED DIRECTLY for the garage manager's office to claim her loaner car. As she stood, waiting for the valet to deliver the vehicle, she wondered about Pizer, what sort of person he was. In the elevator, he'd seemed kind, even empathetic.

Then she recalled Robert telling her about Pizer's various marriages, prenups, and divorces. His original wife, long gone, had been replaced by a series of trophy wives. A couple of years ago Robert had told her that Wife Number One had reemerged to demand more money. When she came into the office to negotiate, she'd called Pizer "a crooked old mobster," before her lawyer, Rice, and Rick Sargosian had hustled her into a conference room and shut the door. She'd gotten her settlement, Robert had said, "a big one."

Thinking of Pizer's billions, Nicole felt that few became that rich without hurting a lot of other people on the way. And that most of the big donors to charity were not contributing in order to "give back" or "make the world a better place" as they were fond of saying, but to satisfy the needs of their own egos. Thinking it over, she realized that was a pretty broad generalization. There had to be some exceptions.

The media didn't recognize her in the company's loaner car, and she drove home unimpeded. She was planning to pack enough clothes for a couple of weeks, although she had no plan, no idea where she was going. Staying with her sister was out of the question. Now that she was sure the media had hacked her phone, it would be easy for them to figure out where Stephanie lived. She called Steph daily. All the paparazzi would need was a reverse phone directory. Child's play. They'd camp outside Steph's apartment, disrupt her life, and infuriate her neighbors.

When Nicole reached her building, a mob of paparazzi was already in front, waiting for her. She wondered if the partners had wasted any time telling them she was leaving the office. Probably not, judging by the gathering of TV vans and cameras. She'd left her garage door opener in her car, so using the building's underground parking was out of the question. She parked on the street and got out, making sure to bring her purse and tote bag with her. Leaving anything, even a grocery bag, in a parked car was an invitation to the paparazzi, not to mention thieves, who specialized in smash and grab "retrieval."

She walked through the crowd, ignoring questions, and went into the building without even attempting to disguise her displeasure or tell them to call Sue. A couple of men with cameras rushed her as she opened the door, as if they planned to push past her into the lobby, but she was quicker than they were. She closed the door, and it locked before they could get there.

She took the elevator to the second floor, opened the door of her condo, and quickly stepped back. The place had been torn apart; everything was on the floor. Even the cushions on her couch had been slit open, and some of the foam filling was falling out. She quickly checked the second bedroom, where she kept her computer. It was gone. Luckily, her important files were backed up on the cloud––not that she had anything crucial on her computer, but it did have her address book, email, and other items that would have taken a lot of work to reassemble.

In her bedroom, the drawers and closets were all open, her clothes scattered on the floor. The mattress had been pulled off the bed and was tipped on its side, leaning against the box springs. The chair to her vanity table was upside down. She righted it and sat down, trying to collect her thoughts.

Finally, she picked up her purse, got out her phone, and called 911. Then she called Sue.

"How dreadful," Sue said. "When the police leave, pack a few things and come to my office. It doesn't matter if reporters follow you. They already know I'm your attorney, and it's not hard to figure out where my office is. Once you get here, I should be able to sneak you out of the building without anyone following us.

By now Nicole could hear police sirens. She was thinking of how thrilled the horde outside would be with this new development. Their immediate hope, of course, would be that she was being arrested. But a break-in would satisfy some of their blood lust, provide another day's headlines, and stir up speculation about what the burglar had been after.

This break-in was another sign that Detective Miller had been right. Whoever had killed Robert and trashed his house was now targeting her. She thought of the man who'd tried to run her down with his car and attempted to force her into a head-on collision. It was all tied together.

The intercom rang: It was the police. She buzzed them into the building. Once inside the condo, they wandered around looking at the mess.

A cop with a goatee and a beer belly seemed to be in charge. He introduced himself as Sergeant Gibbs. When she identified herself, she could tell from his expression that he recognized her name. He picked up the remains of the sofa cushions and asked her to have a seat while he called headquarters. When he was done with his call, he said, "Is anything missing?"

"So far the only thing I've noticed is that my computer is gone. I'll know more when I sort through this mess."

"When did it happen?

"I stayed at my sister's last night and went directly to work from there. So it could have been any time since noon yesterday."

The cop nodded. "Has the building got surveillance?"

It did. She gave them the phone number of the property management firm used by the condo association. The firm took care of security. When Sergeant Gibbs was done with his questions, he told her that he and his partner would wait with her until Detective Miller arrived. Headquarters had notified Miller about the break-in, since she was involved in a case he was handling.

She explained that she was packing up so she could stay somewhere else for a few days. The policeman seemed to think this was a good idea.

She started picking up clothes to take, folding them neatly and placing them in a suitcase. She had just finished packing when the buzzer from the front door sounded. She went to the intercom: It was Detective Miller.

After he arrived at her door, she let him in, and the two uniformed cops left.

Looking around at the mess, Miller said, "Well, you're a real magnet for trouble, Ms. Graves. Anything missing?"

"So far, I think it's just my computer."

"What's on it? You work from home?"

"Well, yes, sometimes. I work for a law firm, and things do come up after hours. All of my work-related stuff has encrypted passwords. But you're right; I'll have to let the firm know the computer was stolen."

He didn't seem much interested, instead making a tour through her condo, emerging back in the living room "So, this must have happened in the last twenty-four hours, right? You stayed with your sister last night."

She nodded, not bothering to ask how he knew.

"Any idea who did this?'

"No."

"Know what they're looking for?"

"Not a clue."

"Going back to stay with sis?"

"I guess."

"We may want to talk to you again. I'd consider it a favor if you didn't leave town." He was silent a moment, then added, "You sure you don't want to share anything with me?"

"Talk to my attorney," she said.

He lifted his arms in an exaggerated shrug, as if asking himself what he was supposed to do with someone so unreasonable.

Nicole was tempted to tell him about the car that had almost run her off the road, but she knew what would happen. First he'd ask if she'd gotten the license number, which she hadn't. Then he'd repeat what he'd said before—that she had to tell him what she knew about Robert. Well, now she did know something. But she certainly wasn't going to tell Miller about Robert's envelope. If she did, he'd say it was vital evidence and demand that she hand it over.

She didn't believe the police were capable of protecting her. She'd read too often of witnesses who were killed or went missing. In particular, she didn't trust Miller. He'd been hostile and suspicious of her from the start. Handing over the envelope would be a mistake; her lawyer had warned her not to give Miller any more information. Besides that, she'd had a bad feeling about law enforcement ever since her experience in England the previous year. In that case, the police hadn't believed her when she told them she was in danger. Their refusal to take her seriously had almost gotten her killed.

Once the detective was gone, she took her suitcase, with some clothes and Robert's envelope inside, and went down to the car. She had to pull it slowly away from the curb to avoid hitting the paparazzi clustered around it. She drove directly to Sue's office, followed by a motorcade of reporters and TV vans. The guard at the garage had Nicole's name on his list. The long line of cars following her were refused admission; they found themselves stuck in line, bumper-to-bumper, and they all started sounding their horns. Nicole got her suitcase out of the trunk, then took the elevator up, glad to get away from them.

Sue was waiting for her. She ushered Nicole into her office and sat her down.

"Here," Sue said, pulling a white envelope out of a drawer and pushing it across the desk. "Your firm wants you to have this, and I'm going to drop you off at Hertz. I've reserved a car for you. Before we leave, I'll give you a big hat so the mob out there doesn't spot you."

Nicole picked up the envelope. Inside was an American Express Platinum card with her name and the firm's name just below it. All at once she remembered something Reinhardt had told her when they first met, when she'd stumbled into the middle of an undercover investigation he was working. "When you're in a perilous situation, and don't know who to trust, trust no one." It occurred to her that, as honest and honorable as Sue might seem, her real allegiance was probably not to her, Nicole, but to the people who were paying the tab: Bascomb, Rice, Smith & Di Angelo. And their generosity in these arrangements was making Nicole uneasy.

"You're going to have expenses in the next couple of weeks," Sue was saying, "and your firm is footing the bill. Charge everything to this credit card. You have carte blanche. Just keep track of your expenses."

After studying the credit card for a moment, Nicole put it back on the desk. "Listen, Sue, you bill the firm for any expenses related to my case, right?"

Sue nodded.

"I'm not comfortable using a credit card," Nicole went on. "Is it possible for you to get me cash instead? Say, $3,000?"

"But why?" Sue said. "I don't understand your thinking."

"It's just a feeling I have. Anyone with computer smarts could look up my charges on the credit card and keep track of where I am and what I'm doing. I have a hunch the people who killed Robert are the ones who trashed my condo. I don't think I'm safe, and I need to make myself scarce for a while."

Left unsaid was the bad vibe Nicole had picked up when she met with the partners earlier in the day. It didn't make sense—all four of them congregated there, just for her.

"Well," Sue said slowly. "We can let the firm know you need a bodyguard. I'm sure they'll be willing."

"No," said Nicole. "I'll be fine if I can just disappear and get off the grid. Can you get me the cash?"

"Of course," Sue said. "But $3,000? That's not enough to live on for a couple of weeks. You'll have lodgings to pay for, meals…"

"Make it $6,000 then. I'm not going to stay at the Four Seasons."

"We'll make it $10,000," said Sue. "I'll send my secretary to the bank right now with my authorization." She pulled a checkbook out of her desk and wrote a check. Then she scrawled a note on a piece of paper and went out to deliver it to her secretary.

When Sue was back, Nicole said, "I also want to do something about my phone. That's another way I could be tracked, but I'll need to stay in touch with you. On our way to the rental car agency, could you stop at an electronics store? I'll run in and get some prepaid, disposable phones. That way you'll be able to reach me, but no one else will."

A little crinkle had appeared on Sue's forehead. "If you really think you're in that much danger, please don't go off by yourself." She paused a moment, then said brightly, "I know! You can stay with me. No one will know where you are."

"Thanks," Nicole said. "But I do have a plan. I'll be fine."

"I'm sure you will, Nicole," Sue said, "But first let's make sure." She got up from her desk and opened a closet where her purse hung on a hook. She reached into it and pulled something out. When she turned around, she was holding a small silver gun.

Nicole jumped to her feet, hand at her throat.

Sue looked at her in surprise. "It isn't loaded. Here, I'm going to get some bullets. Do you know how to load it?"

Nicole could feel herself flush. "I thought—"

"You thought I was going to shoot you?" Sue laughed. "Nicole, I'm on your side. You have to trust me. This gun belonged to my aunt. She died a couple of years ago, but it's still registered to her. So if anything happens, and you need to use it, don't worry. It can't be traced back to me or you, for that matter. Here, I'll show you how to load it."

Nicole went over to her and watched.

"Have you ever shot a gun?" Sue asked.

Nicole remembered, all at once, when Reinhardt had asked her the same question. It was just after he'd kissed her for the first time. They were hiding in a stable on the Scottish coast, waiting for his squad to make a drug bust. He had to leave her there and join his team, and he'd insisted on giving her a quick lesson in using a gun. After he'd left, she'd abandoned the stable, unable to endure the wait. She'd left the gun behind, choosing instead a flare gun he'd left so she could signal for help if she needed it. The flare gun had, in fact, done a perfectly adequate job of protecting her. She shivered, not wanting to think about it.

"I don't want it," Nicole said. "I don't like guns."

"You sense you may be in danger, and I agree," Sue said. "So it's your choice. Either you take the gun, or you're not getting the cash you want. It's as simple as that."

Nicole sighed and walked over to get yet another lesson in the care and handling of a gun.

"This is a Smith & Wesson compact revolver," Sue explained. "It's small enough to carry in your purse, but it only holds five bullets, so it's important to have extras if you need to reload."

When Sue was done demonstrating the weapon and showing how to set it so it wouldn't fire accidentally, Nicole put the gun in her purse, along with a small jewelry bag Sue had found and filled with bullets. By now, the secretary had returned with an envelope of cash. Sue counted it, handed it to Nicole, then went into the closet and pulled down a large, black, floppy-brimmed hat. Nicole put it on, but it was so big that it slipped down, almost covering her eyes. Laughing, Sue pulled it off and took it over to her desk to adjust the hatband. She placed the hat back on Nicole's head, then flipped the brim at an angle. "Perfect," she said. "Now put on your sunglasses, and we're good to go."

TWELVE

IT WAS DARK BY THE TIME Sue dropped her off at the car rental agency. Nicole—still wearing her sunglasses and Sue's hat—waved goodbye and carried her suitcase into the agency. Two people were already waiting in line. There was only one agent, and it took almost twenty minutes before she reached the counter.

She used the time to check email and messages. There was nothing, of course, from Reinhardt. But there was a text message from Josh. "Thinking about you. Call me."

Nicole started to answer, then stopped. The paparazzi, and maybe others, had hacked this phone. She couldn't reply without attracting their attention. She and Sue had stopped on the way here to get disposable phones; she'd given one to Sue, and her own was in her purse. But she didn't want to use it to call Josh. Disposable phone to disposable phone—that was the rule if you didn't want your number traced.

She'd have to figure out another way to let Josh know she'd be off the grid for a while. She turned off the phone and dropped it into her purse. She couldn't use it anymore. It was too much of a liability. Even with location services turned off, it still could be used to track her. Her smart phone was essential in her daily life. She was always in touch, aware of the latest headlines. Most of all, she loved the way it gave her access to the web and immediate answers to just about any question. She was going to miss it.

At last Nicole made her way to the counter. More waiting for the paperwork to be filled out, then printed. Finally, she was handed two keys on a ring and the number of the parking space of the car Sue had reserved for her. It was at the back of the lot under a yellow sign that said HERTZ PRESTIGE COLLECTION. Somewhat to her astonishment, it was a sleek silver Mercedes sedan, not exactly the sort of car that would easily blend in. Besides, it occurred to her that the rental agency and others with an interest in her whereabouts would be able to track her through the vehicle's GPS.

She went back to the office, where three people were now waiting in line. She told the agent she'd changed her mind and put the keys on the counter. He asked her to wait—gesturing toward the line—because she'd have to sign some forms. Remembering how long it had taken for him to process the rental in the first place, she said, "No thanks," and walked out of the agency, ignoring his shouts of protest.

She headed toward the nearest bus stop, several blocks away. It was starting to get dark. Passing a convenience store, she noticed two pay phones on the wall outside. She had to call Josh, and here was her chance. She went to the first phone and picked up the receiver. It was dead, but the second one had a dial tone. She got out her coin purse, fed in three quarters, and punched in his number.

"Hello?" he said, somewhat uncertainly.

"It's me," she said.

"Oh, you!" She could hear the smile in his voice. "Hey, where are you? I don't recognize the number."

"I'm at a pay phone."

"I didn't know they had those anymore."

"I didn't either," she said. "Listen, I said I'd call, so here I am. I had to turn off my cell because the tabloids hacked it. I just wanted to let you know that I'll be out of touch, without a phone, for a bit."

"Hey, I read those stories," he said. "You're not—"

He was interrupted by a woman's recorded voice, saying, "To continue with this call, please deposit seventy-five cents."

"I'm out of quarters," Nicole said. The phone went silent.

She hung up. It rang almost immediately, and she picked it up.

"I saw the number on caller ID," Josh said. "As I was saying, I read today's stories. You aren't—I mean, are you going off to meet that English guy who was in that photo with you? Is he the one you had a relationship with?"

She could tell he was jealous and trying not to be a jerk about it. "No. I'm not seeing him. A lot of what the tabloids are saying is a distortion of the truth," she went on, "but I was involved with him, and he did stand me up. He hasn't contacted me since. I'm done with him."

"Good," Josh said. "Come stay with me. Tell me where you are, and I'll pick you up. Without a cell phone, you'll be off the grid. You can keep out of sight, and no one would ever guess where you are."

She was quiet a moment, thinking how nice that would be—if only it were that simple.

"Look," she answered, "there's something I have to do." She was choosing her words carefully. "And—well, it's complicated. I don't want to drag anyone else into it."

"It's about the guy who was murdered, isn't it?" he said.

When she didn't answer, he said, "Hey, that guy was mixed up with some very dangerous people. Nicole, you're scaring me."

She tried to think of a way to reassure him. Finally, she said, "I'm sorry, but I can't tell you any more than that. I promise I won't put myself in danger. I'm going to say goodbye now. It will just be a day or two. The minute I'm done, I'll call you. I promise."

She could hear him protesting as she hung up the phone. She began walking toward the bus stop. Behind her, the phone was ringing again. She walked faster, sorry she'd upset him. But she did have a plan. It wouldn't take long, and once she'd taken care of it, she'd call him.

As she reached the corner, one of the big blue buses that ran along Pico Boulevard appeared. She climbed on and paid the fare; it hauled her through a slightly seedy area of small storefront shops, some vacant, others occupied with marginal businesses that were so bereft of customers she wondered if they might be money-laundering operations.

Next, the bus entered a strip of more prosperous establishments bordering Beverly Hills. This ran through a residential neighborhood mainly occupied by orthodox and ultra-orthodox Jews. She looked out the window as the bus passed delicatessens, kosher eateries, and markets, mixed with various other businesses that served the area's thriving population. Onward they moved along the congested street, stopping and starting, toward Santa Monica.

It struck her now, in a way that it never did when she was driving, how empty the sidewalks were. Occasionally, she'd spot an elderly man or woman in a motorized wheelchair, tooling across a street, up the specially-designed curb, and along the sidewalk. But, while auto traffic was dense, pedestrians were few. From her own experience, she knew that walking—even in her own relatively safe neighborhood—was problematic.

Although she did her running on a treadmill at the gym, Nicole had to walk her dog in the neighborhood surrounding her condo. Almost invariably she'd find herself being panhandled by one of the homeless—usually male, but sometimes female—who camped on the sidewalks and in storefront doorways. Sometimes she'd cross the street to avoid an obviously deranged person who was screaming or making menacing gestures at passersby. And there was also the issue of the Westside's hyper-aggressive drivers who had no intention of stopping for pedestrians.

Spotting the freeway overpass ahead, she pulled the cord for the bus to stop. She knew exactly where she was headed. The Rent-a-Wreck auto agency was now a nationwide franchise. As a girl, she'd been aware of it as the one-of-a-kind brainchild of a freethinking entrepreneur. He'd built a steady business by renting cars that really did look like wrecks—old, dented and dirty but usually perfectly drivable. It was rumored that movie stars and other famous people rented them because of the anonymity they afforded. In the agency's heyday, Marlon Brando was said to be a regular customer.

Rent-a-Wreck had come a long way since then. It now rented cars that were just a few years old and in pretty good shape. What made the agency attractive to Nicole was that they accepted cash customers, while major brands like Hertz and Avis demanded credit cards. She went in, produced her driver's license, and put down a $350 deposit and a week's advance rental in cash. She left in a nondescript three-year-old beige Toyota and drove a mile east to a Best Western motel. It was on Sepulveda, a wide boulevard of commercial ugliness lined with cracked sidewalks and palm trees. The motel or inn, as it was called, occupied several clunky-looking white buildings in the middle of a block of cracker-box apartment houses.

She checked in, again using cash, and was surprised by the hefty room rate—almost $200 a night. But the place was nicer inside than it appeared from the street, with a swimming pool, gym, and free Wi-Fi. Her room was attractive with yellow walls, soft lighting, and a comfy-looking, king-sized bed. The clock on the nightstand said it was 7:30 p.m. She hadn't had dinner but was too exhausted to feel hungry; she lay down and promptly fell asleep.

Nicole awoke at 7:00 a.m., her stomach growling in protest at the missed dinner. Checking in, she'd noticed a sign in the lobby announcing that a full breakfast, included with the room, was available from 6:30 a.m. until 9:30 a.m. She brushed her teeth, pulled on her clothes, ran her fingers through her hair, and went down to the tiny dining room. The only other people there were an elderly Asian couple who looked up briefly when she walked in, then focused back on their meal. At the breakfast buffet, she served herself scrambled eggs and bacon, then popped a slice of bread into the toaster and poured herself a cup of coffee. The food was lukewarm and tasteless, but she was so hungry she went back for seconds.

Back in her room, Nicole made more coffee in a small automatic coffee maker stationed on a counter outside the bathroom. Then she got out the envelope Freeman had given her and sat down at the desk to go over its contents more carefully. She'd noticed before that Robert's notes about his house seemed to mainly be an inventory of its furnishings and their cost. His handwriting was small and sketchy, written in pencil, and a bit hard to make out. Robert was a great one for pencils. He was the only person she knew who preferred to write by hand and kept a container of sharp pencils on his desk. On the other hand, he was a whiz with the computer and seemed to know a lot about programming and how to hack into other people's computers.

As she leafed through the pages, the words *safe room* jumped out at her. She did a double take, then turned back to the gridded rendering of his floor plan. Sure enough, between the two bedrooms was a room marked SR.

Of course he'd have a safe room, she thought. He had good reason to be paranoid. And he was a secretive person—that was the defining characteristic of his personality. The safe room was probably where he'd keep his computer.

She turned back to the page of descriptions. And there it was: "How to open SR." The room was behind a wall of bookshelves in the master bedroom. The button that made the wall swing open was hidden behind the molding around the bookcase. It was located on the bottom shelf near the fireplace. The note cautioned that anyone entering the room had to stand back because the bookcase swung outward when it opened. It gave instructions for securing the safe room from inside, so no one else could enter. It also noted that the walls were reinforced with half-inch steel and were bullet proof.

She read the rest of the inventory and instructions for the house's many features: the garbage compactor (this stopped her for a moment while she considered whether people really used trash compactors in this era of recycling), controls for the home theater, and the password and instructions for the security system. But the safe room was what interested her. If her theory was right, and the computer was in the safe room, neither the police nor the killer could have found it without these instructions.

Originally, her plan had been to drive up to Robert's cabin and see if his computer was there. But now she realized it might be a lot easier than that. If the computer was in his safe room, all she had to do was go up to his house. She could check it out, copy his computer files, and be back in a single day. More than a week had passed since Robert's murder, and she was fairly certain his house would no longer be taped off as a crime scene. Even if it was, it wouldn't be guarded at this point. She had the key, and besides she was—while not quite the owner—heir to it. She'd hardly be trespassing.

First she had to figure out a way to get into the house without attracting notice. She couldn't enter by the front door because someone might see her. She remembered the broken surveillance camera. Had the police fixed it? Were they keeping an eye on the house? She got out her iPad and opened a map in "earth view" to get a look at the streets surrounding Robert's house. It appeared that the property could be reached through an empty lot on the street below. She studied the map. There was no indication of how steep the hill might be. She figured it would be possible—though perhaps a bit of a hike, given the area's hilly terrain—to climb up to Robert's rear fence. She was fairly certain she'd noticed a gate in that fence the day she went to his house and found his body. She also had to assume that one of the house keys in the envelope would open the gate, which was certain to be locked.

Before she did anything, she had to make herself not just unrecognizable but able to fade into the background, so ordinary-looking that no one would notice her or remember she was there. Putting on Sue's floppy black hat and sunglasses, she glanced in the mirror. The hat and glasses were completely over the top, certain to draw attention. The disguise Sue had rigged up made her look like a celebrity trying—not very hard—to avoid the paparazzi or at least prevent them from catching her without makeup.

She went down to the parking area, got her car, and drove less than a half mile to a discount store to find a more appropriate outfit. She picked out a long silk scarf, a pair of jeans, and tennis shoes. Then, in the men's department she found a T-shirt and a beige windbreaker, both large enough to pretty much hide her figure. Finally, she chose a backpack and a gray baseball cap. She made sure the cap was adjustable. In the hardware department, she picked up a small but powerful flashlight with an adjustable beam.

This accomplished, Nicole returned to her car and drove two blocks to a big-box discount store. She bought a couple of flash drives so she'd be able to copy Robert's files if she did find his computer. Along with these, she chose a connector that would allow her to use the flashdrives on her iPad, since she didn't have access to a computer. She also bought another disposable phone like the one she'd gotten for Sue and herself.

She arranged for the store to send it—same-day delivery— to Stephanie, checking the box on the delivery form requiring a signature. She didn't want it falling into the wrong hands.

She enclosed a gift card, with her disposable phone's number, explaining to Stephanie that she'd be gone a couple of days, that the phone was for emergencies only, and no one else should know about it. She paid cash for everything.

By now it was 1:00 p.m. She hadn't eaten lunch, and she was hungry. But she couldn't possibly make an appearance in one of the area's casual eateries in her celebrity headgear. She headed back to the motel to change. Her first step was to wrap the long silk scarf she'd bought around her chest to flatten her figure. Then she put on her new jeans, T-shirt and the windbreaker. As a final touch, she tucked her hair into the baseball cap.

She found a full-length mirror on the back of the closet door and was so surprised by her reflection that she laughed out loud. She looked like a teenage boy, except that she was wearing lipstick. She went into the bathroom and used a washcloth to scrub it off.

She took the pouch with the diamond ring out of Robert's envelope and put it, along with the cash Sue had given her and her cell phone, in an almost hidden, zippered compartment inside the backpack. Next, she put in her disposable phone, the flashlight, Sue's gun, her iPad, and Robert's envelope with the information about his houses. On top of everything else, she put the newly purchased flash drives, and other essentials she carried in her purse. No sense leaving this stuff in a motel room. Then she went down to her car and once more drove a few blocks to a strip mall with several fast-food restaurants. She chose Mexican and ordered fajitas and a Coke. It was 2:00 p.m. by the time she was on her way to Robert's house.

THIRTEEN

NICOLE WAS CONFIDENT that no one would recognize her or the Rent-a-Wreck car. Even so, she kept a careful watch to be sure she wasn't being followed. Traffic was light, and she reached the street below Robert's in twenty minutes. There was no activity, no one in sight but a couple of gardeners tending a house on the corner. She parked at the empty lot below Robert's and got out. The gardeners, intent on their work, weren't looking in her direction. The hill was fairly steep, covered with tall, dry grass. She started up the hill and was soon sweating with the effort. Although she was fit from her morning runs, she wasn't used to negotiating this much of an incline. It wasn't long before the backs of her thighs ached with every step.

By the time she reached the fence behind Robert's yard, her hair was drenched under her cap, sweat running down her face. She walked over to the gate and stared at it. There was no latch on the outside, but it did have a keyhole. She got out the keys and tried them. The third one fit; she turned it and heard the lock click open. She pulled, then pushed the gate, but nothing happened.

She pressed her face to the bars of the fence to get a look at what was on the other side. There was a simple latch holding the gate closed, but it was almost at the top of the gate, perhaps six feet from the ground. She stepped up on the horizontal bar at the bottom of the fence and stretched out her arm. She still couldn't reach it. She got down, foraged through her backpack, and pulled out the flashlight. After a few tries, she was able to use it to push the latch up until it disengaged, and the gate swung open.

Nicole found herself on a path leading around the reinforced terrace that supported the swimming pool. She used the house key to get in the back door. Finding herself in the laundry room, she stopped when she saw the kitchen. Pots, pans, broken dishes, and glassware were scattered all over the floor. As she made her way through, she had to be careful not to step on broken shards of china and glass.

Beneath the mess, she could see that the kitchen was beautifully designed, the floor and backsplashes in tiny turquoise tiles. There were white marble countertops and light wood cabinets with frosted glass panes. The Sub-Zero appliances included a refrigerator that looked big enough to walk around in. She opened the door, and the smell hit her. Food, spilled from containers, was rotting on the bottom of the refrigerator. The killer had overlooked nothing in his search. She quickly closed the door.

She continued through the house, picking her way through discarded objects and overturned furniture. Sometimes she had to stop and clear a path. But the mess couldn't hide the fact that the house was truly gorgeous. The living room was gigantic, and the side of the house with a view had floor-to-ceiling windows. Wrapped around the exterior was a redwood deck. The late afternoon light, streaming in from the west, made the house seem to float above the city.

Just past the living room, she found the hall leading to Robert's bedroom. Here, as in the rest of the house, everything had been turned upside down and tossed on the floor. Nicole immediately spotted the fireplace and bookcase he'd described in his notes. She went over and cleared furniture and books from the floor near the bookcase.

She got the envelope out of her backpack and reread the instructions for opening the safe room. She located the button behind the molding at the bottom of the bookcase, then pressed it and stepped back. Silently, the bookcase moved toward her, providing entry to the dark space beyond. She went in: The safe room was warm and smelled musty.

She felt around on the wall for a light switch but couldn't locate it. Stepping back into the bedroom, she picked up her backpack and pulled out the flashlight. She waved the beam around the safe room until she located the light switch and turned it on. Once the light was on, the room was a disappointment: an ordinary twelve-by-twelve office with a couch, a desk and chair, some cabinets, and bookshelves. But, yes, here was Robert's missing computer. It looked new. Next to it was a CCTV console that showed eight different views of the house fed by security cameras inside and out. One of the screens was blank, and she realized it must be connected to the camera on the carport, the broken one she'd seen when she first came looking for Robert.

With a start, she noticed the pictures on the wall. They were large, perhaps four-by-six feet, printed on canvas and framed, and they were of her. Five photos in all. There she was in her wedding dress, beaming with happiness. Brad, her ex, had been in that photo, but all traces of him were now gone. Another showed her in her late teens, looking down from the branches of a tree that stood in her parents' backyard. It was where she used to go when she wanted to get away from the noise of her parents' house, always overflowing with extended family and friends. That photo was in her high-school scrapbook, which she now kept in a box in the closet of her spare bedroom. Her wedding pictures were there, too. She hadn't been able to bring herself to throw them away.

The next two pictures were more recent, and these were unfamiliar. One was of her sitting at her desk; another of her outside, walking near the office. When her gaze fell on the last one, she recoiled. It showed her standing at her bedroom mirror, trying on the filmy nightgown she'd bought for her trip to Majorca with Reinhardt, the very gown Robert had stolen. The photo was taken from behind, so it showed the back view of her, as well as the front, reflected in the mirror. She might as well have been naked.

Her face burning with outrage, she yanked it from the wall, threw it face down on the floor and stamped on it. Along with everything else, he was a peeping tom. Wait, she thought, how on earth had he taken this picture? Her condo was on the second floor, and her bedroom wasn't positioned near the wall the paparazzi had climbed to get a view of her bathroom. Had Robert hidden a camera in her bedroom? Had he actually been there? Hiding in her closet, watching? The thought of it made her feel sick. She grabbed the remaining pictures and threw them on the floor face down.

All at once she was aware of noise outside. She went back into the living room and looked out the window. The sound was just a neighbor coming home, but it made her realize how vulnerable she was. She consulted Robert's directions again.

She got her backpack and took it into the safe room. Then she closed and secured the door by turning three deadbolt locks, evenly spaced up the edge of the moving wall. She noticed there were four brackets on the moving wall—one on either side of the opening and two in the center—for a locking bar. She found the bar leaning against the wall. It was heavy, but she managed to lift it into place.

Consulting the instructions again, she went to the control panel next to the light switch and disabled the mechanism that opened the door. Then she turned on the air conditioner and took a look around. Aside from the other furniture, the room held a water cooler, and, on top of a small cabinet next to it, a bowl with a large assortment of energy bars.

Sitting in one corner was a square, white piece of furniture she couldn't identify. She went over to take a closer look. It was sealed in its original plastic wrapper and bore a label reading, "Porta Potti Portable Toilet." Clearly Robert had prepared this room in case he had to hole up in here a while.

Next, Nicole went through the desk drawers. They were empty except for the center top drawer, where she found another Swiss Army knife. He did like those, didn't he? There were the usual office supplies: pencils, paper clips, rubber bands, a few pens. She turned on the computer and plugged in one of her flash drives. The computer asked for a password. She took another look at Robert's instructions. He'd told her to delete his files, but hadn't given her the password to log on to the computer. It occurred to her that perhaps he'd made it easy, something he knew she'd figure out. After a moment's thought, she typed in Nicole. She had to enter it twice because he'd used all lowercase letters, no capital N. The computer instantly logged her in. When it was fully loaded, she could see he had quite a few files in his documents folder. She began copying them onto one of the flash drives. She didn't bother reading them. Her goal was to copy everything, get out as quickly as possible, and read them later.

Nicole was so intent on what she was doing that she jumped when she heard a noise. It sounded like someone was walking around inside the house. She couldn't tell because the sound was muffled by the safe room's thick walls. Heart thumping wildly, she went to the CCTV console. One camera view showed two figures moving around. They must have closed the blinds because the room they were in was almost dark, and it was hard to make out their faces. After studying the view for a moment, she realized they were in the master bedroom, the room she'd just gone through to get into the safe room.

She looked more closely at the console itself. There was a knob under each monitor that looked like the kind used to adjust sound on old-fashioned TV sets. She turned the knob under the bedroom view. There was a click, and all at once she could hear their voices. She quickly lowered the volume. "Where do you think it is?" said a man. With a shock, she recognized the voice: It was Rick Sargosian.

A second voice, this one unfamiliar, answered, "According to the floor plan, there were originally three bedrooms. Now there are only two, so we figure he converted one of them into a safe room. It should be on the other side of this wall."

She held her breath as they started pounding on the wall. She could hear the noise from the security console as well as the muffled sound through the wall itself.

"Does that sound hollow to you?" the second man said. "Not really," Sargosian said. "They would have used a pretty thick wall, and a good safe room is usually reinforced with steel. I doubt it would sound hollow.

"Listen," he went on, "about Nicole. I don't think she knows anything. It was stupid trying to intimidate her and planting those stories about her."

"Well, guess what?" said the other man. "He doesn't want to take any chances. He's put out a hit on her."

"Holy Christ," said Sargosian. "That's the stupidest thing I've ever heard. The paparazzi are riveted by this story. Nicole has become a celebrity. What do you think would happen if she got murdered, too?"

"It's not going to look like murder," the other man said. "It'll be arranged to look like an accident."

"An accident? Who's going to believe that? It's too much of a coincidence. Think of the conspiracy theories it'll inspire. Not just the cops, but every journalist in America will be looking into this case. Leave her alone; she's harmless."

"Why? You got a thing for her? It doesn't matter. It's all been arranged."

"When we're done with this," Sargosian said, "I'm going to call Rice. I can't believe he'd be party to this. I'm telling you—it would be a terrible mistake if anything happened to her. In fact, he should hire a bodyguard to protect her."

"Very funny," the other guy said. "I doubt you're going to change his mind. The chief assigned it to one of his buddies— those guys who smoke cigars with him in the special yard he had fenced off behind headquarters. It's probably too late already."

Inside the safe room, Nicole had begun pacing around. Hearing them discuss the hit on her made her knees go weak, but she was too jittery to sit down. If only they'd leave, she could sneak away. But what if they somehow managed to get into the safe room? She couldn't bring herself to imagine what would happen.

"Just tell me this," the man was saying. "Why are you here? Things would have been a lot easier if I'd just brought my partner."

"Because my boss doesn't want another screw-up," Rick said. "The media coverage of Blair's murder is getting the firm a lot of negative publicity. And the big guy is worried it might stick to him. It was really stupid to make Robert's death look like a mob hit. That's what set everything off. If anyone had been thinking, they would have made that killing look like an accident. Whose idea was it?"

"How the hell do I know?" the man said. "Let's get down to business. The button that's supposed to open the safe room. It should be on this wall somewhere, right?"

The two disappeared from the monitor. She realized they were leaning down, inspecting the lower part of the wall and bookshelf.

"Hey, I think I found it," said Sargosian. "So push it."

"I am, but nothing's happening. Maybe it's stuck."

She could hear them banging against the wall. The banging went on for perhaps five minutes.

"For Christ's sake," the unknown man finally said. "I'm going to use my gun on it. That ought to break something loose."

"Wait," Sargosian said. "If the wall is lined with steel, that might not—" He was interrupted by a loud bang.

"Goddamn it!" the other man shouted. "The fucking bullet bounced off. It just missed me, and it broke the button clean off. Wait! There's a little lever inside." He was quiet a moment, then said, "I can flip it, but nothing happens."

Sargosian pointed his flashlight downward. "We're going to have to get something to break through the wall," he said.

"Yeah," said the second man. "Pickaxes, something like that. We'll go to the police equipment warehouse over in Van Nuys. They'll have what we need."

"They open at this hour?"

"Twenty-four seven."

Nicole couldn't see them actually leave, since the camera in the front yard was broken. Even though she wanted to get out of the safe room and run for her life, she knew she had to wait a little while before she did anything. They still might be in front, talking about what they were going to do. She decided to give it ten minutes. With shaking hands, she used the time to copy the rest of the files from the computer onto the second flash drive. When she was done, she popped both drives into her backpack, slung it over her shoulder, and went to work unlocking the door. She had to look at Robert's instructions again to find out how to open it from inside the room. His directions told her to release the locks and then push the button under the light switch twice.

She did as instructed. The mechanism made a grinding sound, but nothing happened. She pushed it again and again. Nothing but that sound. She had a sickening realization. The bullet that hit the button on the other side of the wall must have jammed it closed. She got out Robert's instructions again, hoping there'd be some hint about how to handle a situation like this—another exit, perhaps. But there was nothing. This was one contingency that Robert hadn't anticipated.

Nicole thought of one last option—calling the police. She pulled the burner phone out of her purse, then hesitated. If Sargosian's companion had access to the police equipment warehouse, did that mean he was on the force? Would he be able to hear an alert directing officers to the house?

Whatever happened she couldn't let the two men find her when their boss wanted her dead. She tapped 911 into the cell's keypad but nothing happened. She looked at the little screen on the phone. At the top, in tiny letters, it said "no service." She remembered the two men discussing the steel reinforcement that usually lined safe rooms. Was the steel blocking the telephone signal, or was this part of the house a cell-phone dead zone?

Whatever the case, there was nothing more she could do. She was trapped.

FOURTEEN

NICOLE LOOKED AROUND the room. There was nowhere to hide, nothing to do but wait for them to return. Eventually, they'd figure out how to open up the room. And—surprise!— there she'd be. She went over to the water cooler and, with shaking hands, poured herself a paper cup of water. She drank it, refilled the cup twice more and drank that, too.

She had to calm down and think this out. From the self-defense class she'd taken several years before, she could remember one thing: She had to stay calm and, whatever she did, not show fear. The instructor had also said it sometimes helped to address a would-be assailant in a take-charge manner, as if she expected him to do what she said.

It struck her that she had to get rid of anything that might suggest she knew she had reason to be afraid. It had to look as if she'd come here at Robert's request to get the computer. She'd say she heard Rick and the other man enter the house and thought it was the murderer returning. That would explain why she was in the safe room.

She took Sue's gun out of her backpack. To hide it, she tried tucking it into the back of her jeans, but quickly realized how uncomfortable that would be if she had to sit down. She shifted it to the right side of her waistband. Her oversized T-shirt covered it. That might work, as long as nobody thought to pat her down.

She also had to do something with the flash drives, which now contained all of Robert's computer files. Her best option was to hide them somewhere on her person. She loosened the shoelaces of her sneakers and slid a flash drive under the tongue of each shoe, then pulled the laces up again—not too tight—and tied them.

Her next step was to change the password on Robert's computer. If the password wasn't an easy guess like nicole—and how dumb was that?—she could claim she hadn't been able to crack it and was completely ignorant of its contents.

Maybe Sargosian would be able to protect her. She could see he understood that it would stir up a hornet's nest if she disappeared or turned up dead. Even an accident would be suspicious. The tabloids would have a field day, and the LAPD would be on the spot to explain her death. It could get ugly for a lot of people.

She changed the computer password to D9l7oN5r3A1, one of her go-to passwords, nearly impossible to figure out, except by an expert. It was her dog's name, Arnold, spelled backward with odd numbers from one to nine, also backwards, between the letters and some capitals thrown in.

To keep from thinking about her situation, she decided to take a closer look at what was on Robert's computer. Flipping through the folders, she found one named Pizer. For a moment, she stared at it, remembering the billionaire she'd shared the elevator with. What possible connection could Robert have with him? The first file she opened listed amounts of money Robert had apparently received from Pizer over the past five years. Adding in her head, she was astonished. Pizer had forked over several million dollars to Robert, but why? For services rendered? What kind of services?

Another file acknowledged receipts of the same amounts deposited in a company called the ABC Corporation, located in the Seychelles. This must be Robert's offshore account. She was even more stunned when she read the next files, which contained Robert's notes on Pizer. They included documents Robert had apparently scanned in, letters and official documents dating back decades. Put together with the notes, they showed that, early in Pizer's career, he'd made the capital to start his first venture by working for the Romano-Valdecci crime family operating in New Jersey. He managed operations like drug dealing, prostitution, and so-called protection. So this was it, she thought. Robert was blackmailing Pizer, and this was what Robert had on him.

She read on, astonished to learn that, after all of these years, Pizer had never completely separated himself from Romano-Valdecci, which now had legitimate businesses as well as criminal enterprises. A Pizer company under the aegis of USBG—purportedly a hedge fund—was actually a money-laundering operation for the mob.

These files, on this computer, were the reason Robert had been killed. Pizer was afraid the information would get out. If it did, it would ruin him.

Another file contained encrypted messages, which Robert had somehow unencrypted, saving both versions. Even if he was nuts, Nicole thought, he really was clever. How had he figured all this out?

She was surprised, then shocked, to see that most of these messages were between Pizer and Jonathan Rice of Bascomb, Rice, Smith & Di Angelo. She'd known Rice was Pizer's attorney, but it appeared that Rice was also knee-deep in illegal activities on Pizer's behalf. Even unencrypted, the messages between them were couched in euphemisms and fairly hard to understand. She read, then reread them before she grasped the broad outlines of their discussions. They showed how the two men used Pizer's "special relationship" with various officials to put in the fix whenever Pizer wanted something done, such as permits for developments and property tax breaks. He also used these connections when his executives, top clients, friends, or loved ones ran afoul of the law.

She opened another folder. It contained lists of officials Robert was blackmailing. Many of them were receiving bribes from Pizer through Rice. At the top of the list was the LAPD police chief, who'd accepted large "stipends" from Rice on behalf of Pizer for special favors. In addition, several judges, city council members, and quite a few state legislators were on the list. Another file contained names of ordinary citizens Robert was blackmailing for various transgressions. He'd probably picked these up while he was on the vice squad, although some of them appeared to be more recent. They ranged from suspected involvement in child pornography to frequenting prostitutes.

It appeared that Robert had hacked some of this information through this computer. Like any competent hacker, he would have done his best to disguise his identity and location, making it difficult to trace this activity back to him. He probably imagined they'd never find him. But apparently they had. A recent email, from an anonymous source warned him that he'd been identified and that his "victim"—no name was mentioned—would no longer pay. In Robert's letter to Nicole, he'd mentioned that he'd brought his "projects to a conclusion and cut all ties, no matter what the risks." Perhaps he'd told Pizer or Rice, whoever that message was from, that he'd hand over the computer for a final payout. And perhaps they'd agreed, but had sent a hit man instead.

Nicole knew that the only way she could get off Pizer's hit list was to make this information public. If it were exposed, Pizer's criminal enterprise would be brought down, along with the police chief. She also knew it would ruin the law firm she worked for.

Once she finished looking through the files, she logged out of the computer, leaving the startup screen with the cursor blinking in the empty password field. The house was still quiet. Sargosian and his buddy hadn't returned.

She was no longer in a panic. An eerie calm had taken over. She knew she was trapped and in danger, but the threat seemed somehow remote, as if she were watching the scene from a distance. Every once in a while, she got up, tried the phone, and attempted to open the door again, but it was no use. It wouldn't budge. By now it was 1:30 a.m. and she was exhausted; she lay down on the couch and fell asleep.

The racket woke her up—earsplitting crashing and banging. From the sound of it, they were going at the wall with pickaxes. Her heart was pounding as she checked the monitor and realized she was right. Nicole could see the men wielding the pickaxes. Through the speaker, she could hear them grunting. It was undoubtedly hard work, but she doubted the pickaxes would get them through the steel reinforcement. Then she realized that wouldn't be their plan. They were breaking down the outer wall so they could get to the steel reinforcement. Undoubtedly, the police would have equipment that could cut through steel.

As she watched them on the monitor from the CCTV's view of the bedroom, she had a sudden realization. She had to disable the surveillance console. She couldn't let them know she'd been listening in, had heard their conversation, the incriminating things they'd said. She rushed over to Robert's desk and grabbed his Swiss army knife. Besides its electrical cord, the console had a cable connecting it to another type of wall outlet. She disconnected the cable from the console and went to work on it. Her breath was coming in short, panicky gasps, and it was an effort to keep her hands steady. She shredded the cable until little wires inside were exposed. She cut some of these off, then reattached the cable. Sure enough, she'd broken the console's communication with the house's security cameras. The monitors now only showed swirling gray snow.

While she was doing this, the thumping and crashing on the other side of the wall continued. Now the only thing left to do was wait.

At last the banging stopped, and another noise took its place, an electrical whining sound. It wasn't long before she saw the tip of a blade appear a couple of feet below the ceiling. It was some kind of saw designed to cut through steel. The work was slow, but steady, throwing off sparks while it cut a fairly straight line down to the floor. The saw blade was removed, then began again along the bottom for about two and a half feet. The next cut was along the top, then the final vertical cut began. As the saw blade reached the floor, the steel sheeting fell inward, toward Nicole. She was sitting in Robert's desk chair, which she'd pushed against the opposite wall so the sheeting wouldn't hit her.

"Holy Christ, Nicole," Sargosian said, when he saw her. "What the fuck are you doing here?" She was surprised by how disheveled he was, how unlike his usual well-groomed self. His face was sweaty, his hair covered with plaster dust and other debris. His shirt was dirty and sticking to him. He looked completely exhausted.

"I should be asking you the same question, Rick," she said. "This is my house, remember? Robert left it to me."

The two men looked at each other. "But what are you doing in the safe room?" Rick said.

Nicole explained that she'd panicked when she heard them enter the house and that she knew about the safe room from the notes Robert had left for her. She reached into her backpack and pulled out the envelope that held Robert's property information. She got up and handed it to Rick. He went over to sit on the couch while he looked through it. The other man plopped himself on the floor, glowering at her.

Rick looked at the man, then at Nicole. "Nicole," he said, "this is Earl. Earl, Nicole."

"How do you do," Nicole said, as if this were a perfectly normal introduction. Earl looked away without responding. It took Rick a while to look through the material. Finally, he said, "Blair told you to erase the computer's hard drive. Did you do that?"

"No, I was going to hand the computer over to the police," she lied. "I did want to see what was on it. But the computer is password protected, and he didn't give me the password." She gestured toward the papers in Rick's hand.

He looked at them again. "Yeah," he said. "I see that."

"So," she said, "you still haven't told me what you're doing here."

"We're here to take the computer into evidence," Rich said. "This is still a crime scene." He'd gotten up and was taking a close look at the computer screen. The cursor was still blinking in the empty password field.

"It's all yours," she said. "Good luck figuring out the password. I still don't get why you're here, though, Rick. I mean, if this is police business."

"It's like I explained before," Rick said, quite reasonably. "The firm wants to make sure confidential information involving our clients isn't handed over wholesale to the police. Rice had a talk with the police chief, and he said I could supervise the handling of this piece of evidence."

Nicole regarded him. *Rick is a good liar*, she thought. *Or maybe he isn't actually lying.* With the police chief in their pocket, the firm could do just about anything.

Earl got up. "OK, buddy," he said to Sargosian, "Let's step into the other room and have a talk. Oh, and I almost forgot. You'd better search your little friend here. Make sure she's not armed."

She stiffened as Rick moved toward her, and not just because she thought he'd find the gun tucked into her jeans. But his search was quick and impersonal. He simply patted lightly down her body. He immediately located the gun. He held it up, then gave a little laugh. "Seriously?" he said. "Do you even know how to use this?"

"Sargosian?" Earl was getting impatient. "We have to talk."

Rick dropped the gun in his pocket, and the men retreated out of the safe room and into a far corner of the master bedroom, where they murmured in low voices. Whatever Sargosian was proposing, Earl didn't like it. Nicole wished she had a way of listening in. She had no idea what they planned to do with her. Her best guess was that she should keep her mouth shut, listen to whatever she could pick up from them, and watch for a chance to escape.

Soon they were back. "I'll take the computer to the car," Earl said. "You bring her."

Nicole opened her mouth to protest, but Rick took her arm. With his other hand, he grabbed her backpack and slung it over his shoulder. "Please don't argue," he said in a low voice. "It's going to be OK."

"Yeah," said Earl, "you're safe with us. We're just going for a little ride."

They marched Nicole out of the room, through the house and out the front door. Parked at the curb was an unmarked police car, a beige Dodge Charger, fairly new. The men put the computer and Nicole's backpack in the trunk. Earl took the driver's seat, while Sargosian got into the back seat with Nicole. She expected them to head downtown. But when they got to Mulholland, the road that runs along the crest of the Santa Monica Mountains, they went west toward the San Diego Freeway and, after merging onto it, headed north and away from L.A. One thing was clear: They weren't going to police headquarters.

FIFTEEN

THEY CONTINUED NORTH. Nicole had checked her watch when they first got into the car. It was 3:00 a.m. Once the car doors closed, the interior light went off, making it impossible to keep track of the time. The longer she sat there, trying to figure a way out of her situation, the more terrified she grew. The only hope she had was that Sargosian would continue to take her side and that he actually had the power to protect her.

After what felt like hours, she was getting drowsy. Sargosian, himself, was fast asleep. She must have dozed off, too, because she was suddenly surrounded by fog, running from someone who was chasing her, gaining on her. She was jolted awake when she felt someone grab her shoulder.

When she was more fully awake, she realized it was just Sargosian. In his sleep, his head had dropped onto her shoulder, intruding into her nightmare. She pushed him away.

He jerked awake with a loud, "Huh?'

"What's going on back there?" Earl said. He slowed and pulled the car to a stop at the side of the road. She looked around. The night sky had lightened enough for her to make out the desolate landscape surrounding them. They seemed to be in the middle of nowhere, surrounded by untilled fields and what looked like mountains up ahead, or they might have been clouds. It was hard to tell.

Earl got out of the car and opened the door on Sargosian's side. "You drive for a while," Earl said. "I need to catch some shuteye."

Earl got into the backseat, leaned against the door, and promptly fell asleep. Nicole closed her eyes again. Her heart was still pounding from the nightmare, and her mind was abuzz with everything that had happened since she'd locked herself in Robert's safe room.

At least they hadn't tied her up. Earl had favored it, but Rick had argued that she'd never get away. It was two against one. "Look at her," he'd said. "What's she weigh? Not much more than a hundred pounds, and she's not armed. Don't tell me you're afraid of her."

"Oh, for Christ's sake," Earl had said, "Have it your way." But when they'd started out, with him in the driver's seat, he'd announced that he was setting the locks on the rear doors so they couldn't be opened from the inside.

There was nothing she could do until they stopped the car and got her out. She'd have to pretend to cooperate in hope they'd let down their guard. She must have fallen asleep again, because when she opened her eyes, the car had pulled to a stop, and the sun was out. She glanced at her watch. It was 8:00 a.m. They'd been driving five hours, and she felt as if her bladder was about to burst.

Through the car window, the scenery was lovely, lush with wild grass and fir trees. There were also a good number of liquid amber, cottonwood, and aspen, now almost bare of leaves. They were in the foothills somewhere, probably the Sierras. Sargosian came around from the driver's side and let Earl out. Through the open door she could see a cabin, a familiar cream-colored

A-frame with red trim. It was the same cabin she'd seen in the photo from Robert's envelope. They'd brought her to his place in the Owens Valley.

After looking through the envelope—containing the key and directions to the cabin—the two men must have decided to bring her here. It occurred to her that these isolated foothills would make the perfect place to bury a body.

Once Earl was out of the car, he reached in, grabbed her by the arm and pulled her out. He wasn't gentle about it. Outside it was windy and incredibly cold, as if it might be about to snow. Nicole, whose only outer layer was a windbreaker, had started to shiver. The two men herded her toward Robert's cabin. Sargosian unlocked the door, and the three of them stepped inside, where it was even colder.

Nicole told them she had to use the bathroom. Earl gave Sargosian a look, and Rick said, "OK. I'll keep an eye on her." He made her leave the door open a bit and stood outside until she was done. Then he delivered her back to Earl and went to use the bathroom himself.

"Sit!" Earl told her, pointing to the couch. They were in the living-room area of the one-room structure. In the center of the room was a pot-bellied stove. The bathroom, just a toilet, sink, and shower, was the only room walled off from the open floor plan. Nicole was now actually shaking from the cold, her teeth chattering. Spotting a blanket draped across the back of the couch, she pulled it off and wrapped it around herself, but it wasn't much help.

Before long, Sargosian was back. "I saw some logs stacked outside," he said. "I'll get some, and we can start the stove. This place is freezing."

He went outside while Earl searched the cupboards in the kitchen area. Next to the refrigerator was what looked like a closet door, secured with a sliding lock. Earl unlocked it and disappeared inside. By now, Sargosian was back, carrying a couple of logs. He opened the door in the belly of the stove and shoved them inside.

Earl emerged from the closet and hurried over. "God's sake," he said with some disgust. "Don't you know how to do anything? You gotta put paper and kindling in first so you can get a fire going. Here, let me." He was already pulling the logs out of the stove. He took some sheets of newspaper from a nearby stack and wadded them up. Then he looked around. "No kindling. This will have to do." He put the logs on top of the paper, then took a lighter out of his pocket and lit the paper.

He adjusted a handle on a pipe leading from the top of the stove to the peaked ceiling in the center of the cabin. Then he opened a drawer at the bottom of the stove. The fire was already crackling, flames leaping up over the logs. He closed the door in the belly of the stove.

Earl stood up and gestured toward the kitchen. "Blair kept his food supplies locked up in that closet," he said. "Probably to keep stuff safe in case a bear broke in. But there isn't much to eat—and there's no booze. We passed a store a while back. I'll go get some provisions." He pulled some long strips of black plastic out of his pocket. "I'm going to cuff her so she can't pull anything while I'm gone."

"For God's sake," Sargosian said. "We've already been over this. Cuffing her is a bad idea. I'll watch her. Besides, if she escaped, where would she go? You're taking the car. The two of us are stranded here."

"I can't figure out why you keep trying to protect her," Earl said.

"I'm not protecting her," Sargosian said. "I'm protecting us. Technically, we haven't actually kidnapped her. We didn't threaten her or point a weapon at her. We could argue that she came with us willingly, that we brought her here to protect her from someone who's trying to kill her. OK? The minute we tie her up that changes everything. We're using force to hold her. Then it becomes kidnapping. If that plastic cuff bruises her or cuts her wrist, a prosecutor could make it kidnapping with bodily harm. That violates the Little Lindbergh Law, a federal offense. You get it?"

"Who do you think you're kidding?" Earl said with great sarcasm. "Of course we kidnapped her. I'm a cop, remember? You're already in the soup, and you know it. That's why we have to get rid of her."

"It won't be me," Sargosian said. "I won't be party to murder. In fact, I'm going to talk to Rice and make sure he knows there is a hit out on her. I can't believe he'll go along with it."

"So call him!" Earl snapped back. "Nobody's stopping you!"

Sargosian got his phone out of his pocket and turned it on. Then, after looking at it a moment, he headed for the door.

"Where are you going?" said Earl.

"There's no reception in here. I'm going to see if I can pick up a signal outside."

A few minutes later, he was back. "Well?" said Earl.

"He wasn't there. I had to leave a message."

"Fine," said Earl, putting out his hand. "Now give me the car keys. I'm going to the store." Sargosian handed them over. After Earl left, Nicole and Sargosian sat on the couch in front of the stove, which was slowly warming the room. She was exhausted, and so apparently was he.

Finally, she said, "Listen, Rick. Why don't you let me go? I can make a run for it. Tell him you fell asleep, and when you woke up, I was gone."

"It's no use," Sargosian said. "You'll never get away. We passed a few cabins on the road here, but they were all boarded up for the winter. Who knows which way you'd have to go to find the nearest year-round resident. The store Earl is headed for is fifteen miles away. I'm sorry about this, Nicole. I've done my best to protect you. But I'm not running the show; there's only so much I can do."

Nicole looked at him, feeling sick. She thought about her sister, then Josh. Would she ever see them again? They'd both be worried by now, afraid something had happened to her. She hadn't told anyone where she was going or what she was planning to do. If Stephanie tried to reach her on her disposable phone—now in her backpack in the trunk of Earl's car—she wouldn't get an answer. As for Josh, she'd promised him she'd be gone only a day or two. This was day three. And Sue, her lawyer, what about her? Nicole hadn't been sure of her loyalty. But if Sue knew nothing of the firm's criminal involvement, then she, like Stephanie, might report her missing.

She thought, suddenly, of Reinhardt. If he was still alive, would he ever find out what had become of her? Had the British tabloids picked up the story?

With nothing to do, the two of them sat without talking, deep in thought. As the room grew warmer, Sargosian took off his jacket and got up to hang it on a hook in the cabin's sleeping area. It held a bed, a single, neatly made up with military corners. He went into the bathroom for a few minutes and came back to sit next to her. He'd washed his face, and his hair was wet and slicked back. His beard, unshaven, was now a two-day stubble, and his clothes were wrinkled and dirty. Aside from the grooming issue, he looked exhausted and upset. She could see that he was in over his head and almost as terrified as she was.

He'd just dropped off to sleep when she thought of Sue's gun. She tried to remember what Sargosian had done with it when he'd taken it from her. She thought she'd seen him drop it into a pocket. Was it in his jacket? She rose as quietly as she could and started to tiptoe toward the wall where the jacket hung. She was half way across the room when she heard him stir. She hurried back to the couch.

After a few minutes, he relaxed back into sleep. She was thinking of making another try for his jacket when she heard a key turn in the lock. Sargosian was immediately awake and on his feet. Earl opened the door and came in, toting a couple of large grocery bags, some newspapers, and two six-packs of beer. He put them on the table, then went back to the car and brought in two more six-packs.

The men each opened a beer and—ignoring Nicole—sat down at the kitchen table to read the papers. Rick paled when he saw the front page of the *Times*. From where she was sitting, she could make out the three-column headline, "Woman in Murdered Ex-Cop Case Missing." She got up to join the men at the table, hoping to look over Rick's shoulder and see what the papers had to say.

"Sit down," Earl said, pointing to the couch. "You get your turn when we're done." He got up and helped himself to a second beer.

The men finished the papers. While Earl opened yet another beer and began drinking it, Rick brought the papers over to Nicole. She thought it odd that there was no discussion between them about the stories, no speculation about what the news meant or whether they thought law enforcement outside of L.A. might be on their trail. As she understood it, this was a real possibility since her disappearance wasn't just a missing person's case; it was related to a murder.

As she started reading the *Times*, Earl turned to Sargosian. "Come on outside, pretty boy," he said. "I want to have a little chat with you." Sargosian followed him out and closed the door.

Nicole considered getting up and making another try for Sargosian's jacket but vetoed the idea. The men might walk back in at any time. She could hear them arguing out there. Earl, having downed three beers by now, made no effort to keep his voice down.

"You lied to me," Earl fairly shouted. "On my way back from the store, I called Rice. He said you did reach him. He told you they were sending somebody up here to help me get rid of her."

Rick murmured a reply, his voice too low for her to hear.

"He said you're supposed to take this dude's car and head back to L.A.," Earl ranted. "You're related to one of those lawyers, aren't you? Guess they don't want you getting your hands dirty." His voice was bitter. "But they don't give a crap about me—after all I've done for them. For all I know, this guy is going to off me, too."

Rick's response was low, placating. Nicole figured he'd lied about the phone call because he knew his own free pass would rile up Earl. And it had. Now that Earl knew what was coming, he was scared, and that was making him all the more volatile.

Half listening to the continuing argument, she gave the newspaper a closer look. The article under the main headline of the *Times* reported that her sister, as well as her attorney, Sue Price, had filed missing persons reports the evening before. It quoted a police spokesman who said they were working on some leads but that they "refused to speculate on an open, ongoing case."

Sue told the paper that she'd last seen Nicole when she dropped her off at the Hertz lot. "Nicole was worried about her safety and wanted to go somewhere to turn off her phone and 'get off the grid.' She gave me a disposable phone with her number, but she hasn't answered in the last twenty-four hours. I'm very concerned."

The paper described Stephanie as being in an "emotional state." She, too, was quoted. "I haven't any idea where she might be or what happened to her. That's all I can tell you. We're worried sick." The story went on to repeat the circumstances of Robert's murder and that he'd left everything to Nicole.

The Owens Valley's local paper had a brief item about her disappearance then went into a few of the more lurid details of Robert's murder, describing it as "a gangland-style assassination."

At that moment, the two men walked back in, and Earl announced he was going to make lunch. It was 11:00 a.m., and none of them had eaten since the day before. While puttering around the kitchen, Earl guzzled yet another beer: his fourth. Nicole had been counting, wondering how much it would take to incapacitate him. So far, except for shouting at Sargosian, he showed no signs of intoxication.

She and Sargosian were sitting at the table when Earl brought over the platter of food, as well as his fifth beer. The presentation was less than appealing—three blackened steaks and three microwaved potatoes. Nicole cut into her steak. It was pretty much inedible, burnt on the outside, raw inside. The potatoes were undercooked.

Nicole picked up her plate and stood up. "Where do you think you're going?" Earl said. "This steak's raw," she said. "I was just—"

"Sit the fuck down," Earl said.

"Earl," Rick said. "I like my steak medium rare. This needs more cooking."

"Then you do it," Earl said. "I'm not going to sit here with her at the stove. No telling what she could do with a hot pan." Nicole looked at him. What a good idea, she thought, and it hadn't even occurred to her. She was too scared, too tired, too depleted to think.

Rick got up with his plate, took Nicole's, and went to the stove to put the steaks back on. He located a bottle of ketchup and a can of baked beans in the closet. He found a pan for heating the beans and, after a few minutes, returned to the table with their plates. Nicole, imagining what was going to happen next, couldn't eat. She pushed the beans around on the plate a bit then put down her fork.

Earl, starting his sixth beer, was pretty much into his own head, smoking a small, very smelly cigar between sips. Rick, himself, had put away three beers. At no point had they offered any to Nicole. Not that she would have accepted it. She didn't even like beer.

When they were done eating, they left the dishes on the table. At that point, both men complained how tired they were from their long night breaking into the safe room and driving to the cabin. Soon they were arguing about what to do with Nicole while they napped.

Earl wanted to cuff her to a kitchen chair, but Rick wouldn't hear of it. Earl was finally showing signs of the alcohol he'd consumed and could hardly keep his eyes open. Rick suggested each take a turn watching Nicole while the other one napped. "I'll take the first watch," he told Earl.

Earl found this agreeable. "Good man," he slurred. The beer had not only made him sleepy, but also seemed to have mellowed him.

Nicole returned to the couch, but she found it impossible to sit there with nothing to do, alone with her terrible thoughts. She noticed a jigsaw puzzle on a nearby bookcase—a kitschy English village scene that looked like a painting by Thomas Kinkaid. She retrieved it, dumped it out on the coffee table, and began to assemble it. Rick was seated across from her in a recliner chair. He'd lowered it until he was almost horizontal while he kept tabs on her. On the other side of the room, Earl had begun to snore.

She focused on the puzzle, glancing up at Rick every once in a while. After about fifteen minutes, he was fast asleep. She got up from the couch and tiptoed across the room toward where he'd hung his jacket. It was just a few feet from the bed where Earl was sleeping. When she got to Rick's jacket, she reached into the right-hand pocket. The gun wasn't there. She took out her hand, and the jacket fell to the floor with a clunk. Nicole froze. Earl had stopped snoring. She looked around, holding her breath. Earl turned over and was now facing away from her. Rick was still in the recliner. As far as she could tell, he hadn't moved.

Quietly, she picked up the fallen jacket, reached into the other pocket, and pulled out—not the gun—but Rick's cell phone. She carefully hung the jacket back on the hook and tiptoed into the bathroom. She turned on the phone and was disappointed to see the tiny words "no service" in the top left corner of the screen. She waved it in different directions, but there was no reception.

As she left the bathroom, she noticed Earl's jacket draped over the back of a chair near the bed. She lifted it to search the pockets. That was when she saw what was under the jacket; it was a holster containing his service weapon. Silently, she pulled it out. It was twice the size of the one Sue had given her and much heavier. If Earl noticed it was gone, he'd go crazy. She had to be ready.

She went back to the couch and, after checking to make sure both men were still asleep, put Rick's phone on the table next to where he was lying. Once she was seated again, she examined the gun more closely. It was a Glock, like the one Reinhardt had given her, and she vaguely remembered his instructions. She located the safety lock and disabled it. Then she carefully placed the gun next to her, nestled between the cushions of the couch.

Her hands were shaking when she started on the puzzle again. She listened intently for any stirring from Earl's corner of the room. She wondered what had happened to Sue's gun. Had Sargosian left it at the house? Or did he have it with him? Maybe it was in his pants pocket.

She jumped at the sound of a vehicle pulling up in front. Then she realized it couldn't be the killer Rice was dispatching. This place was five hours away from L.A., and he wouldn't have had time to get here. A car door slammed, and a moment later someone knocked on the front door. Earl sat bolt upright in bed and said, "What the—" Still drunk and half asleep, he got out of bed and shuffled to the middle of the room. Meanwhile, Rick got slowly up from the recliner. The knocking on the door persisted, but neither man made a move to get it.

SIXTEEN

WHOEVER HAD BEEN KNOCKING at the door was now banging on it. At last, Earl seemed to pull himself together. He made an impatient waving gesture at Rick, indicating he was to take Nicole and stand against the cabin's front wall, so they'd be behind the door when it opened.

Getting up from the couch, Nicole picked up Earl's gun. She held it at her side, slightly behind her, so the men couldn't see it. Not that either was paying attention to her. They were both staring at the door where whoever was outside was calling, "Open up! I know someone's in there."

Once Sargosian and Nicole were against the wall, Earl opened the door. "What can I do for you?" His voice was mild, conciliatory.

"I'm Tommy Green," the man said. "The residents association has me check these cabins for squatters. You the owner here?"

"No," Earl said. "I work with him. He told me we could use his place for a few days."

There was a silence and a rattling of papers. Then Green said, "Hey! It says here this cabin belongs to Robert Blair. Isn't that the guy who got murdered? It's been all over the news."

As the man talked, Earl reached for his holster. Realizing he'd left it hanging on the chair, he lifted his right pants leg and pulled a small gun from a leg holster.

The man stopped talking. The next sound was a gunshot, followed by another. Earl disappeared for a moment, apparently checking to make sure the man was dead. Then he was back, the gun still in his hand. He looked at Sargosian, then he let out a little laugh. Sargosian had pulled Sue's gun out of his pants pocket and was pointing it at Earl.

"Don't be stupid, Sargosian," Earl said. "Put Minnie Mouse down. You don't even know how to use it. I'm not going to shoot you. I need your help putting this guy back in his car so I can hide him somewhere."

Nicole had a flash of realization. Earl was planning to take them up into the foothills, make Rick help him dig a grave, then shoot them and bury them both with the man he'd just killed.

Perhaps Rick was thinking the same thing. "You killed that man," he said, as if he couldn't believe what he'd just seen. He was still pointing Sue's gun at Earl—but as Earl suspected and Nicole knew—Rick had no idea how to use it. The safety lock was on. The gun wasn't going to fire even if he did try to pull the trigger.

Earl raised his gun and pointed it at Rick. "I'm warning you, Sargosian," he said.

It was a standoff. Neither of them was paying attention to Nicole. She took several steps away from Sargosian before she raised the Glock she'd taken from Earl's holster. Her only thought was that she couldn't afford to miss. She aimed at Earl's chest and pulled the trigger. The recoil was powerful, almost knocking her off her feet.

The bullet hit Earl in the head just as he pulled the trigger. His shot, intended for Sargosian, went wild and struck the ceiling.

"Holy shit!" Rick said, lowering his gun.

Earl was now on the floor, a puddle of blood spreading around him. He looked dead, but Nicole, in a rush of adrenalin, hurried over and kicked the gun out of his reach. Then she turned and pointed the gun at Sargosian. Her hands were shaking, and her shoulder ached from the gun's recoil. She tried to avert her eyes from the mess she'd made of Earl's head, the wall next to him spattered with blood and bits of brain. Her mind flashed back to the year before when she'd been forced to bludgeon a man to save Reinhardt's life. She was almost overcome by a wave of nausea. It took all her strength to hold the gun steady.

Sargosian appeared thunderstruck. "Nicole," he said. "You don't want to do this. I tried to save you."

"Drop the gun," she said.

He dropped it. She picked it up, pointed it at Sargosian, and tossed the Glock to the side, well out of reach.

"I'm not going to shoot you, Rick," she said. "Just do what I say." She waved the gun toward the closet. "In there." The inside of the door was unfinished and, from what she could see, made of wood composition. With a little effort, Sargosian could break it down, but all she needed was to contain him until she got away.

Her hands had stopped shaking, and she felt calm enough to do what had to be done. After Rick was in the closet and the door securely latched, she went over to Earl. Trying not to look at the mess the bullet had made of his head, she checked to see if he had a pulse. He didn't. It was a struggle to turn him enough to get the car keys out of his pocket. This done, she pulled the back of his shirt out of his pants and started to wipe his Glock clean of her fingerprints. As she was doing this, she could hear Sargosian hurling himself against the door. After several loud crashes, there was a distinct cracking sound.

She got up, and with the gun in her hand, went over to the closet. "Stop that!" she said. Pointing the gun at the floor, she fired. After the gunshot died away, she added, "If I hear you try that again, I'll shoot through the door. I'll be gone in five minutes. Keep still until you hear me leave. I mean it!"

"Let me out, Nicole," he said. "I'll do anything you say."

She went back to where Earl was lying and finished wiping her fingerprints off his gun. Still holding it with his shirttail, she put it in his hand and curled his fingers around it. Then she tucked his shirt back into his pants.

She got up and went back to the closet. "Your friend Earl is dead," she called to Sargosian.

"He wasn't my friend," he said.

"Look," she said. "I'm taking the car. I'll leave your phone by the front door. Once you get out of there, you should call the firm. They'll figure out a way to make this look as if you were never here."

"I'm no threat to you, Nicole," he said. "Take me with you. Please!"

"Sorry, Rick," she said. "I can't afford to trust anyone at this point. But you'll be OK. You did try to protect me, and I think Earl was planning to kill us both and get away before the man Rice is sending arrives. So, if the police were to show up, you could tell them this: When you realized Earl was going to kidnap me and kill me, you tried to stop him. So he took you prisoner, too. That makes you a victim. And he did shoot that caretaker guy. You can say that I escaped but was so hysterical that I left you behind. I'll back you up. But it probably won't be necessary. As I said, the firm will want to keep this quiet."

She put Sue's gun in her pocket, went to the front of the cabin and, stepping over Earl's body, dropped Rick's phone near the door. Without another word, she walked out of the cabin, got into Earl's car, and drove away.

She pushed the car as fast as it would go toward route 395, the main highway running through the Owens Valley. Even on the 395, traffic was fairly sparse. She'd been driving a while, heading toward the freeway that would take her to L.A., when the car began to slow. She pressed the gas pedal, but the car just kept slowing. She looked at the fuel gauge, and her heart sank. She was out of gas. She managed to pull over to the side of the road before the engine cut out altogether.

Now what? It seemed to her she'd seen a gas station a few miles back. She got out of the car, retrieved her backpack from the trunk, and checked to be sure Robert's envelope was still inside. The only things remaining were the spare tire and Robert's computer, which was now lying on its side. Leaving it to its fate, she closed the trunk and started trudging along the side of the road. It was bitterly cold, still threatening snow. Each passing car whipped up a frigid blast of wind that beat against her. In the distance a big rig truck was approaching. It slowed, then came to a stop about thirty feet beyond her. It backed up until the driver could see her through the passenger's window. "Need a lift?" the man said. "Where you headin'?"

She thought about it. She could ask to be dropped off at a service station. But, no. If this truck was headed for L.A., that would be faster. She wanted to be well away from here by the time Rice's hit man arrived.

"Los Angeles," she said.

"Why, that's just where I'm going," the driver said. "Hop aboard. Wait! That step is pretty high up. I'll come 'round and help you."

Up close, she didn't like the look of him. He had a goatee and his hair was cut short and shaved around the sides like a marine. His neck and hands were covered with tattoos in a way that made her think they probably continued down to his toes.

He stooped, put out his two hands and joined them, interlocking his fingers so she could put her foot in them and hoist herself up. "That's a pretty steep step," he said jovially, "and you're such a little thing. At first I thought you were a boy."

She didn't think this required an answer. Once she was inside the truck, he closed the door and headed around the vehicle to the driver's side. The interior stank of cigarettes and body odor. She already regretted accepting the ride. As the trucker opened his door and climbed in, she reached into her pocket for the gun and released the safety lock, keeping her hand on the weapon. After what she'd already been through, she knew she could handle this guy.

As soon as the man closed the door, she noticed the smell of whiskey. She was quiet, and he seemed to feel a need to fill the silence. He told her about the weather they'd been having. How they could expect snow pretty soon. He wondered why anyone would want to live in L.A. "where all those gangbangers live" when they could just be in the Owens Valley where "things aren't so danged expensive, and it's all nice and peaceful-like." They weren't too far from the freeway when they approached a side road buttressed by trees on either side. He made a wide turn onto the road and pulled to a stop between the rows of trees.

"You don't got a lot to say, do you?" he was saying. "I thought we could stop here for a bit and get to know each other a little better." He turned away from her to reach for a bottle of whiskey in a storage compartment behind him. She pulled out her gun.

When he turned back to her, she pointed the gun at him. "This is loaded and ready to fire. I want you to start the truck and get back on the road. Then you're going to drop me at the first truck stop we come to."

He lunged at her, trying to grab the gun. In the struggle, her finger pulled the trigger, and the gun went off. The bullet shattered the window next to him. He put up his hands.

"Now drive," she said.

No longer talkative, he backed the truck onto the highway. Half a mile later, they merged onto the freeway, and it wasn't long before she saw a huge truck stop ahead.

"Here," she said, waving the gun. "I want you to head down this off-ramp and pull up to the restaurant. Then you're going to give me your phone, let me off, and get out of here."

He didn't answer, but he did follow her directions, taking her right to the entrance of the sprawling restaurant, which was surrounded by big rigs.

"Your phone," she said as she got out, still pointing the gun.

Wordlessly, he handed it over, and she relaxed the gun to her side, watching him drive away and get back on the freeway. When he was out of sight, she dropped the gun into her backpack and tossed his phone into a trashcan standing next to the restaurant's entrance.

She adjusted her baseball cap, making sure her hair was tucked in. Inside the restaurant, she paused to pull out her last two twenty-dollar bills. She tucked one into her pocket for later use. The remainder of Sue's money—$7,000—was still in its envelope at the bottom of her backpack.

She asked the woman at the cash register to change her twenty into ten dollars worth of quarters and a ten-dollar bill. She also asked where the restroom was, as well as the public phones. The woman was tall with brassy blonde hair that looked as if she dyed it herself. Her nametag identified her as Trudy, and she had a kind face. She gave Nicole the change and the directions she'd asked for.

Nicole went into the hallway leading to the restrooms and darted into the women's room. She was still hoping people would think she was a boy, but she wasn't willing to venture into the men's room. She locked the door, washed her face, and took off the baseball cap. In the mirror, she took stock of her appearance, the disheveled state of her hair. She located a comb in her backpack and did her best to smooth out the tangles. Spotting a rubber band on the floor, she rinsed it off, dried it with a paper towel, and used it to pull her hair into a ponytail. She put her baseball cap and sunglasses back on and examined herself in the mirror. During the ride to the Owens Valley, while Sargosian was asleep, she'd taken off the scarf she'd used to flatten her chest. But the windbreaker was big enough to disguise her figure, and she thought she could still pass for a boy. In any case, it was unlikely anyone here would recognize her. They were too busy driving big rigs from one side of the country to the other to pay much attention to TV news, newspapers, or tabloids.

She left the women's room and headed for the phones. Her first call was to the phone she'd sent her sister. Stephanie picked up after the first ring. At the sound of Nicole's voice, Steph broke down and cried. "We've been so worried," she said. "XHN is saying you were killed and buried in the desert."

"Look, Steph," Nicole said, "I'm not out of danger. Do not tell anyone I called. Most especially not the police or anyone from the law firm. Not even my lawyer. No one. Pretend to be upset because you still think I'm missing. Oh—I am going to call Josh, so you can talk to him, if you want. I'll be in touch soon. OK?"

Steph snuffled and said, "But—"

"Listen," Nicole repeated. "I need you to promise to keep this conversation secret. You can't even tell your boyfriend."

"I promise," said Stephanie. "But I have to tell you—"

"I've got to go, Steph. I'll be in touch as soon as I can."

Nicole hung up.

She walked back to Trudy, the cashier, and asked how someone coming from L.A. could get to the truck stop.

Trudy gave her directions. Then, taking a closer look at Nicole, she said, "Why you're a girl, aren't you?"

Nicole looked at her a moment and said, "Yes, but I think it's better if we keep that to ourselves." She paused for effect, then added, "Truckers."

They both laughed.

"And what's the name of this restaurant?" Nicole said.

"Why, it's called Mom's," Trudy said, gesturing to the wall behind her, which displayed several T-shirts with "Mom's" in flowing retro-style script under a cartoon of a steaming cup of coffee.

"Mom's?" Nicole said. "Seriously?" She thought of the Nelson Algren quote Josh had recited on their first date.

"Why, that's always been our name," Trudy said, "going back to the forties. It's famous among truckers."

Nicole's next call was to Josh.

When he heard her voice, he said, "Nicole! My god. I've been so worried. Are you all right? Where have you been? What happened?"

After he was done with his questions, she said, "I'm fine. Can you come and get me? I'm about five hours away."

"Of course," he said. "Just tell me how to get there."

She gave him directions, and when she told him the name of the restaurant, his reaction was the same as hers. "Mom's?" he said. "You're kidding, right?"

"Swear to god," she said.

Almost as an afterthought, she told him that she'd already called her sister and that he couldn't tell anyone he'd heard from her, not the police or even her lawyer.

"Why not?" he said,

"Because this isn't over. I'd like to stay with you and just kind of—well—hide out until I'm sure it's safe."

"Nicole, this doesn't sound good. We should call the police."

"No!" she said. "Don't tell anyone—especially the police. Promise me. I'll explain the whole thing on the ride back to L.A."

"OK," he said. "I'll be there as soon as I can."

After they'd hung up, she sat at the counter and ordered a full breakfast—bacon, eggs, sausage, hashbrowns, and pancakes, all for just $7.99. The food was delicious, but she barely made a dent in the heaping platter the waitress placed in front of her. When she was done, she left a tip, then went over to the cashier to pay.

"You'll be waiting a while if your ride has to drive all the way from L.A.," Trudy said.

Nicole nodded. She was looking around. She'd planned to buy some newspapers and find an unoccupied booth. But the place was packed, and there were few empty seats.

"Tell you what," Trudy said. "We have a break room. I'll show you where it is, and you can wait there. It has a couch, a TV, and a shower. Sometimes the waitresses have a split shift and need a place to rest and clean up. You don't want to be sitting around here half the day."

"Thanks," Nicole said, touched by Trudy's kindness. "That would be wonderful."

"Tell me what your friend looks like," Trudy said, "so I'll know to come get you."

"Well," Nicole said. "He has dark blond hair, and he's tall and good looking. He'll stand out because he doesn't have any tattoos. And he doesn't look anything like"—she gestured around them—"these guys."

"Lucky you," Trudy said, somewhat wistfully.

"Yes," Nicole smiled. "Lucky me."

SEVENTEEN

NICOLE WALKED INTO THE waitress' break room. Her only thought was to take a long, hot shower. She undressed, starting with her shoes, which she hadn't taken off since she'd changed at the motel the day before. She was surprised when she took off a shoe and something dropped to the floor. It was one of the flash drives with Robert's files. She'd forgotten all about them. She stuck them in the toes of her shoes while she showered and washed her hair. Then she put them back in the zippered compartment of her backpack. Feeling a little better, she lay down on the couch and thought about all that had happened and everything she had to do to get clear of the mess she was in. She must have dozed off. The next thing she knew, Trudy poked her head in and said, "Your boyfriend's here!" Then she was gone.

Nicole was only a few feet from Josh before he recognized her. "Wow," he said, "that is some disguise!" He put an arm around her and hustled her to the door. She turned to wave at Trudy, mouthing her thanks.

Once they were in the car, Josh put his arms around her and kissed her. "I've been so worried about you," he murmured into her hair. "It was like I'd just found you, and you completely disappeared."

Nicole looked out at the parking lot. A couple of Inyo County Sheriff's cars were driving in. Maybe they were just stopping for coffee, but the sight of them made her nervous. She scrunched down in her seat. "I think we'd better get out of here," she said.

Josh followed her glance and, spotting the patrol cars, gave her a puzzled look. He started the car and took the nearby onramp to the freeway heading west. Nicole lay her head against the back of the seat and closed her eyes.

"So, are you going to tell me what happened?" Josh said. "Where you've been?"

"It's a long story," Nicole said. "I don't even know where to start."

"How about this," he said. "Explain why we can't tell the police you're safe, so they can stop looking for you. Does this have something to do with Blair's murder?"

"Yes," she said, trying to think of a way to simplify the story into a few sentences. She explained there was a hit out on her, and she couldn't trust the police because the police chief was in on it. She also told him about Pizer's involvement. "Pizer? The billionaire philanthropist—and the chief of police?" Josh said. "Holy shit!" He turned to look at her. "But if we can't call the police, what are we going to do?"

"There's a reporter at the *L.A. Times* whose been following the story," she said. "I think he can be trusted. I'm going to give the information to him. Once it goes public, no one will dare touch me."

"OK," he said slowly. "But until you get that nailed down, you're going to stay with me, inside my house, right? You're not going to disappear again. Will you promise me that?"

"I promise."

"And when you meet up with this guy from the *Times*?" he said. "I'm coming with you."

"Sure," she said.

"Now," Josh said, "tell me everything from the beginning."

By the time they reached his house, it was past 10:00 p.m., and Nicole was fast asleep. He opened the car door, released her seatbelt, and was starting to pick her up when she awoke. "It's fine," she said. "I can walk." She grabbed her backpack, which was resting at her feet, and the two of them went into the house.

Josh gave her one of his T-shirts to wear to bed. It reached her mid-thigh. She was freezing. She cuddled against him, and he put his arms around her. Warmed by his body, she promptly fell asleep.

Nicole woke a little past 8:00 a.m., and he was gone. She located her clothes, folded on his dresser, and put them in the washer. Then she saw a note on the kitchen table. Written in neat block letters, it said, *Went to the office to pick up work to do at home. Will stop for groceries. Back around 9:00. If you need anything, give me a call.* He'd added his cell number and, under that, *Love, Josh.* She read the last line twice.

She went back to bed and dozed until she heard the door close downstairs. After a few minutes, she got up and put on a white terry cloth robe she found hanging in his closet. It was so big it almost reached the floor. She padded barefoot down to the kitchen, and there he was, putting away groceries.

He was all smiles. "Good morning," he said. "Would you like some breakfast?"

"Yes, please," she said, accepting the cup of coffee he handed her.

She watched what he was doing, smiling to herself. She loved this about him. He was, in fact, the first man she'd been with who actually knew how to cook and seemed to enjoy it. She thought of her ex, Brad, and the few times he'd gotten stuck preparing a meal. He was helpless in the kitchen, coming out every few minutes to ask her where a pan or an ingredient was. It was clear he was thinking, "If I screw this up badly enough, she'll never ask me to do it again." As for Reinhardt, he had a beautiful kitchen, all stainless steel appliances and black marble countertops. But as far as Nicole could tell, it was never used, except to make coffee and drinks. When she was with him, and they were staying at his place, they invariably went out for meals.

After breakfast, she helped Josh with the dishes. Then, while she shifted her clothes from the washer to the dryer, he disappeared into his study. Nicole went in to watch. He was working on a drawing of a house he was designing.

"This is a schematic," he said, "a preliminary sketch of a house I discussed with my clients." She watched him draw for a while, surprised that this part of the work was still done with pencil and paper instead of a computer. He explained that it was just a quick sketch, but she was impressed with his skill at drawing. He made it look easy.

She set up her iPad in the dining room. The battery was depleted, and she had to wait a bit before she could fire it up. She used the time to look at the *LA Times*, which had been delivered to Josh's front porch that morning.

The front page led with an article about Earl's death, and the spin they'd put on it made Nicole laugh out loud:

SUSPECTED KILLER OF
MURDERED EX-COP FOUND DEAD

Los Angeles police officer Earl Murray, the prime suspect in the Robert Blair murder case, was found dead, an apparent suicide, late Sunday night in the victim's cabin in the Owens Valley. Murray had once worked with Blair on the LAPD vice squad.

Another body, found at the scene, was that of Thomas Green, a local resident who apparently had been making rounds for the neighborhood watch. Pending the outcome of forensic evidence, police speculate that Murray shot Green, then shot himself.

At an impromptu news conference late Sunday evening, Police Chief Ray Spalding said that the police had been searching for Murray since Friday.

According to Spalding, Blair had been blackmailing Murray for years based on Murray's misconduct when he was a member of the vice squad. Blair had evidence that Murray had pocketed money and drugs he took from suspects he arrested. At the press conference, Spalding said, "As for motive, it appears Murray was no longer willing to pay blackmail."

"After killing Blair, Murray took property from Blair's house," Spalding said, "including the key to Blair's Owens Valley cabin. When Murray realized we were searching for him as a suspect in Blair's murder, he went up to the cabin. He used his service weapon to kill Green, who had found him hiding in Blair's cabin, before committing suicide. The area is under the jurisdiction of the Inyo County Sheriff's Department, and the LAPD is cooperating with Inyo County on the investigation."

Chief Spalding said, "We are happy to announce that we are closing the Robert Blair case. The people of Los Angeles, especially in the Sunset Hills residential area, can be assured that the murderer is no longer at large."

There was more, mainly a rehash of Blair's murder. It took Nicole several readings to digest this and fully grasp the disparity between the information in the newspaper account and what had actually happened. When it was clear to her, she realized that the prediction she'd made to Rick had come to pass. The firm had managed—no doubt with the help of the LAPD—to cover up the facts of the case, including Rick's involvement. The whole Robert

Blair affair was tied up in a neat package, solved in a way that was convenient for them all.

A shorter story, at the bottom right corner of the front page, bore the headline, "Nicole Graves Still Missing." A kicker above the headline read "Day Four." The story was a rehash of her connection to the case and the fact that two missing persons reports had been filed after her disappearance, putting her on a national search database. A police spokesperson said they had opened a "tip" line, but so far had no solid leads as to her whereabouts.

She went into Josh's study, where he was still at work, and handed him the paper. "Here," she said, "take a look at this. Oh, and what's your Wi-Fi password?" He told her, then unfolded the paper and held it up, apparently mesmerized by the banner headline.

Nicole went back to her iPad, joined Josh's network, and pulled up XHN. The site had the story about Earl's "suicide." A video of the police cars gathered around Robert's cabin ended with the scene of two covered bodies being loaded into coroner's wagons.

The second story, which occupied a good amount of space, led with the headline, "Where's Nicole?" Under it was a cartoon map of the world, patterned after the "Where's Waldo?" series. The map was distorted, squeezed into a box to show Los Angeles, London, and Majorca, with not much space in between. Tiny cartoon figures were crowded into each destination. She scrolled past the graphic and encountered a list of places where she'd supposedly been spotted since her disappearance, as reported on the XHN "news tip" bulletin board. It was a long list. She'd been seen everywhere from Juneau, Alaska, to Hong Kong, to (of course) Majorca, with plenty of sightings in Los Angeles and London. One person reported seeing her near Roswell, New Mexico, being escorted by two men in black suits. The men, according to the tip, had pointed ears. She couldn't tell if this was meant to be a joke.

Nicole next went onto the *Los Angeles Times* website, looking for a phone number for Greg Albee, the reporter who'd written the only nice story that had ever appeared about her. No phone numbers were available for *Times* staff members. There was a "news tip and ideas" form, which required her to state her identity and news tip, with the caveat that the paper did not acknowledge each tip. Great, she thought, just what I need—to have this story disappear into the void.

The only way to contact a *Times* reporter, it appeared, was to send an email message to the address listed at the end of each story. She was stumped. How would she do this without giving away her identity? After a bit of thought, she established a new email account as wendybarrett@quicklink.com. Wendy had been her best friend in high school, and it was the first name that came to her. In her message to Greg, she wrote, "I can get you an exclusive interview with Nicole Graves. Please answer this message so we can make arrangements."

Almost immediately, she got an answer. But her heart sank when she read it. "Greg Albee is on vacation through Monday, November 23. If this is urgent, please contact Derek Schiff..." She groaned, then looked at the calendar. Today was the 23rd. My god, she'd completely lost track. She could try him again tomorrow, if he hadn't responded by then. Maybe he checked his messages when he was out of the office. She imagined reporters might be compulsive that way. And she was offering him an incredible scoop, which would become a lot bigger when she handed over Robert's files.

At that moment, Josh appeared in the doorway of the dining room, holding the paper in front of him, a puzzled look on his face. "You've got to explain this to me," he said. "What's going on? You said you shot that guy, but the paper says—"

"It looks to me like my firm, on Pizer's behalf, got the whole thing covered up and sanitized. It solves Robert's murder and, at the same time, explains Earl's death in Robert's cabin. As for

Rick—the attorney who helped kidnap me but tried to talk Earl out of killing me—they must have cleaned up any evidence he was there. He's Di Angelo's stepson and protégé, so they wouldn't want him implicated in this. I guess I'm in the clear, too, although I only shot Earl in self-defense. I'm sure Rick would testify to that."

"Does this mean you're safe? They'll call the dogs off?"

"Not a chance," she said. "I know too much. I'm the remaining loose end. They wouldn't want my version of the story to get out. Here, come look at what XHN posted about my whereabouts. It's pretty funny."

They both read it, laughing and shaking their heads at the things people had written on the bulletin board. There were hundreds, if not thousands of people who claimed to have seen her just about everywhere. When they grew tired of reading them, Josh went back to his work. On a living room bookshelf, Nicole found a copy of *The Way We Live Now*. It was one of the few Trollope novels she hadn't read. She got it down and settled on the couch with it.

Still tired from her ordeal, she found herself dozing off. She put the book down, got up, and went into Josh's study. She put her arms around his neck, her cheek against his. "I'm sleepy," she said. "I'm going back to bed."

He turned to look at her. "You want company?" he said.

"Oh, no," she said, nuzzling her face against his neck. "I can see you're way too busy."

"Are you kidding?" he said, dropping his pencil on the desk and getting up. He raced her up the stairs, both of them laughing, until they reached Josh's room and fell into bed.

Later, Josh got up and went back to his office to work. Nicole fixed dinner: macaroni and cheese—a special favorite of her ex-husband's—and a green salad. After the nightmare she'd just lived through—so little sleep, so few meals—she was enjoying the quiet moments of domesticity with Josh. He always seemed to be in a good mood, always ready for a chat, always interruptible. And she loved the quiet of his house.

They talked companionably at dinner, lingering over a glass of wine. Then Josh went back to his office to work on his project while she lay on the living room couch watching mindless TV. Finally, around 11:00 p.m., she got up. She stuck her head into his study. "I'm going to bed," she said. "Are you coming?'

"I can't," he said. "I have to finish this. It's due tomorrow morning, and I promised the clients I'd have something to show them along with an estimate."

"I'm sorry," she said. "I had no idea. I shouldn't have interrupted your work this afternoon."

Josh smiled at her. "Do you hear me complaining?" he said. "No worries. I'll get this done, but I do have to meet these people in my office tomorrow morning at 11:00. I'll be home around 1:00. You all right with being alone for a bit?"

"Of course," she said. "I'll be fine. I'll fix lunch and wait for you."

"You're becoming quite the little housefrau," he said.

"You forget," she said. "I have long experience being a housefrau. I was somebody's wife for a number of years. I'm an old hand at this. After all the insanity I've been through, it's great just hanging out, doing practically nothing."

At some point in the night Nicole felt Josh climb into bed and put his arms around her. But when she woke at 7:00 a.m., he was already up.

EIGHTEEN

BEFORE GETTING UP, Nicole took her iPad from the night table and checked her new email account for a reply from Greg Albee. There was none, but this was his first day back from vacation, and she had no idea what time reporters got to work. She sent him another message, typing the words "Urgent! Re: Nicole Graves" in the subject line.

She put on Josh's robe and went downstairs. She found him already dressed and in his study, hard at work. She'd solved her lack of wardrobe by washing her jeans, T-shirt, and underwear at night and putting them in the dryer during breakfast, using Josh's robe and T-shirts while her things were in the wash. If this went on much longer, she thought, she'd have to order some clothes online.

She got busy in the kitchen, fixing scrambled eggs, bacon, toast, and coffee. Since Josh was still working, she located a tray on top of the refrigerator and brought his breakfast to his study. He looked up from his work, surprised. "You didn't have to do that," he said. "I can take a few minutes to eat with you." He took the tray from her and followed her back into the kitchen.

During breakfast, the two of them shared the front section of the *L.A. Times*, holding it up so they could both read the latest on the Robert Blair case. The paper had more details about the alleged murderer's "suicide." There was also a reaction story consisting of comments by the police commissioners, the mayor, and members of the city council about the case's implications. Some were interested in reviving the failed plan to monitor the bank accounts of members of "high temptation" police units, like the vice and narcotics squads. The article also included pro-and-con quotes from experts in the law enforcement field, as well as from privacy advocates. A small story at the bottom of the front page noted that Nicole Graves was still missing. It said that police had investigated an apparently solid tip that her body was buried in the desert outside Lancaster but had failed to turn up anything.

The articles occupied a good part of the front page and two pages inside. A row of photos ran along the bottom of one inside page, a rogue's gallery of people, dead and alive, mixed up in the case. Nicole herself was shown in the often-used bikini pose.

She checked her email again. Then, still finding nothing, scrolled through the tabloids. XHN quoted several experts in criminology who thought it "highly likely" she was dead, based on the period of time she'd been missing, and that her body might never be found. It mentioned several prominent, unsolved missing-persons cases, as well as cases where murderers had been convicted even though their victims were never found.

The tabloid also had a man-on-the-street reaction story, which analyzed online responses from readers about Nicole's possible fate. Choices included: "in-hiding," "kidnap victim," "suicide," "murder victim," or "amnesia victim." There was also a box where readers could fill in another possible fate for, as the tabloid put it, "this enigmatic figure." Seventy-five percent of the respondents thought she'd been murdered. Among the write-in votes, five percent thought the whole thing was a hoax.

Reading this, Nicole could see the tabloid had reached the bottom of the barrel. She couldn't imagine how they could keep the story alive much longer without a new development. After breakfast, Josh disappeared into his study. Then, at 10:30, he went upstairs to change clothes for his meeting. A short time later he reappeared, looking handsome in khakis, a yellow polo shirt, and a black sports coat. He went into his study and reappeared, carrying a zippered leather folder with his proposal inside. He kissed Nicole goodbye and said he'd be home by 1:00 or 1:30 p.m. "Whatever you do," he said, "don't answer the door or the phone." Then he added, "If I need to call you, I'll let it ring three times, then hang up and call again. Then you pick up."

She made tuna salad for their lunch and put it in the refrigerator. That done, she poured herself some coffee, found the book she was reading, and settled down on the living room couch. For privacy, they'd been keeping the blinds closed night and day, and she had to turn on a lamp to read.

It was 12:30 when the doorbell rang. She got up, thinking it must be Josh, finished early with his meeting. Then she realized that he wouldn't be ringing the doorbell. He had a key, and he'd told her not to answer the door. She sat down again, feeling a little shaky. This wasn't about her, she told herself. It was probably a realtor or a FexEx delivery. Nobody knew she was here.

The bell rang several more times, there was a loud knock, and a few moments later a familiar voice called, "Nicole!" She immediately dropped her book and hurried to the door to look through the peephole.

It was Reinhardt. When she opened the door, his face lit up with a smile. Speechless, she took a step back.

His smile faded, and he regarded her uncertainly. "I think we need to talk," he said.

She finally found her voice. "I guess we do."

She invited him to sit on the couch. Once he was seated, she settled at the other end. "First of all," she said, "how did you find me?"

"When I arrived from London, I contacted your sister. She invited me to her apartment so we could talk. While I was there, you called, so of course I overheard. She tried to tell you I was there, but you hung up.

"I told her I thought I could help you," he went on, "and we tried to figure out where you might be. That was when she told me about your," he hesitated, then said, "friend Jude—"

"Josh," she corrected.

"Right, Josh. She said he was an architect in this area, and she had his phone number. With that information, I didn't have any trouble finding him."

"Oh, no," Nicole said. Her mouth had gone dry, and it was hard for her to form the words. "She didn't tell that to the police, did she?"

"She didn't tell them anything. She called them when you first disappeared—several times. The detective working the case said he'd get back to her. But he never did. Quite a police force you have here. I believe I'm the only one who knows where you are."

He looked around the room and then back at her. "Am I right in assuming that you and this Josh chap are more than just friends?"

"Yes," she said.

"Good god, Nicole. I thought—I mean, I assumed that we— How long have you known him, anyway? Just a few weeks, I gather, from what Stephanie told me."

"She didn't have any business telling you anything. I was going to tell you—if you ever turned up."

"Yes," he said. "I truly apologize about London. My work— well, what I was doing at the time made it impossible for me to contact you. But here I am. The British tabloids picked up the story about Blair's murder, and I could see you were in trouble. As soon as I could extricate myself, I came."

She heard the sound of a key in the lock, and Josh walked in. He froze when he saw Reinhardt. Both Reinhardt and Nicole stood up.

"Um," she said, "I guess I should introduce you. Josh, this is Ronald Reinhardt. Ronald, this is Josh Mulhern." She could feel herself flush. She watched them regard each other with open dislike. Reinhardt was, of course, more classically handsome. But Josh was just as good looking in a less conventional way. He was the taller of the two and more athletically built. He was also a decade younger than Reinhardt, who would turn forty on his next birthday.

Nicole shivered slightly. It was almost surreal seeing them together like this—comparing them, knowing she'd already chosen one over the other.

At last Reinhardt broke the silence, addressing Josh, "Pardon me for the intrusion." His voice was chilly, and he was wearing the same expression he had when Nicole first met him. He'd been a police inspector at the time, working a case that involved the people Nicole and her husband had swapped houses with. At that first meeting, Nicole recalled, Reinhardt had seemed sinister. She had, in fact, been afraid of him.

"Nicole and I need to talk," Reinhardt was saying, "and, given the issue of her safety, I can't very well take her out. I wonder if you'd mind leaving us alone for a bit." He looked at his watch. "An hour perhaps? We have some matters to discuss."

Nicole was mildly surprised to see that he'd put on his cop persona, making the conversation they were about to have sound like police business.

Instead of answering Reinhardt, Josh turned to Nicole. "You sure you want to be alone with this guy?"

Nicole stifled a nervous giggle. She knew Reinhardt would take exception to the idea that she might not be safe with him. And he certainly wouldn't like being referred to as "this guy."

"I have to talk to him, Josh," she said. "You know I do. He's come all this way."

"Fine," Josh said. "I'll go back to the office. I have some work to do. I'll be back in—well, you have my number." He paused and gave Reinhardt an unfriendly look, then glanced back to Nicole. "Give me a call when you want me to come back."

He picked up his leather folder and jacket, which he'd tossed on a chair. Then he walked over to plant a kiss on the top of Nicole's head.

As Josh turned to go, Reinhardt moved toward him and put out his hand. Reluctantly, Josh put out his own, and they briefly shook hands.

"Pleased to meet you," Reinhardt said.

"Yeah, right." Josh didn't bother to disguise the sarcasm in his voice. Opening the door, he gave Nicole an unhappy glance.

When Josh was gone, and they'd settled back on the couch, Reinhardt turned to her and said, "Why, he's just a boy. How old is he?"

"He's four years younger than I am," Nicole said. "What's your point?"

Reinhardt shook his head, as if to dispel the thought. "Where were we?" he said. "Oh, yes. I was explaining why I didn't meet you in London and couldn't contact you."

"You didn't really explain anything, but it's not important," Nicole said. "Well, maybe it is. It gave me a clear view of what our future would be. You know, we really did have something. The time I've spent with you was wonderful. And I still have feelings for you. I do. Up until the last few weeks, I thought we could just keep on seeing each other every month or so, and that would be enough. Now I realize it's not.

"You told me when we first met that someone in your line of work made poor marriage material. Now this new position you've taken—whatever that is—makes any relationship impossible. I can't live with that kind of uncertainty. I'm thirty-four, Ronald, and I want children and a stable home life. I'm not ever going to have it with a spy who lives half the world away."

"I could change that," he said.

"You'd resent it; you'd come to resent me."

"No, no," he said. "I've already made inquiries. I could take a job at the British Embassy. Right here in the States, in New York. Or at the British Consulate in L.A., if you'd prefer."

"Are you saying you'd give up being a spy?"

He looked at her for a long moment. "I never said I was a spy," he said carefully. Then he cleared his throat and went on, "If I took a position with an embassy or consulate, some of my duties would involve travel, sometimes at short notice."

"You see?" she said. "That's exactly what I'm talking about. Maybe you can't tell me what you do, but can you answer a hypothetical question? Suppose someone is a spy with, say, MI6. And suppose he moves in with a woman or marries her. Would he ever admit to her that he's a spy?"

"They—I mean, I've heard that anyone who signs up for this type of work agrees not to tell anyone, friends or family."

"That's what I thought," she said. "But your work isn't the only reason I'm breaking things off. I've met Josh. It's too soon to be sure, but I think I'm falling in love with him. I feel close to him in a way I never felt with you. There's a part of you that is very closed off, Ronald. Maybe it's the spy thing."

"I wish you'd stop saying that." Now he sounded annoyed. "I'm not a spy."

"Right," she said. "But if you were, you wouldn't tell me, would you?" She smiled at him.

"No, I wouldn't." He didn't return her smile. "But I'm not."

"Well, I guess that about sums it up," she said.

She started to get up. But he said, "Wait. You haven't told me why you're hiding like this. What makes you think you're in danger?"

She told him the whole story, then, at his request, took him into the study, where she plugged Robert's flash drives, one at a time, into Josh's computer.

Reinhardt looked the files over and asked a lot of questions. Then he said, "I agree that you can't go to the police with this, given the police chief's relationship with Blair and Pizer. What are you going to do?"

She told him her plan to go to the papers.

"Well, that has its own risks," he said. "You don't know this reporter or who he's allied with. You don't know what he's going to do with the information you'll give him, or even if he'll write a story. Nor do you know the editors who would be working with him. Something could leak out that would help these people figure out where you are.

"But," he went on, "I have to admit that this may be your best option. Perhaps I can help. I do have contacts with people who have some knowledge of your police department. I'm pretty sure they'll know what your police chief has been up to. It might be to their benefit to have him exposed without their direct involvement. If a reporter is willing to write an article, why don't you give him my number? I'll be around for a couple of weeks."

He paused to look at her. "I wasn't planning to spend my holiday alone, but I might as well see the sights here. And if you need my help, all you have to do is call." He pulled out a card and wrote his latest cell number on the back of it, then handed it to her.

"How are you going to handle the meeting with this reporter?" he added. "Of course you can't meet him here."

"I'll meet him somewhere out in the boondocks," Nicole said lightly. "And make sure no one follows me."

"Good." He looked at her for a long moment. "This certainly isn't the reception I expected. But I do understand. I'm going to miss you, Nicole."

He pulled her into a hug, kissed the top of her head, and held her against him. She realized, to her surprise, that he was trembling. "Truthfully," he said. "I can't say I blame you. I'm terrible at long-term relationships." He relaxed the hug and held her by the shoulders, giving her a long look. "And marriage?" He shook his head. "But I do wish you well. You and Jude."

"Josh," she said, laughing.

For the first time, he laughed, too. "Josh," he repeated. "You and Josh."

As soon as he was gone, she called Josh and told him the coast was clear. He could come home.

NINETEEN

NICOLE CHECKED HER EMAIL again. This time there was a message. "Willing to meet," Greg Albee wrote. "Tell me where and when. Also, can you let me know if I'm actually going to interview Nicole Graves at that time?"

She was thinking about where they should meet. It had to be in a completely different part of town, not the valley, not anywhere near Josh's house. She remembered, suddenly, a restaurant in Arcadia, east of the city. Her parents used to take Stephanie and her there as a special treat when they were kids. The Derby was a throwback to another era, with dark wood paneling and red-leather upholstered booths. She remembered its decor had a racetrack theme, and the place wasn't far from the Santa Anita racetrack. She hadn't thought of it in years.

On her iPad, Nicole did a search for the Derby and found several reviews. Not only was it still in business, it was getting good ratings. She was pleased. Some things in L.A. did endure, despite what people said. She messaged Albee back, but told him nothing about whether he'd get the interview or if this was just a preliminary meeting to schedule it. He'd have to wait and see. All she said was, "Meet me at the Derby restaurant near Santa Anita at 11:30 a.m. tomorrow. Please confirm that you received this message and will be there."

Just then she heard the front door open. She sent off the message, then rushed into the living room to meet Josh.

"He's gone?" Josh said.

"Gone," she said.

"Holy shit," Josh said, pulling her into a hug. "That was one scary guy. Did you say he's a cop?"

"I don't remember telling you anything about him," she said.

"Well," he said, "I was kind of avoiding the subject, hoping it would go away. What does he do for a living?"

"He was a police inspector with Scotland Yard when I first met him," she said. "But he changed jobs and wouldn't tell me what he's doing."

"Those cold eyes," he said. "I just can't picture you with him."

"It takes a while to get to know him. There's the chilly hit-man person you saw. Then he morphs into proper British politeness that makes your skin crawl. But when you really get to know him, he's—"

Josh let go of her to put his hands over his ears. "Stop!" he said. "I want to forget about him. I want you to forget about him."

She laughed. "Oh, I heard from the *Times* reporter," she said. "I told him to meet us at 11:30 tomorrow at the Derby. It's near the Santa Anita racetrack. Does that work for you?"

"Sure," he said. "But couldn't it be a little closer? Santa Anita is a long drive."

"That's the idea. We don't want him to know where I'm staying. We have to meet in a completely different part of the city."

"You're right," he said, then added, "Guess what? I'm taking the rest of the day off. We can loaf around and do nothing."

It was already 2:00 p.m. and neither of them had eaten lunch. While Josh changed, Nicole pulled the tuna salad out of the refrigerator and made sandwiches. He reappeared in shorts and a T-shirt and set the table.

After lunch, they spent a lazy afternoon. Both were worn out—Josh from working most of the night, and Nicole from her encounter with Reinhardt. They watched a movie on TV, made love, then watched another movie. Josh, she noticed, seemed to need to be fed every couple of hours. At one point, he got up and made popcorn, drenched it with melted butter and brought it into the living room in two heaping bowls. Later, he warmed some chocolate chip cookies, topped them with vanilla ice cream and gave the larger serving to her.

"You're going to make me fat," she said

"I'm building you up," he said. "You lost weight while you were gone. Do you know that?"

"No surprise," she said. "Those kidnappers were terrible cooks. And food was the last thing on my mind."

Around 8:00 p.m., too lazy to make dinner, they sent out for pizza. When it arrived, they ate in the dining room and made plans for the next day.

Nicole, who'd thought out what preparations were needed, explained them to Josh. She'd already copied Robert's files from the flash drives onto Josh's computer, since she'd be giving the originals to Albee. In the morning, they'd need to buy a disposable phone for Albee, so she could communicate with him without being traced. And, finally, she asked Josh to rent a car for the drive to the Derby. She didn't want him to take his own car, she explained, in case the reporter or someone else tried to trace his license plates.

"I'll pay for everything," she said. "The firm gave me quite a bit of cash when they made me take a leave of absence. I've still got most of it." She smiled at him. "We're all set."

That night, despite the confidence Nicole had expressed earlier, she was too anxious to sleep. She kept thinking of things that could go wrong. Her worst fear was that Albee wouldn't believe her story or that he'd tell her the information on the flash drives lacked the proof necessary to get a story in the paper. And that was true. All she had were the financial records from Robert's computer, the blackmail lists, and his notes. There were no witnesses, no corroborating evidence. That meant Albee would have to find ways to check out the information she was giving him, and that could take time. Finally, around 3:00 a.m., she got up, made coffee, and tried to think of people who might be able to verify the story. She came up with just two names but she thought that might do.

This completed, she started looking through the tabloid websites. They were now speculating whether she would actually be able to inherit Robert's money (if she turned up alive), since the police had discovered some of it was obtained from the crime of extortion. They hypothesized that perhaps all of it was.

The article quoted a law professor, who said that Robert could leave his ill-gotten gains to anyone he wanted. "Since Blair was never convicted of a crime," he said, "the government wouldn't be able to claim the money for victim restitution. He is considered innocent until proven guilty in a court of law. And he can never be convicted, since he is now dead. The IRS, however, will probably want to collect taxes from the estate. And his extortion victims could sue for restitution in civil court. But that's unlikely, since it would publicize whatever behavior they were paying Blair to keep quiet."

Nicole found the article interesting, although she considered the legal concept convoluted and somewhat wrongheaded. And she still couldn't see herself actually accepting Robert's money.

Nicole and Josh hit heavy traffic on the drive east, and it took an hour and a half to get to the Derby. They were twenty minutes late. The hostess showed them through several rooms of the restaurant to a booth at the back.

Albee was sitting there, nursing a beer. She'd envisioned him as a fit, energetic embodiment of an investigative reporter, like Bob

Woodward, as played by Robert Redford in the movie classic, *All the President's Men*. Albee was none of this, but a pudgy, middle-aged, balding man with lots of freckles and a slump. He looked anything but energetic.

He seemed equally disappointed when he saw Nicole and Josh. Nicole had worn her teenage boy disguise, with a T-shirt, windbreaker, and sunglasses. Her hair was ponytailed inside the baseball cap. They both nodded at Albee and sat down. The hostess handed them menus, and a waitress hurried over to take their drink orders. They were silent until the servers had left.

Then Albee turned to Josh, and said, "So, let me understand this. It's just a set-up meeting, right? You had me drive all the way out here to make arrangements for the actual interview. Or is this a hoax?" He was clearly annoyed.

Josh gestured to Nicole. Glancing around, to make sure no one was looking, she took off her glasses and baseball hat.

"It's you!" Albee exclaimed. "You're actually here!"

Already, Nicole had her cap and glasses back on. "Yes," she said. "It's me."

"And who is this?" Albee gestured at Josh.

Josh seemed about to introduce himself, but Nicole reached over to give his thigh a squeeze. "Let's just say he's a friend. I have some information—"

She stopped talking. The waitress had appeared with her order book. The three of them glanced quickly at their menus and placed their orders: Cobb salads for Nicole and Albee, a hamburger for Josh.

As soon as the waitress was gone, Nicole continued, "I have information about the Robert Blair murder that will give you a huge scoop. It's bound to upset some of L.A.'s most influential people. It might even ruin some of them. But first you have to promise that you won't let word out that you've seen me until after the story appears. The people involved in this have a hit out on me. That's not going to go away until they're exposed. I'm hoping you can make it happen."

Albee's eyes got very big. "Sure," he said, "I'll do my best."

"And you won't tell anyone you've heard from me."

"I promise," he said solemnly. "I always protect my sources. Always." He'd taken out a notebook and started to write as Nicole explained how she'd copied Robert's files and what they contained.

She pulled the flash drives out of her pocket, placing them on the table and pushing them toward him. She explained that, besides information on Ernest Pizer and the chief, the drives contained lists of other people Blair had been blackmailing. Then she unfolded the list of contacts and put it down, too. "These are names and numbers of a couple of people who might be able to help corroborate the information from Robert's computer." She tapped the first name on her list, Ronald Reinhardt. "He's a friend of mine with the English—um—law enforcement. He has contacts he thinks can find out about the L.A. police chief."

She looked up as a busboy appeared with their food. None of them spoke while it was placed on the table and the busboy refilled their drinks. When they were alone again, she went on, pointing to the second name on her list, Rick Sargosian. "This guy is a partner at Bascomb, Rice, Smith & Di Angelo," she said. "He sat in on an unusual event at the firm, a second property settlement between Pizer and his first wife, Angela. They've been divorced for at least twenty-five years. Pizer's been married and divorced several times since, always with a prenup."

Nicole continued, "Originally, Angela received what a lot of people would consider a good amount of money, but she ran through it, and a couple of years ago she came back demanding another settlement. She got it. I don't know exactly how much, but one thing I do know: She came into the firm screaming about how Pizer was a 'crook' and a 'mobster.' Blair told me about it.

Pizer's attorney, Jonathan Rice, and her own attorney ushered her into the conference room and closed the door.

"Here's the thing," Nicole said. "I'll bet she knows plenty and you might be able to get her to talk. She certainly hates Pizer, and he was willing to part with a good amount of money to shut her up. And this guy Rick?" she tapped the name. "He'll know how to find her. Just tell him that Nicole says he owes her a favor. That should get his cooperation."

"I thought you said not to tell anyone I spoke to you."

"Yes, but Reinhardt can be trusted, and Rick would have to be really stupid to mention this to anyone. It's going to scare him, but he'll keep quiet. Now, I may be wrong, but it seems to me that if you verify the information about Pizer and the police chief, or even just one of them, you have a story. Is that right?"

"Well, yeah," he said. "We wouldn't have to talk to all the people Blair was blackmailing. But the two big guys—if I can nail that down—would make one hell of a story."

"This is probably a stupid question," she said, "but do you have any idea how long this will take?"

Albee shook his head. "No idea," he said. "It could be a week or two or even a month or longer. It could be a few days. I have to see what you've given me, talk to my editors, then call these two guys and see what they can tell me."

"Oh," Nicole said. "Is there any way you can limit the number of people who know about this? Maybe you can go to the editor of the paper and work directly with him. I've heard that sometimes he'll personally handle a really big story."

"I'll talk to him," Albee said. "I can't promise he'll do that, but I probably can get him to assign a single editor I'll work with. We can keep it quiet."

"One last thing." Nicole pulled the new disposable phone out of her backpack and handed it to him. "If it's not too much to ask, I'd like you to let me know how it's going. Can you do that? Don't use your office or cell phones." She added her own name to the contact list with the number of her burner phone.

"Sure," Albee said. "I'll call you every day or two, and if you don't hear from me, you call me."

"I guess that's it," Nicole said.

"Thanks for the story," Albee said, "But I'm wondering: Why me? There are a lot of other reporters you could have gone to."

"I gave it to you because you were the only one who ever wrote anything nice about me."

He looked puzzled, as if he had no idea what she was talking about.

"When you interviewed my friends and my ex-husband? Every other story made me sound like a gold-digging tramp."

He laughed and actually flushed. "Well, I'm glad you were happy with it," he said. "There was a lot of comment about it on the website. I think your public image has improved now that people think you're dead."

"Well," she said. "I'd sure like to think I'm going to outlive this mess I'm in. It would be great if you could get this story out soon."

"I'll do my best," he said.

On the way home, Nicole was quiet. She felt let down, depressed by the thought of waiting days, maybe weeks, before her situation became tenable.

After ten minutes of silence, Josh asked, "You okay?"

"I guess. I'm just tired. Couldn't sleep last night, and now all the air has gone out of me."

"That was one hell of a performance," Josh said. "I mean the way you told that guy what the story was and how to handle it. You'd figured it out from every angle. You were pretty amazing."

"Thanks," she said. "I've been thinking about what to say to him for days. I hope he can pull it into a story, or I don't know what I'm going to do."

He put his hand on her leg. "You can stay with me as long as you need to," he said. "Longer, if you want."

She put her hand over his and squeezed it. Then she lapsed into silence again, thinking of the long wait ahead.

TWENTY

ONCE THEY WERE BACK at the house, Nicole decided to do something about her wardrobe. If she was going to stay at Josh's for a while, she needed more than a single pair of jeans and a T-shirt. What better use for the money the firm had given her? She still had seven thousand dollars left and no more intention of giving them back than she did of ever working there again. Besides, once Albee's story came out, the firm would face so much fallout, she doubted it would survive.

Josh had to go to his office for a few hours, so she borrowed his credit card and got busy on her iPad, going straight to the Bloomingdale's website. She treated herself to some high-end casual separates: a couple of pairs of designer jeans, some T-shirts and blouses, a cashmere cardigan, and an oversized, zip-front hoody. Then, getting into the spirit of things, she picked out some frilly bra and panty sets, a couple of stunning nightgowns and—most expensive of all—a gorgeous coral, orange, and white print robe of lightweight cashmere. She added slippers, boots, colorful running shoes, a dozen pairs of socks, and a small Kate Spade bag.

When the total reached $3,200, she decided she was done. She was just filling in the payment and delivery information when she heard a distant ringing. It took a moment for her to realize it was her disposable phone. She got up from the table and rushed to the hall closet, where she'd left her backpack with the phone inside.

It was Albee, and he sounded excited. "I talked to the editor. He's really jazzed about this story. I'm going to work directly with him. We had to add three investigative reporters. But don't worry. They're real pros, used to keeping their work under wraps. You don't have to worry about a leak."

Nicole felt let down. She'd hoped the story would be limited to Albee and a single editor. "Okay," she said. "If you're sure no one will find out I'm your source."

"No worries on that score," he said. "But I do want to level with you: This is a big investigative story, and we can't just run it. We have procedures. As you know, we have to verify the information you gave us. Then legal has to go over it, and we may have to go back and dig up more information. Before the story runs, we also have to ask the police chief, Pizer, and his lawyer for a response to what we've written about them."

"A response?" she said. "For heaven's sake! They'll deny everything! They'll threaten to sue you!"

"This is the process, Nicole," he said. "That's why we have to verify the information and have our lawyers take a careful look at the article before it appears. The truth, backed up with the proper documentation, protects us against libel. Even if the people we've written about deny everything, we can run it. We print their denials or say they refused to comment. Then we're covered."

"You realize, don't you, that my life is in danger?" Nicole said. "People want me dead because they're afraid I'll tell what I know.

They have no idea I've already done that. At this rate, I'm not sure I'll live long enough to see this in print."

"All you have to do is stay out of sight," he said. "No one knows where you are. Even I don't know. Believe me. It's going to be okay. I'll remind the team how urgent this is, and we'll get it out as soon as we can."

"All right," Nicole said, but she felt like crying. She hadn't realized investigative reporters moved at such a glacial pace. If this was the way they worked, it was a miracle these stories ever appeared in the paper.

"I've already set up an interview with Sargosian," Albee went on. "He wants to meet late tomorrow night as far away from his office as possible—some dive in Carson. You were right about him. I had to call three times before his secretary would put me through. But when I finally got him on the line, and said you told me to call, he was falling all over himself to cooperate. Of course I had to promise not to mention his name in the paper. Thanks for putting me in touch with him and thanks for the story."

"Did you call Reinhardt?"

"Yeah, but he didn't pick up. I had to leave a message. I'm hoping he'll get back to me soon."

"Thanks for the call, Greg," she said.

After Nicole hung up, she stood in the entry hall, her stomach churning with anxiety. She forced herself to go back and finalize her online purchases—at least that was something concrete she could accomplish. Then she called Reinhardt and was put directly through to voicemail. This gave her pause. She hoped he hadn't gone back to England and disappeared into another assignment. She left the number of her disposable phone and asked him to call her as soon as possible.

The next morning, when Josh went out to get the paper, he brought in a huge stack of boxes, her purchases from the day before, which she'd arranged for overnight delivery. After breakfast, Josh went into his study to work, and Nicole brought the packages up to the bedroom so she could try on her new clothes in front of the mirror.

Her phone rang, and this time it was Reinhardt.

"I got your message," he said. "I just landed at Heathrow."

"Were you called back to work?"

"No," he said. "I decided seeing L.A. by myself wouldn't be much fun, so I'm back in London."

"I'm sorry," she said.

"Don't be," he said. "I'll be fine."

"Did you call the *Times* reporter?"

"I handed it over to my contact," he said. "He's looking into the matter. He'll be in touch with the reporter. He said it would just take a day or two to get the information."

"Good," she said. "I really appreciate your help."

After a long moment's silence, she realized there was nothing left to say.

"Goodbye, Ronald," she said, "and thanks for everything."

"Goodbye, Nicole. Good luck."

There was a click, and he was gone.

The next four days passed slowly. After all she'd been through, handing off the investigation to someone else left her feeling helpless and depressed. She was itching to be part of the action. Instead, she was not only confined to the house, but completely out of the loop, with no idea what was happening.

While Josh was at his office for a meeting, Nicole wandered aimlessly around the house, hardly knowing what to do with herself. She tried getting back into the novel she'd been reading but was unable to focus. When she found herself reading the same page over and over, she closed the book and put it back on the shelf. She went into Josh's office and sat down at his computer. Even though it made her feel guilty, she took another look at his email. With a start, she noticed that Elle had sent another message the day before. Josh had already opened it and she could tell, from the icon next to the message, that he'd sent a reply. Elle's message was short: "Call me," it said. "Please."

Josh's reply was also short. "Don't hold your breath," it said. "I've met someone else." After reading it, Nicole flushed with pleasure and, for a few minutes, forgot her worries.

She gave up trying to do anything that required concentration. She watched daytime TV, something she'd never done before, at least not as an adult. She also called her sister, sometimes several times a day, and they chatted. When Josh was free, they talked and played cards, as well as old games he'd squirreled away in a closet: Scrabble (at which she beat him), Monopoly (at which he beat her), and Operation (which was a draw).

They took up running after dinner, when it was dark. She pulled her hoodie up to avoid being recognized. And they spent a good amount of time upstairs in bed. Those runs and Josh's companionship kept Nicole from going stir crazy. But underlying her thoughts was the constant worry about Albee's story, when it would appear, and whether it would have the effect she was hoping for. Another concern had begun to eat at her: Even if the police chief and Pizer were exposed, would the hit man be called off? And how could she be sure?

The tabloids had pretty much gone silent about Robert Blair since the police had identified the man they claimed was responsible for the murder. Never mind that he was the wrong man. For all intents and purposes, the case was closed. And, since the supposed killer was dead, there wasn't even a trial for the media to speculate about.

The *Times* ran a brief story about the investigation into Earl Murray's death. The Inyo County sheriff had released a statement that the evidence—fingerprints and gunpowder residue—wasn't consistent with suicide. Nicole read the story several times.

The article didn't go into detail, but she was pretty sure why the coroner would have doubts. Earl hadn't been shot at close range, as he would have in a suicide. She'd been four or five feet away when she shot him, so there wouldn't be gunpowder residue where the bullet entered his head. Furthermore, she'd wiped the gun clean before placing it in his hand. That would be another red flag. The coroner would expect to see the gun covered with fingerprints, since it was Earl's service weapon, and he would have handled it daily. Since he had used his second gun to shoot the man who knocked at the door, Earl would have gunpowder residue on his hand. But investigators would wonder why he'd used two different guns. This evidence would confuse anyone. Even if Inyo County law enforcement had suspicions, she doubted they'd ever be able to figure out what really happened.

Nicole's disappearance had dropped out of the *Times* altogether. The tabloids were still running briefs, tracking the number of days she'd been missing, but this had shifted toward the bottom of their websites. XHN had taken down the reader discussion topic "Missing Nicole," which had served the purpose of accepting news tips and reports from readers who claimed to have seen her. Apparently the tabloids, the paparazzi, and their readers had lost interest. Headlines now focused on an old comedian, long retired, who was accused of child molestation, and a couple of divorcing movie stars in the throes of a bitter child-custody dispute.

On the fifth day, Albee called her from the airport. He was on his way to Florida to talk to Pizer's first wife. "The research is going well," he said. "Your English friend really delivered on the police chief. We've got that pretty much written. Now I have to nail Pizer. He's the biggest fish in this story. If I can get him—" He paused, and she could hear a voice on a loud speaker in the background. "I've got to go," he said. "My flight is boarding."

It was another three days before Nicole heard from Albee again. "Sorry I've been out of touch," he said. "It took me a long time to convince Angie Pizer to give me what I'm looking for. She's one smart cookie. When they first got divorced, she hired a forensic accountant, who assembled a paper trail of Pizer's financial dealings, including those with the mob. She keeps it in a vault—I'm talking about a vault in an actual bank."

Nicole was quiet.

"You wouldn't believe the security she has in her house," Albee continued. "An alarm, of course, but also a bodyguard and dogs. Thing is, she wouldn't let me remove the documents from the vault. She had a couple of dozen key pages scanned for me. With the rest, I had to take notes by hand. But now I'm done and heading for the airport. So I'll be back at work, finishing up the research and getting ready to write the story."

"How long do you think it will take?" Nicole said.

"It depends on what the other reporters have dug up and whether legal has any objections. It might be as soon as next week or maybe ten days. I can't say for sure. This story is going to blow the lid off," he said. "The editor thinks it could win a Pulitzer."

"When I gave you the story, Greg," she said, "I knew you couldn't just run it in the paper the next day. But I'm in terrible danger here, and this is taking too long."

"What are you saying?"

"I'm saying that this story has to run pretty soon or I'll take it elsewhere."

"Listen Nicole," he said. "Please! Just sit tight. I'll see what I can do."

Not long after Albee's call, Nicole and Josh had their first argument. Nicole was in the room when Josh's mother called, and she overheard his side of the conversation.

After an exchange of affectionate greetings, he was quiet, listening. "I can't come for dinner tomorrow night, Mom," he said, "I've got a date."

He was silent another few moments, then said, "The weekend isn't going to work, either. Um—I've met someone. We're going to Laguna."

Josh's mother was so excited that she almost shouted, "That's wonderful, Josh! Tell me all about her!" Her voice was so loud even Nicole could hear her. Josh held the phone away from his ear and rolled his eyes.

"This isn't a good time, Mom," he said. "I have company."

Another silence on his end. Then, "Yes, she's here now. We'll talk later in the week, OK?"

After he hung up, Nicole said, "You really should visit your family, Josh. I'll be fine here on my own."

"I'm not leaving you until I'm sure it's safe," he said. They argued about it until he said, somewhat testily. "You don't get to tell me what I should or shouldn't do with my family." His jaw was set and there were spots of pink on his cheeks.

Nicole regarded him with surprise. She'd never seen him angry before. Was the sweet nature he always displayed just courtship behavior? Or was she being too pushy? That had been one of her ex-husband's complaints.

"You're right," she said. "You know your parents, and I don't. Thanks for taking such good care of me. But I can't imagine what your family will think when they find out who your new girlfriend is."

"They'll be thrilled," he said. "They'll love you."

She wasn't so sure. Ever since the paparazzi had set their sights on her, she'd felt as if her reputation was forever tarnished. She thought of her various misadventures—becoming heir to a murdered man's millions, getting kidnapped and having to kill a man to escape. There was the photo of her that appeared in the tabloids, the one in a barely-there bikini—courtesy of expert photo manipulation by the tabloids—sunning herself with Reinhardt. The media had also revealed that her ex-husband was a jailbird.

She thought about her earlier experience that had somehow escaped the British tabloids' notice—her previous year's escapade in the UK. These kinds of things didn't happen to other people. Had she just been unlucky, or was there something about her that invited trouble?

In this case, the tabloids had done a pretty thorough job of making her out to be someone who was "mad, bad, and dangerous to know." She couldn't imagine that Josh's parents would be pleased to find out he was mixed up with her. If she were Josh's mother, she wouldn't be happy about it at all.

Late in the afternoon, Josh told her he had to go in to the office to meet with clients. "I'll be back at 5:30 at the latest," he said.

"Do you want to go for a run before dinner?" she said.

"Sure. This shouldn't take long."

But at 5:45, he called and said that the clients were ready to sign the final contract for the house he'd designed, and he probably wouldn't be back before 7:00. "Why don't you go ahead and eat," he said.

"No, I'll wait," she said.

"Promise you won't go for a run without me. It's too dangerous. I don't want to come home and find you gone."

"I promise."

After they hung up, Nicole looked at the clock. She was dying to get out of the house. It was so tempting. How good it would feel to take a run in the crisp evening air.

No. I can't do that. I promised, she thought, She just had to suffer through until this damned story ran. She went upstairs and changed out of her running gear. Leaving the bedside lamp on, she lay down on the bed, and tried to think of a way to endure this interminable wait. She'd dozed off when she heard a car pull up in front. Her first thought was that it was Josh. He was early. They could go for a run after all. She got up and looked out the window. It was too dark to see out with the lamp on. She turned it off.

The car was a dark SUV. She couldn't make out the color, but it looked like the one that had been following her. The doorbell rang. She tiptoed downstairs and into the living room. The lights were off and the blinds closed so no one could see in.

There was a knock at the door. A man called out, "Federal Express." She tiptoed into the entry hall and looked out the peephole in the front door. The man outside was under the porch light. She recognized the large, shaved, bullet-shaped head she'd seen in her rearview mirror when the SUV tried to run her off the road.

Somehow he'd tracked her down. Her car was parked out in front, a tipoff that she was here. The bell rang again. Nicole quietly opened the hall closet door, reached into her backpack, and pulled out Sue's gun. The man knocked several more times, repeating that it was Federal Express, and that he needed a signature. When this produced no results, he disappeared from the peephole. What was he going to do now? The backyard was secured by a six-foot fence. There was a gate the gardener used to get in. It was padlocked, but how hard would it be for an expert to dispose of that obstacle? If he managed to get into the backyard, though, the house was fairly burglar-proofed. Somehow she doubted he'd smash a window or kick in a door. From what Earl had said, the hit man was under orders to make her death look like an accident.

Her hands were shaking as she picked up the phone in the entry hall and called Josh's cell. When she heard it ring in his study, she realized he'd forgotten to take it with him.

She peeked through the slit at the side of the blinds in the living room. The SUV was still parked across the street, but the man had disappeared. She walked back upstairs, hoping to spot him from the bedroom window. Just then she heard a scrambling noise and a thud. She stopped just outside the bedroom door and peeked in. Through the French doors that led to the small deck outside the bedroom window, she could see a man's silhouette. She'd stepped out on the deck earlier in the day and hadn't engaged the deadbolt. She could hear soft, clicking sounds as the man worked on the lock. He'd make short work of that.

Nicole turned and ran downstairs. When she'd looked outside before, the neighboring houses were dark. She could leave the house by the front door, but where would she find safety? She doubted she could grab her car keys and make it to her car before he caught up with her, and she had no way of knowing if any of her neighbors were home. She had to find somewhere in the house to hide. Then she remembered the storage closet under the stairs. The wall was finished with white-painted vertical boards. When Josh had showed it to her, he'd explained he was going for a seamless look. Instead of a doorknob, he'd used a latch that popped open when it was pushed. This made the door almost invisible. Nicole slipped into the closet, carefully moving aside the vacuum cleaner to avoid making any noise.

She silently closed the door. Waiting in the darkness, she fought a tickle in her throat, barely daring to breathe.

Nicole could hear the man walking around upstairs, opening doors, looking for her. Soon he came downstairs, searched the kitchen and laundry room before heading toward the front of the house. Her heart was beating in her throat when he passed the closet where she was hiding.

Just then, she heard Josh's car pull in the driveway. Her terror escalated. What would happen when Josh walked in? Was this man going to shoot him? I have the gun, she thought. I'll come out with it pointed at the intruder and distract him before Josh opens the front door.

Nicole heard the jingle of Josh's keys and reached for the closet door. At that moment, the man reversed directions and dashed back up the stairs. She could hear him run through the bedroom and onto the deck. Just as Nicole stepped out of the closet, Josh walked in and flicked on the light.

"What are you doing in there?" Josh said. "And what's with the gun?"

"I don't know how, but he found me," Nicole said. "He broke into the house through the deck outside the bedroom. This was the only place I could think to hide."

"Holy shit," Josh said.

"Look outside," she said. "He was driving an SUV. He parked it across the street. It's the same one that almost hit me the day we met.

They both went to the front door and looked out the small window. The intruder was just getting into his car. He revved the engine and, with a screech of tires, sped off. His lights were off, making it impossible to see the license plate.

They retreated into the living room and sat on the couch in stunned silence. Josh put his arm around Nicole. She rested her head on his shoulder.

"What do you think made him run away?" Josh said.

"When I was kidnapped, I heard Earl talking about the hit on me. He said the killer was instructed to make it look like an accident. When you showed up, I guess that ruined his plan. How could he invent an accident that would explain two dead bodies?

"We'll have to call the police," she went on. "I didn't want them involved, but I don't see that we have much choice."

"Wait a minute," Josh said, "I just thought of something. I know a guy who works as a bodyguard. I should have called him days ago."

"Who is it?" she said.

"Carlos, my personal trainer at the gym. Big guy who does security for visiting celebrities, stuff like that. He'll either take the job himself or find someone else to do it."

He got out his phone and made the call. It took him a while to explain the situation.

Meanwhile, Nicole went in the other room and put in a call to Greg Albee.

"What's up?" Albee said. In the background was the sound of a busy newsroom, a low roar of voices and the clatter of people moving about.

"The hired killer has found me, Greg. I can't wait for you to vet this story. Something has to run now, tonight, or I'm taking it to XHN."

"Please don't do that, Nicole. You can't trust those—"

"I don't care. I've talked to David Griffen. He's dying to get my story. XHN is just irresponsible enough to run it without checking it out or asking the chief and Pizer what they have to say."

"Please!" Albee sounded desperate. "Just give me a little time. I'll call the editor and see if we can make it happen. Maybe we can get at least part of the story in the paper right away."

"It has to be enough to get the hit man to back off," she said, glancing at her watch. "I'll give you an hour. It's 8:15 right now. You've got until 9:15."

"An hour!" he complained. Then, "Okay, okay, I'll get back to you."

When she rejoined Josh in the living room, he said, "Carlos is on his way."

Nicole told him about the call she'd put in to Greg Albee.

"Good," Josh said. "I never could figure out what was taking so long. Those guys are slower than the department of building and safety."

In less than ten minutes, the doorbell rang again. Josh went over to look out the window, then opened the door. A huge Latino man in his late thirties nodded at Josh. He was at least six-foot five and built like a truck. "Hi, bro," he said.

Nicole stood up, and introductions were made. Then Carlos walked around the house, inspecting the locks on the doors and windows. He went outside and looked around. When he came back, he said, "The gate to the back was open. That lock on it is pretty lame. You'll have to pick up something better." At

Josh's invitation, Carlos sat on a big upholstered chair near the couch. The men started talking sports, and Nicole tuned out their conversation.

She glanced at her watch. Forty-five minutes had passed since she'd talked to Albee, and she was beginning to think she really would have to put in a call to XHN.

It was another five minutes before Albee finally rang. He was a little breathless. "We're running the story about the chief on our website late tonight, and it will be in the morning paper," he said. "Legal is giving it a final once over. The story gets the police chief, Pizer, and his lawyer. It proves they've been bribing the chief on a regular basis. We'll keep working on Pizer's mob connections and, hopefully, have that out in a few days. This story will say that it's the first in a series, and that we're continuing to work on information about Blair's other blackmail targets."

"Thanks, Greg," she said. But her enthusiasm was muted. Why in the hell hadn't they done this in the first place? The story could have run a week ago, even before Albee went to Florida.

"Now, there's just one piece of this story I'm missing, and that's what I want to talk to you about," he said.

"What's that?"

"My exclusive interview with Nicole Graves. The story in your own words. How you found out about Blair, the attempts on your life, everything you've been through. Remember? You promised you'd do that when you first contacted me."

She had forgotten, but she said, "No problem." She put her hand over the phone and whispered to Josh, "He wants to interview me. Is it okay if he comes here?"

Josh nodded.

Albee agreed to come to the house, and she gave him the address.

"I'll have to bring another reporter with me and a photographer," Albee said. "Is that all right with you?"

"Sure," she said. Mention of a photographer grabbed her attention. As soon as they hung up, she got up from the couch and, with renewed energy, hurried upstairs to change.

By the time Albee and his crew arrived, it was 10:00 p.m. Carlos and Josh both went to the door. Josh looked out and, recognizing Albee, gave a nod to Carlos before opening the door. Albee greeted Nicole and Josh enthusiastically, pulling her into a hug and shaking Josh's hand. He introduced his photographer and the other reporter.

Then Albee looked at Josh. "Are you going to tell me your name this time? Or do you still prefer to remain anonymous?"

"I'm Josh Mulhern," Josh said. "This is Carlos Rodriquez, Nicole's bodyguard. I'm Nicole's—uh—significant other." This made Nicole laugh. He looked at her in mock seriousness. "Have I misunderstood the situation?" he deadpanned.

She flushed and patted his arm. "No, silly. It's just such a ridiculous phrase." Then she turned to Albee and said, "I'd rather you not use Josh's name in the story."

"Hey!" Josh said. "Why not?"

"You're not going to like it when everyone you know reads that you're connected to some very unsavory events. Seriously, Josh, you don't need that kind of publicity."

"And I'm saying I want to be with you on this."

When she saw his jaw set in the way it had been during their argument, she realized she was stepping on his toes again.

She gave Albee a shrug. "If you think it's relevant."

Josh went to get chairs out of the dining room for the photographer and the second reporter. Meanwhile, Albee sat on the couch next to Nicole. After he put his phone on the coffee table and turned on its voice recorder, he started asking questions. He wanted to know about Robert, her relationship with him, why she thought he'd left her the money, and what she planned to do with it once she got it. On the last point, she simply said she didn't know.

During the interview, Carlos kept getting up to look out the windows, checking to see if anyone was out there.

Albee asked Nicole how she'd found Robert's computer. Then, backtracking, how she'd discovered the safe room in the first place, and how she'd gotten into the house. And, finally, where she'd been since she'd disappeared ten days before.

At this point she veered from the truth. She told him she'd been kidnapped by the man police later found dead at Robert's cabin and another man whose name she didn't know. She said the two men had fallen asleep after consuming several six-packs of beer. She'd taken the car keys and escaped. She didn't mention Rick because she'd promised him she wouldn't. Nor did she say the man found dead in the cabin wasn't actually Robert's murderer. From what she'd gathered, Robert had been the target of the same hit man who was after her. Maybe this would come out. But there didn't seem much point in going over it. Nor did she admit she was the one who'd shot Earl, that he hadn't committed suicide.

She told Albee that Josh had picked her up at the truck stop and that she'd been staying with him ever since, avoiding going out in public.

"Do you mind if we take your picture?" Albee asked her.

"No, not at all," she said.

The photographer then swung into action, taking a couple dozen shots of Nicole from various angles. Then Albee said, "It would really add to the story if I could get a photo of the two of you together."

"Fine with me," Josh said.

"I don't know, Josh," Nicole said. Even if it annoyed him, she felt obliged to point out the downside of having his photo in the newspaper, especially with her. "What about your parents? How are they going to feel when they see you in the paper? And your clients? What will they think?

"They'll be fine about it," he said. "I haven't done anything wrong, and neither have you."

"What is it you do for a living, Josh?" Albee said.

"I'm an architect," Josh said. "I mostly design family homes."

"Listen buddy," Albee said. "This will be the making of you. When those ladies see the photo of a good looking guy like you, and read how you rescued a damsel in distress, they'll beat a path to your door."

Josh and Nicole laughed, and the photographer quickly snapped some shots.

"Just one more thing," Nicole said. She checked her watch. It was 12:00 a.m. They'd been at it for two hours. "What time is this story going to run?"

Albee paused for a moment to do some calculations in his head. "I just have to get back to the office and write up this interview. I'd say it will be up on the website at 3:00 or 3:30 a.m., at the latest."

They said goodbye to Albee and his crew. After he was gone, Carlos continued to monitor the windows, pacing around the house. His watchfulness—not to mention his size—made Nicole feel they were in safe hands.

Then she remembered Josh's family. "You'd better call your parents and tell them about all this," she said.

"They'll be asleep," Josh said.

"I know," she said. "But think how they'll feel when they read about you in the morning paper."

He looked at her a moment, then nodded and picked up the phone.

While he was doing that, she went on his computer, looked up the top ten tabloid websites and the phone numbers for their "tip lines." She also found numbers for the TV channels who'd sent crews out to cover her earlier. She noted the information on two sheets, eight on each list.

When Josh hung up, he looked less than happy.

"How'd they take it?" she said.

"It was a bit of a—uh—surprise," he said. "But they'll be fine. They just have to meet you. That's all."

Nicole wondered if that was true. But there wasn't time to worry about it now. She asked Josh for his cell phone, then quickly downloaded an app that could make his calls appear to be coming from somewhere else. She selected Bishop, California, in the Owens Valley. She'd already done the same to her phone.

She told him what she had in mind. "We're going to call tabloids and TV stations, say we live in the Owens Valley, and that the LAPD has been up there digging near Robert's cabin. We'll tell them there are a bunch of vehicles, including two coroner's wagons. And that people are saying they've located two bodies, including mine. The TV and tabloids will send their people up there, and the paparazzi will follow. They'll be two or three hours out of town before Albee's story appears."

"You want to send them on a wild goose chase," Josh said.

"Right," she said. "Payback. They made my life a living hell after Robert died and left me his money. This will make sure most of the paparazzi are several hours away when Albee's story hits." She looked at him. "Are you up for it? They'll still be able to make a huge deal out of this story. We'll just slow them down—and stress them out a little."

"Perfect," Josh said.

TWENTY ONE

AFTER THEIR CALLS WERE MADE, the paparazzi alerted and on their way to the Owens Valley, Nicole, Josh, and Carlos waited for the story to actually appear. It popped up on the *Times* website at 3:17 a.m. The three of them gathered in front of Josh's computer so they could all read it at the same time. When they were done, they laughed and cheered.

Only then—at 3:40—was it time for bed. Josh gave Carlos a pillow and blankets so he could sleep on the living room couch. Josh and Nicole headed upstairs.

They were awakened by a commotion on the street in front of the house. Nicole looked at the bedside clock. It was 8:00 a.m. Josh got up and peered out the window. "Holy shit!" he said. "There's a crowd of photographers in front and TV trucks are parked all down the block."

Nicole groaned. She hadn't thought of this. Josh had been identified in the story as an architect who lived in Studio City. Of course the paparazzi would figure out where he lived and track them down.

"Your neighbors are going to hate this," she said. "I'll tell the reporters that I'll answer their questions and pose for pictures if they promise to leave when we're done."

"Do you really think they'll go?"

"I don't know," she said. "But now that the chief is on his way out, we can call the police. These people are disturbing the peace in a residential neighborhood. I don't think they get to do that."

She got up and put on her robe. Opening the bedroom window, she called her offer down to them.

There were shouts of agreement. "Give me fifteen minutes," she shouted. "And could you please keep down the noise? You're disturbing the neighbors."

The clamor outside continued while she got ready. Meanwhile, Josh pulled on jeans and a T-shirt. "I think I'll let you handle this one," he said. "I'll go down and make coffee." Nicole wondered if his last conversation with his parents had anything to do with his decision to avoid the paparazzi. She suspected it had. With the cameras waiting, she took some time with her hair and makeup. This was her big appearance, and she wanted to look her best.

When she was ready, she went downstairs. Josh was starting to put together breakfast. He greeted her with a kiss and handed her a cup of coffee. She took a couple of gulps and gave the cup back to him. Carlos, who'd been drinking coffee in the kitchen, put down his cup and followed her.

When they were out on the porch, Carlos took a position four or five feet away from her and started scanning the crowd. "OK. Here I am," Nicole said to the gathered reporters and photographers. There were perhaps fifty of them. They started shouting questions, and she said, "Raise your hands. I'll call on you one at a time. I promise I'll get to everyone."

So, one-by-one, they asked their questions. The first was, "Who's the big guy standing next to you?"

Nicole introduced Carlos and said that he was her bodyguard. Predictably, the next question was why she thought she needed one. She explained that a man had made several attempts on her life, and that was why she'd been in hiding. Now, with the story made public, the people who'd been exposed would have to pray that nothing happened to her. But she wasn't entirely convinced she was out of danger, so she'd enlisted Carlos' help.

For the most part, the reporters and paparazzi asked for information that had already appeared on the *Times*' website and, presumably, in the morning edition of the paper. They wanted her to retell it in her own words on video. As she understood it, some of this was being broadcast live on a couple of the TV channels, maybe even on tabloid websites. It was a good hour and a half before Nicole had answered every question. Then another hand went up. She gave the man a nod, and he said, "Can you ask your boyfriend to come out, so we can get shots of the two of you together?"

"I'm sorry," she said, "but he's not making an appearance today."

"Why not?" someone else shouted. "He let the *Times* run his picture."

"And that was quite enough," she said. "Thank you for your time this morning." She turned and headed back into the house, dismissing them.

True to their word, the reporters, paparazzi, and TV crews immediately packed up and got into their vehicles. In fact, they cleared out in such a hurry that she figured they must have a tip on a hotter story.

Josh had cooked them a huge breakfast. Waffles, eggs, and sausages were in the oven keeping warm. On the table, he'd placed a pitcher of fresh-squeezed orange juice and a bowl of mixed berries.

The three of them had just sat down when the doorbell rang. Carlos went to get it. He was back almost at once.

"Who was it?" Nicole said.

"Paparazzi," he said. "Three of them. They told me to smile for the cameras, so I did." They all laughed. "Looks like everybody else is gone," he added.

"Thank god!" Nicole exclaimed. She'd just begun to serve herself breakfast when her phone rang. She'd turned it back on, and it was in its charger on the kitchen counter. She picked it up. Detective Miller was on the line. "I called to both thank you and apologize," he said. "So don't tell me to call your lawyer. Just listen, okay?"

"Go ahead," Nicole said.

"First of all, I'm sorry I didn't believe you when you first told me you weren't involved with Blair. But more importantly, I want to thank you for exposing the chief. A lot of us on the force knew about him, but nobody was willing to step forward. There's a code of silence—I'm sure you've heard of it—but the truth of the matter is that no one had the balls to take on the chief."

Detective Miller paused then continued, "I also want you to know that our squad arrested him and his inner circle at their homes early this morning. They're being charged with murder and conspiracy in the case of Robert Blair. They're also facing a number of other charges, including accepting bribes. We met with the D.A. as soon as the *Times* story appeared, and he was completely onboard. At this very moment, our men are bringing them into police headquarters. So you don't have to worry about your safety anymore."

"That sounds great," Nicole said, "but how can I be sure you got the man who was trying to kill me?"

"Turn on Channel Nine right now," he said. "You'll see the men being brought in. Hurry or you'll miss them."

She went into the living room, followed by Josh and Carlos, and turned on the TV, switching to Channel Nine. Sure enough, a "breaking news" sign appeared on the screen, and a perp walk was taking place as men were marched into police headquarters. She didn't see the man who'd been following her. But photos of the arrested men and their names were running along the bottom of the screen. There were nine of them, including the police chief. The man who'd been after her was third from the left. He was shown in his police uniform, which made him look even more menacing. "That's him!" she told Miller. "The guy in the third photo."

"Hank Kozlowski. We'll need you to come in and identify him," Miller said. "Then we can add the charge of attempted murder."

"Can we give it a couple of days?" she said. "I have a lot to catch up with."

"Call me tomorrow, and we'll make an appointment," he said. "By the way, if you happen to stop by your old law firm at 3:00 p.m. today, you might run into something of interest. Please keep this to yourself. And, again, thanks. A lot of the guys down here are really grateful to you. I mean it."

Back in the kitchen, Josh was reheating the food in the microwave. By now every phone in the house was ringing—all of their cell phones, as well as Josh's home phone.

They tried to ignore the ringing, but it was too insistent, stopping only to start up again a few seconds later. They got up and turned off the phones, and Josh disconnected the jack of his home phone. Then they sat down at the table and started to eat, happy to have the story out and Nicole's safety assured. For the first time since she'd found Robert's body, she felt safe. She pretty much cleaned her plate. Carlos couldn't get over Josh's cooking, and he went back for a heaping plate of seconds.

After they were done, Carlos said, "Looks like you guys don't need a bodyguard anymore."

Josh and Nicole walked him to the door. "Thanks for being here for us Carlos," Josh said. "Send me a bill and I'll settle up."

"No way," said Carlos. "This one's on me. You guys did a huge public service. I'm not going to charge you for it."

As Carlos left, Nicole found herself thinking, Now what? What was she going to do about a job? What was she going to do about her inheritance? And, even more pressing, what about Josh? She could move back to her own place now. She'd been waiting for this day, but now she had mixed feelings about it. This time with Josh had been lovely.

"Listen," Josh said. "We need to talk."

She followed him into the living room where they both settled on the couch. Nicole was quiet.

"First, you have to make peace with this inheritance you keep saying you don't want," Josh said. "I really do think you should accept it, Nicole. Blair's behavior—stalking you and then leaving his money to you, which made you a suspect—his whole obsession with you blew your life apart. You've said you're not going back to the law firm, so you're also out of a job. You've gone through all kinds of traumatic experiences because of Blair. You've earned this money."

When Nicole was still silent, Josh continued, "As for that diamond ring you showed me, I'll bet Tiffany's will take it back. If not, you can donate it to a charity. They can raffle it off or use it in a silent auction. And think what you can do with Blair's money. You tell me your sister is living in a rundown apartment, driving a beat-up, old car. Once you sell Robert's house, you can buy sis a house or a condo and a new car. It will change her life. And this money will buy you time to figure out what you want to do next. You can give some of it away to causes you care about. You can even put some away for our kids' college funds. What do you think the government would do with it if you refuse to take it? They'll use it to build a couple of inches of a new freeway on-ramp or half a prison cell."

Nicole's mind was still stuck on the college funds. "Our kids?" she laughed. "Surely you're not proposing to me! We've only known each other a few weeks."

"Oh, I am going to marry you," Josh was saying. "But that conversation's for another time. Here's what's going to happen:

You're going to your place today to pack up some of your things and start the process of moving in with me."

"That's completely crazy," she said. "What person in her right mind would give up Westwood for Studio City?" She looked into his eyes for a long moment and grew more serious. "I think we may have a future together, but we need time to find out. Right now we're in the first flush of romance. We don't know each other very well, or whether we'll get along once the courtship phase wears off. And what about your family? I gather they weren't too thrilled when you told them who you're seeing."

"They'll be fine once they know you," he said. "Right now, all they have to go on is what they've read in the paper."

"Well," Nicole said, "before we do anything rash, I want to meet your family and, hopefully, get them to like me. And what about your friends? We don't even know each other's friends. Let's be sensible. I mean, I've loved staying here with you, but actually moving in is a big step. And—well—I need some time to process what's happened and sort myself out."

Josh looked dashed. He was silent until Nicole said, "It's not like we're going to stop seeing each other. Let's revisit this conversation in six months. Okay?"

He smiled, and they sealed the bargain with a kiss. Josh was up for more, but Nicole said, "Later. I need to spend the day out and about, tending to things I've had to let slide. I'll take the rental car. I left mine in the garage at work. By now, they've probably had it towed. I'll have to find out where it is."

"Take my car," he said. "I'll return the rental. The agency is just a short walk from my office, and I usually walk to work anyway." Then he added, "Hey—let's go out to dinner tonight."

"Café Marie? I'd love that!"

Nicole made some phone calls to set up appointments, then called her sister so they could discuss the good news. They didn't talk long; Nicole had too much to do. First, she stopped by Daniel Freeman's office to sign the papers accepting her inheritance.

Freeman said it would be in her bank account the next day. He gave her the phone number of an accountant who could figure out the taxes owed on Robert's unreported blackmail earnings and arrange for her to pay it. As for Robert's house, he said he'd have the deed transferred over, but that would take several weeks. Of course she couldn't put it up for sale before it was cleaned up and "staged" to help it sell. She could use the time to start the process.

Next, Nicole called on her lawyer. Sue was wearing a pale pink dress, which made a dazzling contrast with her red curly hair. Nicole had forgotten how beautiful she was.

Sue was clearly hurt that Nicole had dropped out of sight without telling her. Nicole apologized. "I'm really sorry, but I just didn't know who I could trust, and the firm was paying you."

"I understand, Nicole," Sue said, "but I thought you knew I'm on your side, and I've been so terribly worried about you. But let's put it behind us. I'm glad you came by. Now, tell me: What are your plans now that this mess is behind you?"

Nicole explained that she didn't know, but she had accepted Robert's bequest, and she and Josh were thinking about the future.

Sue beamed at her. "So something good has come of all of this."

"It has," Nicole said. "It certainly has."

Next, she stopped at her condo. Her mailbox was full, but since it was only big enough to hold a few days' deliveries, she went up to see if her neighbor, Maryann, had taken some in. Maryann always looked after the mail when Nicole was off visiting Reinhardt. Sure enough, Maryann had a small carton filled with Nicole's bills, notices, and junk mail.

"I was just reading about you in the paper," Maryann said. "My god! What a nightmare. Why don't you come in and tell me about it? I just made a pot of coffee."

"I'd love to, Maryann," Nicole said, "but I've got too much to do." She thanked Maryann, then went next door.

The place was still a mess from the break-in, and it smelled of the fruit, now rotting, which she'd left in a bowl on the dining room table. She took it out to the trash and threw it away, bowl and all. Once back inside, she avoided the refrigerator. She'd deal with that later.

In its disheveled state, the place felt spooky, haunted by events of the last few weeks and even before. For the first time, she thought about putting this property up for sale. She'd be able to afford a bigger place now. If things with Josh worked out, maybe he could eventually move in with her. In any case, she didn't want to live here anymore. Too many bad memories—her failed marriage, Robert's stalking, not to mention the two break-ins.

She glanced at her watch. It was 2:40. She hurried down to the car and headed for the law offices of Bascomb, Rice, Smith & Di Angelo.

The media was back in front of the building, the full complement of paparazzi and TV trucks. She pulled into valet parking. As soon as she got out of her car, the cameras moved toward her.

"Hey, Nicole," one of the paparazzi shouted. "You know what's going on?"

She smiled, recognizing him from that morning when she'd seen him in front of Josh's house. "No idea," she said. "I'm just dropping by for a minute. Don't you know what you're supposed to be covering?"

He shrugged and said, "Someone called the tabloids and said something big was going down at this address at 3:00." He gestured toward the street where three LAPD squad cars occupied the no-parking zone. Somehow she hadn't noticed them.

Nicole hurried into the building; she was pretty sure she knew what was coming next, and it made her tingle with excitement. The desk in the lobby was tended by a new security guard, and she had to stop and show identification before he'd let her in.

As soon as she stepped off the elevator, she could see the staff was aware that something big was happening. They weren't sure of the details but understood it was going to affect them, and not in a good way. No one was working or even sitting at a desk. The whole support staff was standing around in clusters, talking. Some appeared to be arguing among themselves. All of them looked anxious and unhappy. Several were standing near the corridor that led to the attorneys' more lavish suites. One at a time, they would step into the doorway for a look down the hall.

Nicole walked forward, greeting those who looked her way. A few people nodded at her abstractedly, but their attention was elsewhere. She went into her glass cubicle and began looking for her things in the closet and desk drawers. Her coat had been replaced by what she recognized as Breanna's. In the desk were new drawer organizers and supplies.

When she looked up, Breanna was standing next to her. "This is my office now, Nicole," she said. Her voice was neutral, neither friendly nor unfriendly. Perhaps she was expecting a fight.

"You're welcome to it, Breanna," Nicole said. "I just stopped by to formally hand in my notice and pick up my stuff."

"Oh," Breanna replied, in a friendlier tone. "I guess you didn't hear. I mean—of course, you wouldn't have heard. What am I thinking? They told me they didn't expect you to come back, so they gave me your job." She flushed. "Sorry, Nicole. I always enjoyed working for you."

Nicole put her hand on Breanna's shoulder. "I know," she said. "Same here."

"Your things are in the storage room," Breanna said. "I'll get them for you."

"So, what's going on?" Nicole gestured toward the lawyer's part of the office.

"All I know is that some cops arrived about ten minutes ago and asked for Rice," Breanna said. "It's possible they're just here to arrest a client who's come in to surrender. But I think it's something more. I'm really scared, Nicole. What if Rice or another of the partners is arrested? Anything like that would put the firm out of business, and we'd all lose our jobs. Do you know anything?"

"Me?" Nicole said. "I've been completely out of circulation. But it doesn't sound good. What about Rick? Is he in?"

"No," Breanna said. "He left the firm last week. Someone said he got a job with a small firm in West Covina, handling DUI cases. I find that pretty hard to believe."

Suddenly, Nicole was aware of voices coming from the lawyers' suite. She stepped out of Breanna's office and pushed through the people standing at the entrance to the connecting corridor. Once there, she stood against the wall and folded her arms across her chest. She was so excited she could hardly breathe.

There was movement as a group of men assembled at the lawyers' end of the corridor. A voice she recognized as Rice's said, "Why can't we take the executive elevator? Then we won't have to go out front and face all those cameras."

"You don't get to sneak out the back to avoid the press," a man answered. "You're going out the front door." Nicole recognized this voice, too. It was Detective Miller.

Another man blustered, "My good man, do you know who I am? You can't treat me like a common criminal!" Nicole was pretty sure it was Pizer.

"I don't care if you're King Solomon," Miller said. "You're going to walk outside and face the public, just like everybody else who gets arrested."

Then Rice again, "Can't you at least take these handcuffs off until we're in the car? We arranged to surrender, and we kept our part of the bargain. We're not going to try to escape. Why in the hell would you make us do a perp walk?"

"Because that's the way it works, counselor," said Miller. "You, of all people, should know that. Now let's stop arguing and get this over with."

The group began walking toward Nicole. She flattened herself against the wall to let them pass.

Miller, who was in the lead, gave her a wink. It was a bit of a shock to see Rice and Pizer with their hands cuffed behind them. When Rice saw her, he stopped abruptly, causing Pizer to bump into him. Miller turned around. "No funny stuff," he said sternly. As they passed Nicole, Rice gave her a look of pure hatred. Pizer, on the other hand, seemed dazed, as if unable to process what was going on. At the rear of the group were three uniformed cops.

They all walked through the support staff's wing and filed into an elevator. Members of the staff stood and watched, each looking stunned. As soon as the elevator doors closed, Nicole went back to Breanna's office and stood at the window to watch what was happening below. The three black-and-whites were now in the valet lane, which had been cleared of other vehicles. Beyond them was the army of cameramen and reporters, which seemed to have doubled since she'd entered the building.

Breanna joined Nicole at the window. Neither of them spoke. After a couple of minutes, the police and their prisoners emerged below. Rice was loaded into the back of one patrol car and Pizer into another. A uniformed policeman held each prisoner's head, so he wouldn't bump it on the way into the caged backseat.

Nicole smiled, thinking that she couldn't remember ever seeing a spectacle quite so satisfying.

ACKNOWLEDGMENTS

I WANT TO THANK my family for their continuing support. I also want to thank my husband Bill for serving as technical advisor on the news business and on tabloid journalism, which he observed close up while covering the O.J. Simpson trials. Special thanks go to my other technical advisors: Jeff Boyarsky, my brother-in-law, a defense attorney, who helped me with information about lawyers and the police; and Cathy Watkins, my P.I. friend, who did double duty as a consultant on private investigators and as a copy editor. Extra special thanks to my sister, Susan Scott, who did the heavy lifting, proofreading each version of this book and helping me keep the plot straight. Thanks to Trish Beall who was also a great help in that department. Thanks to my daughter, Jennifer Doliner, for the title. Others who deserve special mention for their support and encouragement are Chuck Rosenberg, Sue Price, Jeannie Hahn, and other friends who cheered me on.

ABOUT THE AUTHOR

THE BEQUEST: A NICOLE GRAVES MYSTERY is Nancy Boyarsky's second novel, following *The Swap*, which is the first of the Nicole Graves mysteries. Before turning to mysteries, Nancy coauthored *Backroom Politics*, a *New York Times* notable book, with her husband, Bill Boyarsky. She has written several textbooks on the justice system as well as articles for publications including the *Los Angeles Times*, *Forbes*, and *McCall's*. She also contributed to political anthologies, including *In the Running*, about women's political campaigns. In addition to her writing career, she was communications director for political affairs for ARCO. Readers are invited to connect with Nancy through her website at nancyboyarsky.com.

NICOLE GRAVES MYSTERIES
BY NANCY BOYARSKY

The Swap
Book 1

The Bequest
Book 2

...*you might also like*

THE PETER SAVAGE SERIES
BY DAVE EDLUND

Crossing Savage
Book 1

Relentless Savage
Book 2

Deadly Savage
Book 3

Hunting Savage
Book 4

Peter Savage #5
Book 5, coming 2018